KT-103-598

angus, thongs and perfect snogging

Based on the bestselling
CONFESSIONS OF GEORGIA NICOLSON

Further Confessions of Georgia Nicolson:

Angus, thongs and full-frontal snogging

'It's OK, I'm wearing really big knickers!'

'Knocked out by my nunga-nungas.'

'Dancing in my nuddy-pants!'

'...and that's when it fell off in my hand.'

'...then he ate my boy entrancers.'

'...startled by his furry shorts!'

'Luuurve is a many trousered thing...'

Also available on tape and CD:

'...and that's when it fell off in my hand.'

'...then he ate my boy entrancers.'

'...startled by his furry shorts!'

'Luuurve is a many trousered thing...'

Angus, thongs and full-frontal snogging

with

'IT'S OK, I'M WEARING REALLY BIG KNICKERS!'

Louise Rennison

HarperCollins *Children's Books*

Find out more about Georgia at
www.georgianicolson.com

Angus, thongs and full-frontal snogging was first published in Great Britain
by Piccadilly Press Ltd in 1999, then by HarperCollins *Children's Books* in 2005
'*It's OK, I'm wearing really big knickers!*' was first published in Great Britain
by Piccadilly Press Ltd in 2000, then by HarperCollins *Children's Books* in 2005
First published in this two-in-one edition as *Angus, thongs and perfect snogging*
by HarperCollins *Children's Books* in 2008
HarperCollins *Children's Books* is a division of HarperCollins*Publishers* Ltd,
77-85 Fulham Palace Road, Hammersmith, London W6 8JB

5

Copyright © Louise Rennison 1999, 2000
Cover images © Paramount Pictures 2008. All rights reserved.

The author asserts the moral right to be identified as the author of this work.

ISBN-13 978-0-00-727467-3
ISBN-10 0-00-727467-X

Printed and bound in England by
Clays Ltd, St Ives plc

Conditions of Sale
This book is sold subject to the condition that it shall not,
by way of trade or otherwise, be lent, re-sold, hired out or
otherwise circulated without the publisher's prior written consent
in any form of binding or cover other than that in which it
is published and without a similar condition including this
condition being imposed on the subsequent purchaser.

Angus, thongs and full-frontal snogging

To Mutti and Vati and my little sister, also to Angus. His huge furry outside may have gone to cat heaven, but the scar on my ankle lingers on. Also to Brenda and Jude and the fab gang at Piccadilly. And thanks to John Nicolson.

La marche avec mystery

Sunday August 23rd
My Bedroom
Raining
10:00 a.m.

Dad had Uncle Eddie round so naturally they had to come and nose around and see what I was up to. If Uncle Eddie (who is bald as a coot – too coots, in fact) says to me one more time, "Should bald heads be buttered?" I may kill myself. He doesn't seem to realise that I no longer wear romper-suits. I feel like yelling at him. "I am fourteen years old, Uncle Eddie! I am bursting with womanhood, I wear a bra! OK, it's a bit on the loose side and does ride up round my neck if I run for the bus... but the womanly potential is there, you bald coot!"

Talking of breasts, I'm worried that I may end up like the

rest of the women in my family, with just the one bust, like a sort of shelf affair. Mum can balance things on hers when her hands are full – at parties, and so on, she can have a sandwich and drink and save a snack for later by putting it on her shelf. It's very unattractive. I would like a proper amount of breastiness but not go too far with it, like Melanie Griffiths, for instance. I got the most awful shock in the showers after hockey last term. Her bra looks like two shopping bags. I suspect she is a bit unbalanced hormonally. She certainly is when she tries to run for the ball. I thought she'd run right through the fence with the momentum of her "bosoomers" as Jas so amusingly calls them.

Still in my room
Still raining
Still Sunday
11:30 a.m.

I don't see why I can't have a lock on my bedroom door. I have no privacy: it's like *Noel's House Party* in my room. Every time I suggest anything around this place people start shaking their heads and tutting. It's like living in a house full of chickens dressed in frocks and trousers. Or a house full of those nodding dogs, or a house full of... anyway... I can't have a lock on my door is the short and short of it.

"Why not?" I asked Mum reasonably (catching her in one of the rare minutes when she's not at Italian evening class or at another party).

"Because you might have an accident and we couldn't get in," she said.

"An accident like what?" I persisted.

"Well... you might faint," she said.

Then Dad joined in, "You might set fire to your bed and be overcome with fumes."

What is the matter with people? I know why they don't want me to have a lock on my door, it's because it would be a first sign of my path to adulthood and they can't bear the idea of that because it would mean they might have to get on with their own lives and leave me alone.

Still Sunday
11:35 a.m.

There are six things very wrong with my life:

1. I have one of those under-the-skin spots that will never come to a head but lurk in a red way for the

next two years.

2. It is on my nose.
3. I have a three-year-old sister who may have peed somewhere in my room.
4. In fourteen days the summer hols will be over and then it will be back to Stalag 14 and Oberführer Frau Simpson and her bunch of sadistic "teachers".
5. I am very ugly and need to go into an ugly home.
6. I went to a party dressed as a stuffed olive.

11:40 a.m.

OK, that's it. I'm turning over a new leaf. I found an article in Mum's *Cosmo* about how to be happy if you are very unhappy (which I am). The article is called "Emotional confidence". What you have to do is *Recall... Experience... and HEAL.* So you think of a painful incident and you remember all the ghastly detail of it... this is the Recall bit, then you experience the emotions and acknowledge them and then you JUST LET IT GO.

2:00 p.m.

Uncle Eddie has gone, thank the Lord. He actually asked me if I'd like to ride in the sidecar on his motorbike. Are all adults from Planet Xenon? What should I have said? "Yes, certainly, Uncle Eddie, I would like to go in your pre-war sidecar and with a bit of luck all of my friends will see me with some mad, bald bloke and that will be the end of my life. Thank you."

4:00 p.m.

Jas came round. She said it took her ages to get out of her catsuit after the fancy dress party. I wasn't very interested but I asked her why out of politeness.

She said, "Well, the boy behind the counter in the hire shop was really good-looking."

"Yes, so?"

"Well, so I lied about my size – I got a size ten catsuit instead of twelve."

She showed me the marks around her neck and waist: they are quite deep. I said, "Your head looks a bit swollen up."

"No, that's just Sunday."

I told her about the *Cosmo* article and so we spent a few hours recalling the fancy dress party (i.e. the painful incident) and experiencing the emotions in order to heal them.

I blame Jas entirely. It may have been my idea to go as a stuffed olive but she didn't stop me like a pal should do. In fact, she encouraged me. We made the stuffed olive costume out of chicken wire and green crêpe paper – that was for the "olive" bit. It had little shoulder straps to keep it up and I wore a green T-shirt and green tights underneath. It was the "stuffed" bit that Jas helped with mostly. As I recall, it was she that suggested I use Crazy Colour to dye my hair and head and face and neck red... like a sort of pimento. It was, I have to say, quite funny at the time. Well, when we were in my room. The difficulty came when I tried to get out of my room. I had to go down the stairs sideways.

When I did get to the door I had to go back and change my tights because my cat Angus had one of his "Call of the Wilds" episodes.

He really is completely bonkers. We got him when we went on holiday to Loch Lomond. On the last day I found him wandering around the garden of the guest house we were staying in. Tarry-a-Wee-While, it was called. That should give you some idea of what the holiday was like.

I should have guessed all was not entirely well in the cat department when I picked him up and he began savaging my cardigan. But he was such a lovely looking kitten, all tabby and long-haired, with huge yellow eyes. Even as a kitten he looked like a small dog. I begged and pleaded to take him home.

"He'll die here, he has no mummy or daddy," I said plaintively.

My dad said, "He's probably eaten them." Honestly, he can be callous. I worked on Mum and in the end I brought him home. The Scottish landlady did say she thought he was probably mixed breed, half domestic tabby and half Scottish wildcat. I remember thinking, Oh, that will be exotic. I didn't realise that he would grow to the size of a small Labrador only mad. I used to drag him around on a lead but, as I explained to Mrs Next Door, he ate it.

Anyway, sometimes he hears the call of the Scottish highlands. So, as I was passing by as a stuffed olive he leaped out from his concealed hiding-place behind the curtains (or his lair, as I suppose he imagined it in his cat brain) and attacked my tights or "prey". I couldn't break his hold by banging his head because he was darting from side to side. In the end I managed to reach the outdoor brush by the door and beat him off with it.

Then I couldn't get in Dad's Volvo. Dad said, "Why don't you take off the olive bit and we'll stick it in the boot."

Honestly, what is the point? I said, "Dad, if you think I am sitting next to you in a green T-shirt and tights, you're mad."

He got all shirty like parents do as soon as you point out how stupid and useless they are. "Well, you'll have to walk, then... I'll drive along really slowly with Jas and you walk alongside."

I couldn't believe it. "If I have to walk, why don't Jas and I both walk there and forget about the car?"

He got that stupid, tight-lipped look that dads get when they think they are being reasonable. "Because I want to be sure of where you are going. I don't want you out wandering the streets at night."

Unbelievable! I said, "What would I be doing walking the streets at night as a stuffed olive... gatecrashing cocktail parties?"

Jas smirked but Dad got all outraged parenty. "Don't you speak to me like that, otherwise you won't go out at all."

What is the point?

When we did eventually get to the party (me walking

next to Dad's Volvo driving at five miles an hour), I had a horrible time. Everyone laughed at first but then more or less ignored me. In a mood of defiant stuffed oliveness I did have a dance by myself but things kept crashing to the floor around me. The host asked me if I would sit down. I had a go at that but it was useless. In the end I was at the gate for about an hour before Dad arrived, and I did stick the olive bit in the boot. We didn't speak on the way home.

Jas, on the other hand, had a great time. She said she was surrounded by Tarzans and Robin Hoods and James Bonds. (Boys have very vivid imaginations... not.)

I was feeling a bit moody as we did the "recall" bit. I said bitterly, "Well, I could have been surrounded by boys if I hadn't been dressed as an olive."

Jas said, "Georgia, you thought it was funny and I thought it was funny but you have to remember that boys don't think girls are for funniness."

She looked annoyingly "wise" and "mature". What the hell did she know about boys? God, she had an annoying fringe. Shut up, fringey.

I said, "Oh yeah, so that's what they want, is it? Boys? They want simpering girly-wirlys in catsuits?"

Through my bedroom window I could see next door's poodle leaping up and down at our fence, yapping. It would be trying to scare off our cat Angus... fat chance.

Jas was going on and on wisely. "Yes they do, I think they do like girls who are a bit soft and not so, well... you know."

She was zipping up her rucksack. I looked at her. "Not so what?" I asked.

She said, "I have to go, we have an early supper."

As she left my room I knew I should shut up. But you know when you should shut up because you really should just shut up... but you keep on and on anyway? Well, I had that.

"Go on... not so what?" I insisted.

She mumbled something as she went down the stairs.

I yelled at her as she went through the door, "Not so like me you mean, don't you?!!!"

11:00 p.m.
I can already feel myself getting fed up with boys and I haven't had anything to do with them yet.

Midnight

Oh God, please, please don't make me have to be a lesbian like Hairy Kate or Miss Stamp.

12:10 a.m.

What do lesbians do, anyway?

Monday August 24th

5:00 p.m.

Absolutely no phonecalls from anyone. I may as well be dead. I'm going to have an early night.

5:30 p.m.

Libby came in and squiggled into bed with me, saying, "Hahahahaha!" for so long I had to get up. She's so nice, although a bit smelly. At least she likes me and doesn't mind if I have a sense of humour.

7:00 p.m.

Ellen and Julia rang from a phonebox. They took turns to speak in French accents. We're going for a mystery walk tomorrow. Or *La Marche Avec Mystery*.

10:30 p.m.

Have put on a face mask made from egg yolk just in case we see any *les garçons gorgeous* on our walk.

Tuesday August 25th

9:00 a.m.

Woke up and thought my face was paralysed. It was quite scary – my skin was all tight and stiff and I couldn't open my eyes properly. Then I remembered the egg-yolk mask. I must have fallen asleep reading. I don't think I'll go to bed early again, it makes my eyes go all puffy. I look like there is a touch of the Oriental in my family. Sadly not the case. The nearest we have to any exotic influence is Auntie Kath, who can sing in Chinese, but only after a couple of pints of wine.

11:00 a.m.

Arranged to rendezvous with Ellen and Julia at Whiteleys so we can start our *La Marche Avec Mystery*. We agreed we would dress "sports casual" so I'm wearing ski trousers, ankle boots and a black top with a roll neck, with a PVC jacket. I'm going for the young Brigitte Bardot look which is a shame as, a) I am nothing like her and b) I haven't got blonde hair, which is, as we all know, her trademark. I would have blonde hair if I was allowed but it honestly is like *Playschool* at my house. My dad has got the mentality of a Teletubby only not so developed. I said to Mum, "I'm going to dye my hair blonde, what product would you recommend?" She pretended not to hear me and went on dressing Libby. But Dad went ballistic.

"You're fourteen years old, you've only had that hair for fourteen years and you want to change it already! How bored are you going to be with it by the time you are thirty? What colour will you be up to by then?"

Honestly, he makes little real sense these days. I said to Mum, "Oh, I thought I could hear a voice squeaking and making peculiar noises, but I was mistaken. TTFN."

As I ran for the door I heard him shouting, "I suppose you think being sarcastic and applying eyeliner in a straight line will get you some O-levels!!!"

O-levels, I ask you. He's a living reminder of the Stone Age.

Noon
La Marche Avec Mystery. We walked up and down the High

Street, only speaking French. I asked passers-by for directions, "*Où est la gare, s'il vous plaît?*" and "*Au secours, j'oublie ma tête, aidez-moi, s'il vous plaît.*"

Then... this really dishy bloke came along... Julia and Ellen wouldn't go up to him but I did. I don't know why, but I developed a limp as well as being French. He had really nice eyes... he must have been about nineteen, anyway I hobbled up to him and said, "*Excusez-moi. Je suis Française. Je ne parle pas l'anglais. Parlez-vous Français?*"

Fortunately he looked puzzled, it was quite dreamy. I pouted my mouth a bit. Cindy Crawford said that if you put your tongue behind your back teeth when you smile, it makes your smile really sexy. Impossible to talk, of course, unless you like sounding like a loony.

Anyway, dreamboat said, "Are you lost? I don't speak French."

I looked puzzled (and pouty). "*Au secours, monsieur,*" I breathed.

He took my arm. "Look, don't be frightened, come with me."

Ellen and Jools looked amazed: he was bloody gorgeous and he was taking me somewhere. I hobbled along attractively by his side. Not for very long, though, just into a French pâtisserie where the lady behind the counter was French.

8:00 p.m.
In bed.
The French woman talked French at me for about forty years. I nodded for as long as humanly possible then just ran out of the shop and into the street. The gorgeous boy looked surprised that my limp had cured itself so quickly.

I really will have to dye my hair now if I ever want to go shopping in this town again.

Wednesday August 26th
11:00 a.m.
I have no friends. Not one single friend. No one has rung, no one has come round. Mum and Dad have gone to work, Libby is at playschool. I may as well be dead.

Perhaps I am dead. I wonder how you would know? If you died in your sleep and woke up dead, who would let you know?

It could be like in that film where you can see everyone but they can't see you because you are dead. Oh, I've really given myself the creeps now... I'm going to put on a really loud CD and dance about.

Noon

Now I am still freaked out but also tired. If I did die I wonder if anyone would really care. Who would come to my funeral? Mum and Dad, I suppose... they'd have to as it's mostly their fault that I was depressed enough to commit suicide in the first place.

Why couldn't I have a normal family like Julia and Ellen? They've got normal brothers and sisters. Their dads have got beards and sheds. My mum won't let my dad have a shed since he left his fishing maggots in there and it became bluebottle headquarters.

When the electrician came because the fridge had blown up he said to Mum, "What madman wired up this fridge? Is there someone you know who really doesn't like you?" And Dad had done the wiring. Instead of DIY he talks about feelings and stuff. Why can't he be a real dad? It's pathetic in a grown man.

I don't mean I want to be like an old-fashioned woman – you know, all lacy and the man is all tight-lipped and never says anything even if he has got a brain tumour. I want my boyfriend (provided, God willing, I am not a lesbian) to be emotional... but only about me. I want him to be like Darcy in *Pride and Prejudice* (although, having said that, I've seen him in other things like *Fever Pitch* and he's not so sexy out of frilly shirts and tights). Anyway, I'll never have a boyfriend because I am too ugly.

2:00 p.m.
Looking through the old family albums... I'm not really surprised I'm ugly, the photos of Dad as a child are terrifying. His nose is huge... it takes up half of his face. In fact, he is literally just a nose with legs and arms attached.

10:00 p.m.
Libby has woken up and insists on sleeping in my bed. It's quite nice, although she does smell a bit on the hamsterish side.

Midnight
The tunnel of love dream I've just had, where this gorgey bloke is carrying me through the warm waters of the

Caribbean, turns out to be Libby's wet pyjamas on my legs.

Change bed. Libby not a bit bothered and in fact slaps my hand and calls me "Bad boy" when I change her pyjamas.

Thursday August 27th

11:00 a.m.

I've started worrying about what to wear for first day back at school. It's only eleven days away now. I wonder how much "natural" make-up I can get away with? Concealer is OK – I wonder about mascara. Maybe I should just dye my eyelashes? I hate my eyebrows. I say eyebrows but in fact it's just the one eyebrow right along my forehead. I may have to do some radical plucking if I can find Mum's tweezers. She hides things from me now because she says that I never replace anything. I'll have to rummage around in her bedroom.

1:00 p.m.

Prepared a light lunch of sandwich spread and milky coffee. There's never anything to eat in this house. No wonder my elbows stick out so much.

2:00 p.m.

Found the tweezers eventually. Why Mum would think I wouldn't find them in Dad's tie drawer I really don't know. I did find something very strange in the tie drawer as well as the tweezers. It was a sort of apron thing in a special box. I hope against hope that my dad is not a transvestite. It would be more than flesh and blood could stand if I had to "understand" his feminine side. And me and Mum and Libby have to watch whilst he clatters around in one of Mum's nighties and fluffy mules... We'll probably have to start calling him Daphne.

God, it's painful plucking. I'll have to have a little lie down. The pain is awful, it's made my eyes water like mad.

2:30 p.m.

I can't bear this. I've only taken about five hairs out and my eyes are swollen to twice their normal size.

4:00 p.m.

Cracked it. I'll use Dad's razor.

4:05 p.m.

Sharper than I thought. It's taken off a lot of hair just on one stroke. I'll have to even up the other one.

4:16 p.m.

Bugger it. It looks all right, I think, but I look very surprised in one eye. I'll have to even up the other one now.

6:00 p.m.

Mum nearly dropped Libby when she saw me. Her exact words were, "What in the name of God have you done to yourself, you stupid girl?"

God I hate parents! Me stupid?? They're so stupid. She wishes I was still Libby's age so she could dress me in ridiculous hats with earflaps and ducks on. God, God, God!!!

7:00 p.m.

When Dad came in I could hear them talking about me.

"Mumble mumble... she looks like... mumble mumble," from Mum, then I heard Dad, "She WHAT??? Well... mumble... mumble... grumble..." Stamp, stamp, bang, bang on the door.

"Georgia, what have you done now?"

26

I shouted from under the blankets – he couldn't get in because I had put a chest of drawers in front of the door – "At least I'm a real woman!!!"

He said through the door, "What in the name of arse is that supposed to mean?"

Honestly, he can be so crude.

10:00 p.m.
Maybe they'll grow back overnight. How long does it take for eyebrows to grow?

Friday August 28th
11:00 a.m.
Eyebrows haven't grown back.

11:15 a.m.
Jas phoned and wanted to go shopping – there's some new make-up range that looks so natural you can't tell you have got any on.

I said, "Do they do eyebrows?"

She said, "Why? What do you mean? Do you mean false eyelashes?"

I said, "No, I mean eyebrows. You know, the hairy bits above your eyes." Honestly friends can be thick.

"Of course they don't do eyebrows. Everyone's got eyebrows, why would you need a spare pair?"

I said, "I haven't got any any more. I shaved them off by mistake."

She said, "I'm coming round now, don't do anything until I get there."

Noon

When I open the door Jas just looks at me like I'm a Klingon. "You look like a Klingon," she says. She really is a dim friend. It's more like having a dog than a friend, actually.

6:00 p.m.

Jas has gone. Her idea of help was to draw some eyebrows on with eyeliner pencil.

Obviously I have to stay in now for ever.

7:00 p.m.

Dad is annoying me so much. He just comes to the door, looks in and laughs, and then he goes away... for a bit. He brought Uncle Eddie upstairs for a look. What am I? A daughter or a fairground attraction? Uncle Eddie said, "Never mind, if they don't grow back you and I can go into showbiz. We can do a double act doing impressions of billiard balls." Oh how I laughed. Not.

8:00 p.m.
The only nice person is Libby. She was stroking where my eyebrows used to be and then she went off and brought me a lump of cheese. Great. I have become ratwoman.

I wonder who our form teacher will be?

Pray God it's not Hawkeye Heaton. I don't want her to be constantly reminded of the unfortunate locust incident. Who would have thought a few locusts could eat so much in so little time? When I let them out into the biology lab for a bit of a fly round I wouldn't have expected them to eat the curtains.

Strikes me that Hawkeye has very little sense of humour. She is also about a hundred and a Miss – which speaks volumes in my book. Mind you, as ratwoman I'll probably end up as a teacher of biology in some poxy girls' school. Like her. Having cats and warm milk. Wearing huge

♥ 29

knickers. Listening to the radio. Being interested in things.

I may as well kill myself. I would if I could be bothered but I'm too depressed.

Saturday August 29th
10:00 a.m.

M and D went out to town to buy stuff. Mum said did I want her to buy some school shoes for me? I glanced meaningfully at her shoes. It's sad that someone of her mature years tries to keep up with us young ones. You'd think she'd be ashamed to be mutton dressed as lamb, but no. I could see her knickers when she sat down the other day (and I wasn't the only one).

11:00 a.m.

Phone rang. Ellen and Julia and Jas are coming round after they've been to town. Apparently Jas has seen someone in a shop that she really likes. I suppose this is what life will be like for me – never having a boyfriend, always just living through others.

Noon

I was glancing through *Just 17* and it listed kissing

techniques. What I don't understand is how do you know when to do it, and how do you know which side to go to? You don't want to be bobbing around like pigeons for hours but I couldn't tell much from the photos. I wish I had never read it, it has made me more nervous and confused than I was before. Still, why should I care? I am going to be staying in for the rest of my life. Unless some gorgeous boy loses his way and wanders into my street and then finds his way up the stairs into my bedroom with a blindfold on I am stuck between these four walls for ever.

12:15 p.m.
Perhaps as I can't go out I can use my time wisely. I may tidy my room and put all my dresses in one part of my wardrobe, and so on.

12:17 p.m.
I hate housework.

12:18 p.m.
If I marry or, as is more likely, become a high-flying executive lesbian, I am never going to do housework. I will

have to have an assistant. I have no talent for tidying. Mum thinks that I deliberately ignore the obvious things but the truth is I can't tell the difference between tidy and not tidy. When Mum says, "Will you just tidy up the kitchen?" I look around and I think, Well, there's a few pans on the side, and so on, but I think it looks OK. And then the row begins.

2:00 p.m.
Putting the coffee on for the girls. It's instant but if you mix the coffee with sugar in the cup for ages it goes into a sort of paste, then you add water and it's like espresso. It makes your arms ache like billy-o, though.

7:00 p.m.
Brilliant afternoon! We tried all different make-ups. I've been Sellotaping my fringe to make it longer and straighter and to cover up the space where my eyebrows were. Jas said, "It makes you look like you've escaped from the funny lads' home." Ellen says if I emphasise my mouth and eyes then attention will be drawn away from my nose. So it's heavy lippy for me from now on.

We were all lolling about on my bed, listening to the Top

Forty and Jas told us about the gorgeous boy in the shop. She knows he is called Tom because someone called him Tom in the shop he works in. Supersleuth! We all pledged that we would wait until I can go out again and then we will go and look at him.

Talk then turned to kissing. Ellen said, "I went to a Christmas party at my cousin's last year and this boy from Liverpool was there. I think he was a sailor. Anyway, he was nineteen or something, and he brought some mistletoe over and he kissed me."

We were full-on, attention-wise. I said, "What was it like?"

Ellen said, "A bit on the wet side, like a sort of warm jelly feeling."

Jas said, "Did he have his lips closed or open?"

Ellen thought. "A bit open."

I asked, "Did his tongue pop out?"

Ellen said, "No, just his lips."

I wanted to know what she did with her tongue.

"Well, I just left it where it normally is."

I persisted, "What about your teeth?"

Ellen was a bit exasperated. "Oh, yeah, I took those out."

I looked a bit hurt. You know, like, I was only asking...

She said, "I can't really remember. It was a bit tickly and it didn't last long, but I liked it, I think. He was quite nice but he had a girlfriend and I suppose he thought I was just a little thirteen-year-old who hadn't been around much."

I said, "He was right."

10:00 p.m.

My sister Libby kisses me on the mouth quite a lot, but I don't think sisters count. Unless I am a lesbian, in which case it's all good practice probably.

11:00 p.m.

Through my curtains I can see a big yellow moon. I'm thinking of all the people in the world who will be looking at that same moon.

I wonder how many of them haven't got any eyebrows?

Sunday August 30th

11:00 a.m.

Thank God they're all actually going out. At last. What is all this happy family nonsense? All this "we should do things as a family"?

As I pointed out to Dad, "We are four people who, through great misfortune, happen to be stuck in the same house. Why make it worse by hanging around in garden centres or going for a walk together?"

Anyway, ratwoman does not go out. She just hangs around in her bedroom for the next forty years to avoid being laughed at by strangers.

I will never ever have a boyfriend. It's not fair, there are some really stupid people and they get boyfriends. Zoe Ball gets really nice boyfriends and she has got sticky-out ears.

1:00 p.m.
I still haven't tackled Dad about his apron.

1:15 p.m.
God I'm bored. I can see Mr and Mrs Next Door in their greenhouse. What do people do in them? If I end up with someone like Mr Next Door I will definitely kill myself. He has the largest bottom I have ever seen. It amazes me he can get in the greenhouse. One day his bottom will be so large

he will have to live in the greenhouse and have bits of chop passed to him, and so on. *O quel dommage! Sacré bleu!! Le gros monsieur dans la maison de glass!!!*

1:20 p.m.
I may start a neighbourhood newspaper.

1:22 p.m.
Oh dear. I have just seen Angus hunkering down in the long grass. He's stalking their poodle. I'll have to intervene to avert a massacre. Oh, it's OK, Mrs Next Door has thrown a brick at him.

11:00 p.m.
What a long, boring day. I hate Sundays, they are deliberately invented by people who have no life and no friends. On the plus side, I've got six o'clock shadow on the eyebrow front.

Operation sausage

Tuesday September 1st

10:00 a.m.

Six days to school and counting. I wish my mum could be emancipated, a feminist, a working mother etc. And manage to do my ironing.

I thought I'd wear my pencil line skirt the first day back, with hold-up stockings and my ankle boots. I'm still not really resolved in the make-up department because if I do run into Hawkeye she'll make me take it off if she spots it. Then I'll get that shiny red face look which is so popular with PE teachers. On the other hand, I cannot possibly risk walking to school without make-up on. No matter how much I stick to sidestreets, sooner or later I will be bound to bump into the Foxwood lads. The biggest worry of all is the bloody beret. I must consult with the gang to see what our plan is.

5:00 p.m..

We're having an emergency Beret and Other Forms of Torture meeting tomorrow, at my place again. I have got eyebrows now but still look a bit on the startled earwig side.

7:00 p.m.

After tea, when Dad was doing the washing-up, I said casually, "Why don't you wear your special apron, Dad?"

He went ballistic and said I shouldn't be prying through his drawers. I said, "I think I've got a right to know if my dad is a transvestite."

Mum laughed, which made him even madder. "You encourage her, Connie. You show no respect, so how can she?"

Mum said, "Calm down, Bob, of course I respect you, it's just that it is quite funny to think of you as a transvestite." Then she started laughing again. Dad went off to the pub, thank goodness.

Mum said, "It's his Masonic apron. You know, that huddly duddly, pulling up one sock, I'll scratch your back if you scratch mine sort of thing."

I smiled and nodded but I haven't the remotest idea what she is talking about.

11:30 p.m.
Why couldn't I be adopted? I wonder if it's too late. Am I too old to ring Esther Rantzen's helpline? I might get Esther. Good grief.

Wednesday September 2nd
Five days to purgatory
10:00 a.m.
Oh. No, it's here already. As a special "treat" my cousin James is coming to stay with us overnight.

I mean, I used to like him and we were quite close as kids and everything, but he's so goofy now. His voice is all peculiar and he's got a funny smell. Not hamsterish like Libby but sort of doggy-cheesy. I don't think all boys smell like that, perhaps it's because he's my cousin.

2:00 p.m.
James is actually not such bad fun; he seems much younger than me and still wants to do mad dancing to old records

like we used to. We worked out some dance routines to old soul records of Mum's. "Reach out I'll be There" by the Four Tops was quite dramatic. It was two pointy points, one hand on heart, one hand on head, a shimmy and a full turn around. Sadly there's not much room in my bedroom and James trod on Angus who, as usual, went berserk.

Actually, it would be more unusual to say "Angus went calm". Anyway, he ran up the curtains and finally got on top of the door and crouched there, hissing (Angus, that is, not James). We tried to get him down and also we tried to get to the bathroom but he wouldn't let us. If we tried to get through the door he'd strike out with his huge paw. I think he is part cat, part cobra. In the end Mum got him down with some sardines.

7:00 p.m.
After "tea" James and I were listening to records and talking about what we were going to do after we ditch The Olds (as we call our parents). I'm going to be a comedy actress or someone like those "it" girls who don't actually do anything except be "it". The newspapers follow them all day and the headlines say, *Oh, look, there is Tara Pompeii Too-Booby going out to buy some biscuits!! Or Tamsin Snaggle-Tooth Polyplops*

goes skiing in fur bikini. And they just make money from that. That is me, that is.

James wants to do something electronic (whatever that means; I didn't encourage him to explain because I felt a coma coming on). He wants to travel first, though. I said, "Oh, do you, where?" Thinking... Himalayas, yak butter, opium dens, and he said, "Well, the Scilly Isles in particular."

11:00 p.m.
Something a bit weird happened. We went to bed – James slept in a sleeping bag on some cushions on the floor, and we were chatting about Pulp, and so on, and then I felt this pressure on my leg. He had reached out and held my leg. I didn't know what to do so I kept really still, so that he might think he'd just got hold of a piece of the bed or something. I stayed still for ages but then I think I must have dropped off.

Thursday September 3rd
9:00 a.m.
At last the eyebrows are starting to look normal.

2:00 p.m.

James went home. The "leg" incident was not mentioned. Boys are truly weird.

5:00 p.m.

Libby has the flu. She was all pale and miserable. I let her sleep in my bed and she was snuffling, poor thing. Poor little thing, I really love my little sister.

8:30 p.m.

Took Libbs some hot milk and thought she might like me to read *The Magic Faraway Tree*. She said, "Yes, now, more please," and sat herself up in my bed. Then, as I opened the book, she took my duvet cover and blew her nose on it. It's absolutely covered in green snot. Who would have thought such a tiny girl could produce a bucket of snot?

10:00 p.m.

I had to sleep in the sleeping bag. What a life.

Friday September 4th

11:00 a.m.

Emergency Beret and Other Forms of Torture meeting to be held this afternoon. I've decided that my eyebrows have recovered enough to venture out (obviously not on their own). I feel like one of those blokes who have been held in solitary in a cellar and come out into the daylight blinking.

We go to Costa Ricos for cappuccino. I hate cappuccino but everyone drinks it so you can't say no. I haven't been out for weeks – well, five days. Town looks great. Like New York... but without the skyscrapers and Americans. We decide we'll have the meeting and then go and sneak a look at the boy that Jas likes, Tom. He works in Jennings. I said, "What, the grocer's?"

Jas said, "It's a greengrocer-cum-delicatessen," and I said, "Yes, well it sells houmus." And she said, "And yoghurt," and I said, "*Quel dommage*. I forgot the yoghurt. Yes, it's like going to Paris going into that shop, apart from the turnips."

Jas sort of went red, so I thought I would shut up. Jas doesn't get angry very often but she has a hefty kick.

Jools said, "Shall we talk beret plan?" At our stupid school you have to wear a beret with your outdoor uniform.

It's a real pain because, as we know, everyone – and especially the French who invented it – looks like a stupid prat in a beret. And they flatten your hair. Last term we perfected a way of wearing it like a pancake. You flatten it out and then pin it with hair grips right at the back of your head. Still a pain, but you can't see it from the front. Ellen said she had made up a different method, called "the sausage". She showed us how to do it. She rolled her beret up really tight like a little sausage and then pinned it with hair grips right at the back in the centre of her head. You could hardly see it at all. It was brilliant. We decided to instigate Operation Sausage at the beginning of the term.

It has been a constant battle about these berets. The so-called grown-ups will not negotiate with us. We sent a deputation to the headmistress Slim (so-called because she weighs twenty-five stone... at least. Her feet cascade out of her shoes). At the deputation we asked why we had to wear berets. She said it was to keep standards up, and to enhance the image of the school in the community. I said, "But the boys from Foxwood call out, 'Have you got any onions?' I don't think they do respect us, I think they make a mock and a sham of us."

Slim shook herself. It was a sort of habit that she had when she was irritated with us (i.e. all the time). It made her look like a jelly with shoes on.

"Georgia, you have had my last word on this, berets are to be worn to and from school. Why not think about something a bit more important, like perhaps getting less than twenty-one poor conduct marks next term?"

Oh, go on, play the old record again. Just because I am lively.

We did have another campaign last year, which was If You Want Us to Wear Our Berets, let's Really Wear Our Berets.

This involved the whole of our year pulling their berets right down over their heads with just their ears showing. It was very stunning, seeing one hundred girls at the bus stop with just their ears showing. We stopped eventually (even though it really infuriated Slim and Hawkeye) because it was terribly hot and you couldn't see where you were going and it played havoc with your hair.

Meeting over and time for boy-stalking. Jas was a bit nervous about us all going into the shop. She's not actually spoken to Tom – well, apart from saying "Two pounds of greens".

We decided that we'd lurk casually outside and then, when she went in to be served, we'd sort of accidentally spot her and pop into the shop and say "Hi". This would be casual and give us the chance to give him the once-over and also give the (wrong) impression that Jas is a very popular person.

Jas popped to the loos to make herself look natural with panstick etc. Then she went into Jennings. I gave it five minutes and then I was the first one to walk by the shop doorway. Jas was talking to a tall, dark-haired boy in black jeans. He was smiling as he handed over some onions. Jas was a bit flushed and was twiddling with her fringe. It was a very irritating habit she had. Anyway, I stopped in my tracks and said in a tone of delight and surprise (which convinced even me), "Jas... hi! What are you doing here?" And I gave her a really warm hug (managing to say in her ear, "Leave your bloody fringe alone!").

When I stopped hugging her she said, "Hi, Georgie, I was just buying some onions," and I laughed and said, "Well, you know your onions, don't you, Jas?"

Then Ellen and Jools came in with arms outstretched and shrieking with excitement, "Jas! Jas! How lovely! Gosh, we haven't seen you for ages. How are you?"

Meanwhile, the boy Tom stood there. Jas said to him, "Oh. I'm really sorry to keep you waiting," and he just went, "It's cool," and Jas asked him how much she owed him and then she said, "Bye then, thanks," and he said, "See you later." And we were outside. When we got a few metres away we didn't say anything but sort of spontaneously all started running as fast as we could and laughing.

7:00 p.m.

Just spoken to Jas on the phone. She thinks Tom is even more gorgeous but she doesn't know whether he likes her, so we have to go through the whole thing.

I could hear Jas's dad in the background, saying, "If you are seeing each other tomorrow can't you wait and not add to my phone bill?"

Parents are all the same – all skinflints. Anyway, Jas said, "He said, 'See you later.'"

I agreed but added thoughtfully, "But he might say that to everyone, like a sort of 'See you later' sort of thing."

That upset her. "You mean you don't think he likes me?"

I said, "I didn't say that. He might never say 'See you later' unless he means, 'See you later'."

That cheered her up. "So you think he might mean 'See you later', then?"

I said, "Yes."

She was quiet for a bit; I could hear her chewing her chewing gum. Then she started again, "When is 'later', though?"

Honestly, we could be here all night. I said, "Jas, I DON'T KNOW. Why don't you decide when 'later' is?"

She stopped chewing then. "You mean I should ask him out?"

I could see my book sort of beckoning to me, saying, "Come and read me, come and read me, you know you want to." So I was firm but fair. "It's up to you, Jas, but I know what Sharon Stone would do. Goodnight."

Saturday September 5th
10:00 a.m.
Same bat time. Same bat place.

10:15 a.m.

Jas called. She wants to launch Operation Get Tom. We're going to go to Costas for more detailed planning.

10:30 a.m.

Lalalalala. Life is so fab. Lalala. I even managed to put mascara on without sticking the brush in my eye. Also I tried out my new lipliner and I think the effect definitely makes my nose look smaller. In a rare moment I shared my nose anxiety with Mum. She said, "We used to use 'shaders'. You know, light highlights and darker bits to create shadow – you could put a light line of foundation down the middle and then darker bits at the sides to sort of narrow it down." Wrong answer, Mum, the correct answer is, "You are gorgeous, Georgia, and there is nothing wrong with your nose."

I didn't say that, I didn't give her the satisfaction. Instead I said, through some toast so I could deny it if I had to, "Mum, I don't want to look like you and your friends did, I've seen the photos and no one wants to look like Abba any more."

11:30 a.m.

Mrs Next Door complained about Angus again. He's been frightening their poodle. She says Angus stalks it. I explained, "Well, he's a Scottish wildcat, that's what they do. They stalk their prey."

She said, "I don't really think it should be a household pet, in that case."

I said, "He's not a household pet, believe me. I have tried to train him but he ate his lead. There is only so much you can do with Angus."

Honestly, is it really my job to deal with hysterical neighbours? Why doesn't she get a bigger dog? The stupid yappy thing annoys Angus.

1:00 p.m.

I'd better be nice though, otherwise I'll be accused of being a "moody teenager" and the next thing you know it will be tap tap tap on my door and Mum saying, "Is there anything you want to talk about?" Adults are so nosy.

1:30 p.m.

Went next door and asked Mrs Fussy Knickers if she wanted

anything from the shops as I was going. She sort of hid behind the door. I must be nicer. I start out being nice and then it's like someone else takes over. Am I schizophrenic as well as a lesbian?

2:00 p.m.
Jas phones. She wants me to help her with part two of her plan to get Tom. The plan is subtle. Jas and I will pass by Jennings, and as we pass the door I will pause and then say, "Oh, Jas, I just remembered I said I'd get some apples. Hang on a minute." Then I go into the shop and buy the apples. Jas stands behind me looking attractively casual. I smile as Tom hands over the grannies (Granny Smiths) and then – and here is the masterstroke – I say, "School in two days. Back to Stalag 14. Which centre of boredom and torture do you go to?" (Meaning, which school do you go to, do you see?) Then he tells me and then we know how to accidentally bump into him.

4:00 p.m.
Well, we got to Jennings and Tom was in there – Jas went a bit swoony. He is nice-looking, I must say, with sort of

crinkly hair and great shoulders. I said my "Hang on, Jas, I promised I'd get some apples," and we went in, so she could lurk attractively behind me, as planned.

When he saw her Tom looked and smiled. I asked for my grannies and he said, "Sure. Are you looking forward to going back to school?"

(Hang on a minute, those were my lines. Still, I've done drama for four years so I improvised.) I rejoined, "Does the Pope hate Catholics?"

He smiled but I didn't really mean to say anything about the Pope, it just popped out. Tom went on, "Which school do you two go to?" I was just about to tell him (even though in our plan it wasn't really his turn)... when a Sex God came out of the back room.

I swear he was so gorgeous it made you blink and open your mouth like a goldfish. He was very tall and had long, black hair and really intense, dark-blue eyes and a big mouth and was dressed all in black. (And that's all I remember, officer.) He came over to Tom and handed him a cup of tea. Tom said, "Thanks," and the Sex God spoke. "Can't let my little brother slave away, serving apples to good-looking girls without even a cup of tea." Then he

WINKED at Tom and SMILED at me, then he went out the back.

I just stood there, looking at the space where SG had been. Clutching my apples, Tom said, "That's forty pence. Did you tell me what school you both go to?"

I came out of my trance and hoped I hadn't been dribbling. "Er... I..." and I couldn't remember.

Jas looked at me as if I had gone mad and said, "Oh, it's only the one we've been at for four years, Latimer and Ridgley. Which one do you go to?"

7:00 p.m.
I am still in a state of shock. I have just met Mr Gorgeous. And he is Tom's brother. And he is gorgeous. He saw me with my mouth open. But, fortunately, not without eyebrows. Oh God! Quick, nurse, the screens!!

7:05 p.m.
I tried opening my mouth in the mirror like I imagine it looked like in the shop. It doesn't make me look very intelligent but it also doesn't make my nose look any bigger, which is a plus (of sorts).

1:00 a.m.

I wonder how old he is? I must become more mature quickly. I'll start tomorrow.

Sunday September 6th

8:00 a.m.

When I walked into the kitchen Dad dropped his cup in a hilarious (not) display of surprise that I was up so early. "What has happened, George, has your bed caught fire? Are you feverish? It's not midday yet, why are you up?"

I said, "I came down for a cup of hot water, if that's OK." (Very cleansing for the system; I must avoid a spot attack at all costs.)

Mum said, "Well, I'm off, Libby, give your big sister a kiss before we go." Libby gave me a big smacking kiss which was nice but a bit on the porridgey side. Still, I must get on.

10:00 a.m.

I have completed the *Cosmo* yoga plan for inner peace and confidence. I vow to get up an hour before school and go through the twelve positions of "Sun worship". I feel great and two or three foot taller. The Sex God will not be able to resist the new, confident, radiant, womanly me.

2:00 p.m.
Face pack done and milk bath taken. I must try and get the milk stains off the bath towel somehow, it already smells a bit sour.

Jas rang. She thinks we should track Tom tomorrow after school. Tom – what is he to me?

4:00 p.m.
Just discovered that Libby has used the last of my sanitary towels to make hammocks for her dolls.

4:30 p.m.
She has also used all of my Starkers foundation cream on her panda: its head is entirely beige now.

5:00 p.m.
I have no other foundation or money. I may have to kill her.

5:15 p.m.
No. Peace. Ohm. Inner peace.

8:00 p.m.

Aahhhh. Early to bed, early to rise.

9:30 p.m.

Woke with a start. Thought it might be time to get up.

Midnight

Should I wear my pencil skirt or not tomorrow.

Monday September 7th

8:30 a.m.

Overslept and had to race to get a lift to Jas's with my dad. No time for yoga or make-up. Oh well, I'll start tomorrow. God alone knows how the Dalai Lama copes on a daily basis. He must get up at dawn. Actually, I read somewhere that he does get up at dawn.

8:45 a.m.

Jas and I running like loonies up the hill to the school gate. I thought my head was going to explode I was so red, and also I just remembered I hadn't got my beret on. I could see Hawkeye at the school gate so no time for the sausage method. I just rammed it on my head. Bugger bugger, pant pant. As we ran up to the gate I catapulted into... the Sex God. He looked DIVINE in his uniform. He was with his mates, having a laugh and just strolling coolly along. He looked at me and said, "You're keen." I could have died.

9:00 a.m.
My only hope is that a) he didn't recognise me and b) if he did recognise me he likes the "flushed, stupid idiot" look in a girl.

9:35 a.m.
After assembly I popped into the loos and looked in the mirror. Worst fears confirmed – I am Mrs Ugly. Small, swollen eyes, hair plastered to my skull, HUGE red nose. I look like a tomato in a school uniform. Well, that is that then.

4:00 p.m.
The bell. Thank God, now I can go home and kill myself.

7:00 p.m.

In bed. Uncle Eddie says there is an unseen force at work of which we have no comprehension... Well, if there is, why is it picking on me?

Tuesday September 8th

8:00 a.m.

Still no time to do my yoga. Not that it matters any more. I did manage to do the sausage beret and the lip-gloss and the concealer. Nothing like shutting the stable door and tarting up the horse after it's bolted.

8:20 a.m.

Nice and early with Jas. This time we are both ready. We walked up the hill really chatting and laughing. Waving at friends (well actually, waving at anyone, just to give the impression that we are really popular). We walked slowly at the end bit leading up to the gate and although there was the usual crush of Foxwood boys ogling, there was no sign of Tom or SG.

9:30 a.m.

I'd forgotten how utterly crap school is. In assembly there was a bit of chatting going on before Slim took the stage, and do you know what she said? She said, "Settle, girls, settle." Like we were a bunch of pigeons or doves or something. She's already started her fascist regime by saying she has been told that some girls were not wearing their berets as they arrived at school. She would like the older girls to set an example to the younger ones, rather than the other way round. Is this what my life is now? Talking about berets? Whilst a Sex God strolls around on the planet? I felt like shouting out, in front of assembly, "Get a life, Slim!! In fact, get two... there's enough of you!!"

But Hawkeye was looking at me. I know she was thinking about the locusts. She's always watching me. She's like a stoat. I don't think I can stand much more of this and it's only nine thirty.

5:00 p.m.

What a nightmare! Jas, Ellen, Jools and I are NOT ALLOWED to sit together at the back. I CANNOT BELIEVE IT. Instead, I have been placed next to Nauseating Pamela

Green. It is more than flesh and blood can stand. Nauseating P. Green is so boring it makes you want to slit your wrists just looking at her. Plus Hawkeye is our form mistress. *Quelle horreur* and triple *merde*. And it's physics last thing Friday afternoon. What is the point?

Wednesday September 9th
8:40 a.m.
I have perfected putting a little bit of mascara on so that you can't tell I have got any on.

No sign of the lads.

1:00 p.m.
After lunch Alison Peters and Jackie Mathews came by. They were smoking and I must say they are common girls, but obviously I must not say it to them as I do not want a duffing up, or chewing gum in my tennis shoes.

Jackie said, "We're doing a new thing tomorrow, it's a sort of Aleisteir Crowley thing, so you can all come and meet us in 5C form room tomorrow after second lunch."

Cheers, thanks a lot. Good night. It is, of course, strictly forbidden to be in school after second lunch. I sense something... what is it? Oh yes, it's my first poor conduct mark coming along.

6:00 p.m.
Is my life over? Is this all there is? Downstairs my parents are laughing at something and in the other room Libby is playing with her dolls. I can hear her talking to them. It's so sad, that she is so young and she doesn't know the sadness that lies ahead. That is what is so sad. I can hear her little voice murmuring... what is she saying...?

Oh, it's "Poor Georgia, poor Georgia."

Thursday September 10th
5:00 p.m.
Boring day at school, then home to my even more boring home life. I wanted to debrief with Jas but she had to go to the dentist. Jackie and Alison's proposed Aleisteir Crowley extravaganza was put off this lunchtime, thank the Lord. The message got passed along at assembly that Jackie was off sick. She has started taking sickies very early on in term. Anyway, we are spared whatever they had in mind for a few days. I think they take drugs. Horse tranquillizers, probably.

Tuesday September 15th
4:30 p.m.

Absolutely no sign of SG. However, I have found out some gossip because Katie Steadman's parents know SG's parents from some naff card club the really old go to. Apparently he's called Robbie Jennings – his parents, Mr and Mrs Jennings, own the shop – the so-called greengrocer-cum-delicatessen, according to Jas. I don't normally like Katie Steadman that much. She's OK but I get the impression she thinks I am a bit on the superficial side.

She's bloody tall, I'll say that for her, and her hair is nice, but she sort of tries too hard. She puts her hand up in class, for instance. Properly, I mean. She doesn't do the putting your hand up but leaving it all floppy at the end of your arm, so it just flaps around. That is the sign of someone who is obliged to put their hand up because that is the fascist way, but isn't really putting their hand up. I have taken to putting my hand up and pointing one finger forward – you know, like at football matches when everyone points at a chubby player and chants, "Who ate all the pies?" But as usual any sign of humour is stamped down in this place. Hawkeye said, "Georgia, if you are too tired to put your hand up properly perhaps you should go to bed earlier... or perhaps a few thousand lines might strengthen your wrist?"

I may try it out on Herr Kamyer – we have him for German and physics, which is the only bright spot in this hell-hole. He has the double comedy value of being both German and the only male teacher in an all girls' school.

8:00 p.m.
Listening to classical music, I thought it might be soothing, but it's really irritating and has no proper tune.

8:05 p.m.
I love life!!! Jas has just phoned to say we've been invited to a party at Katie Steadman's and... Katie has asked Tom and Robbie. YESSSSS!!!! I must have done a good job of being nice to Katie. WHAT ON EARTH CAN I WEAR??? Emergency, emergency! It's only a couple of weeks away.

8:10 p.m.
I'd better do my yoga.

8:15 p.m.
I'd better start applying face masks now.

8:20 p.m.
I wonder if I slept with a peg on my nose, like Amy in *Little Women*, if it would make it smaller? Why couldn't Mum choose someone with a normal sized hooter to marry?

8:30 p.m.
I asked Mum why she married Dad (he was bowling with Uncle Eddie – I ask you). She thought for a bit and then she said, "He makes me laugh." He makes her laugh. He makes her laugh. Well, Bart Simpson makes me laugh, but I'm not going to marry him.

Midnight
Hahahahahahahaha.

Monday September 21st
8:00 a.m.
Eleven days to the party.

Tuesday September 22nd
9:30 a.m.

Someone farted in assembly this morning (I suspect Nauseating P. Green). Whoever it was, it was really loud and during the silence we were having to think about all the poor people. And it wasn't just a quick one, it was a knee-trembler. Jas, Ellen, Julia and me were shrieking with laughter, well everyone was. I was laughing for most of the day and now my stomach hurts.

Thursday September 24th
5:30 p.m.

In bed. I'm absolutely frozen. I may have TB. Honestly, Miss Stamp is obviously a sex pervert as well as clearly being a lesbian. Why else would anyone make girls run around in sports knickers hitting a ball with sticks? She calls it hockey – I call it the sick wanderings of a sick mind. If I miss this party because of lesbian lust Miss Stamp WILL DIE. SHE WILL DIE.

Friday September 25th

10:00 a.m.

A sighting at last!! On the way to school we saw Tom. He actually stopped to chat, he said, "Hi, having fun?"

I said, "Yes, what could be more fun than being with sadistic loonies for eight hours every day?"

He laughed and said, directly to Jas, "Are you going to Katie's party?"

Jas went all pink and white, then sort of pinky-white apart from the tip of her nose which remained red. I must remember to tell her what she looked like. She managed to reply and he said, "Well, I look forward to seeing you there."

Jas was ecstatic. "Did you hear what he said?"

"Yes."

"He said, 'Are you going to Katie's party?'"

"Yes."

"He said, 'Well, I look forward to seeing you there.'"

"Yes."

"He said, 'I look forward to seeing you there.'"

"We've been through this."

"He said, 'I look forward to seeing you there,'... to me. He said 'you' because he meant me."

"Er, Jas."

"Yes?"

"Will you shut up now?"

5:00 p.m.

She didn't though.

Herr Kamyer didn't take us for physics as he has a cold. Double damn. When am I going to have any fun? *Sacré bleu*.

Saturday September 26th

10:00 a.m.

Went for a moody autumn walk with Libby in her pushchair. She was singing, "I am the Queen, oh, I am the Queen." She wouldn't take off the fairy wings that I had made for her. It was a nightmare getting her into the pushchair. The clouds were scudding across the sky but it was quite sunny and crisp. I cheered up enough to join in the singing with Libby. We were both yelling, "I am the Queen, oh, I am the Queen!" and that's when he got out of a red mini. Robbie. The SG. He saw me and said, "Oh hello, we've met before, haven't we?"

I smiled brilliantly, trying to do it without making my

nose spread out over all my face. It's a question of relaxing the mouth, putting the tongue behind the back teeth but slightly flaring the nostrils so that they don't go wild. He looked at me a bit oddly.

"Apples," I said wittily.

"Oh yeah," he said, "the shop, you and your friend."

He smiled again. He was dreamy when he smiled. Then he bent down to Libby who, true to form, gave him one of her scary "I am a crazy child" looks. She said, "I am the queen," and he said, "Are you?" (Ooohhh, he's so lovely to children.)

Then Libby said, "Yes, I am the queen and Georgia did a big poo this morning."

I couldn't believe it. He could not believe it. Nobody could believe it. It was unbelievable, that's why. He stood up quickly and I said, "Er, well, I'd better be going."

And he said, "Yes, see you later."

And I thought, Think Sharon Stone, think Sharon Stone. So I said, "Yes, well I'll probably see you at Katie's party," and he said, "No, I'm not going, I'm doing something else that night."

7:00 p.m.

"Georgia did a big poo..."

7:05 p.m.

"No, I'm not going, I'm doing something else that night."

7:06 p.m.

Does life get any worse?

8:00 p.m.

Yes it does. Dad has just put his head round the door to say, "James is popping over tomorrow. We thought we'd all go to Stanmer Park for the day."

Sunday September 27th

10:00 p.m.

James tried to kiss me!!!

It was disgusting. He's my cousin. It's incest. I can't even think about it or I'll be sick. Erlack erlack.

10:05 p.m.

It was in my room after a *horriblement* day spent tramping

♥

around a bloody park. How old do they think I am? They made me go on a seesaw. I, of course, snagged my new tights.

So a summary of my lovely day out is... I snagged my tights, then I was attacked by my cousin. *Perfectamondo*. In my room!!!

10:07 p.m.
When we got back James and me were listening to records and reading old joke books and suddenly he switched off the light and said, "Shall we play tickly bears?" Tickly bears!! We used to play that when we were about five. One person would be the tickly bear and they would chase the other person and tickle them and, er... that's it. I was so shocked (and also couldn't see a thing in the dark) that I just sort of went "Nnnnnnnnnn". And then he said, "Grr gotcha!" and started tickling me. It was the most embarrassing thing. But it didn't end there – a sort of wet thing touched my face near my nose. I leaped up like a salmon and stumbled for the light. James sort of stood up and then he picked up a joke book and started reading it. So I did as well. Then he got taken home by my dad. The wet

thing on the nose incident was never mentioned. Like the leg.

I don't think I can stand much more of this.

Monday September 28th
11:00 a.m.

At break I told Jas and Jools everything. They went, "Errgghhhlack, that's truly disgusting. Your cousin? That is sad." Jools said that she had actually seen her brother's "how's your father" quite often. She said, "it's quite nice, really, like a mouse." She lives in a world of her own (thank God). Well bless us, Tiny Tim, one and all, I say.

4:15 p.m.

On the way home. I could kill Jas. She's all excited about the party and I might as well not go now. Jackie and Alison caught up with us on the way home. Jackie had so much make-up on. And her hair was all done. As we passed the loos in the park she made us stand lookout whilst she changed out of her school uniform.

"I'm off clubbing," she said from inside the loos, mistaking me for someone who was remotely interested in what she did.

"I didn't think that clubs opened at four thirty," I said.

She called out, "Don't be dim, Ringo." (I hate her. I hate her.) "I'm off to my mate's first to get ready, put my make-up on and everything." Put her make-up on? If she put any more make-up on she'd hardly be able to hold her head up because of the weight.

She emerged in a sort of satin crop top and tight trousers: she looked about twenty-five.

"I've got a date with the DJ at Loveculture – he's so cool. I think he's about thirty but I like mature men."

After they'd gone I walked on with Jas. "Do you think that Jackie has 'done it'?" I asked her. Jas said, "Well, put it this way... is the Queen Mother really, really old?" Sometimes Jas is quite exceptionally mad. Just to prove my point she went on, "Gemma Crawford was telling me that she knows a boy who gives kissing lessons. Do you think we should go before the party?"

I just looked at her. "Jas, are you suggesting that we go to a male prostitute?"

Jas went on, "He only does kissing and you don't pay."

I just tutted.

10:00 p.m.

I lay on my arm until it went numb and then I lifted it (with the non-numb arm) on to my breasts. I wanted to see what it felt like to have a strange hand on them. It was quite nice, but what do I know? I'm too full of strange urges to think properly. Should I wear my bra to the party?

10:05 p.m.

Urgh, it's horrible when the feeling starts coming back into your arm when it's been numb.

11:07 p.m.

Kissing the back of your hand is no good because you can't tell which is which – which is lip and which is hand – so you don't get a proper sensation from either. Do boys have this trouble or do they just know how to do stuff?

11:15 p.m.

No, is the answer, if the "tickly bear" incident is anything to go by.

Tuesday September 29th
8:30 a.m.

Biology, double maths, Froggie and geoggers. *Qu-est ce que le point?*

In my room
6:00 p.m.

What a fiasco. Jackie and Alison decided that today was the day for the Aleisteir Crowley fandango in the 5C form room.

It's amazing how few people stand up to them, including the teachers.

We all trooped up to 5C after second lunch. This in itself is a fiasco – you have to lurk outside the main door until the coast is clear, then dart to the downstairs loo, check if the coast is clear, then leap up the stairs to floor one and so on, up to the fifth floor.

I was shattered by the time I got up there. There were seven of us all in peak condition – i.e. spluttering and coughing. Jackie said we were going to do a black art act of levitation, calling on the dark forces to help us. Oh goodie, we're summoning the devil. What larks.

Why, I thought, oh why am I here? Maybe if we are going

to be forced to commune with the devil I could strike some sort of bargain with him, swap my dad's soul in exchange for bigger breasts for the party on Friday.

Abby Nicols "volunteered" to be the sacrificed one and she had to lie down on a desk. Jackie went at her head and Alison at her feet and then the rest of us spread out evenly around her. Jackie said, "Please be very quiet and concentrate, we are summoning dark forces. Put one finger of each hand underneath Abby's body and then we will begin."

We all did as we were told. Then Jackie shut her eyes and started chanting in a low, husky voice, "She's looking poorly. She's looking poorly," and we all had to repeat it after her one by one round the desk. Then she said, "She's looking worse. She's looking worse. She's looking ill. She's looking ill."

Actually, she was looking a bit peaky by this time. It went on for about five minutes as Abby's condition deteriorated. Finally Jackie whispered, "She's dying. She's dying..." We all repeated it. "She's dead. She's dead." She certainly did not look at all well and she was as stiff as a board. I couldn't see her breathing.

Then Jackie said, "Help us, oh master, to send Abby

Nicols upwards." And then she said, "Lift her up," and it was really freaky-deaky because I just slightly lifted with my two fingers and she sort of rose up really easily as if she was light as a feather. She was right above our heads. It was weird.

After a couple of minutes we all simultaneously got the jitters and let her down really heavily on to the desk. This seemed to perk her up a bit, because as we ran out I heard her saying, "I think I've broken my bottom."

11:00 p.m.
I woke up with a start because I heard the bedroom door open. It just opened by itself...

Wednesday September 30th
7:30 a.m.
I can't move my head from side to side because I sat up in bed all night and I have cricked it now.

1:00 p.m.
Gemma said her friend Peter Dyer, the professional kisser, is going to be around tomorrow after school. All you have to do is go to his house and knock on the door after four thirty

and before six thirty when his parents get home. Apparently it's first come first served. Has it come to this? No it has not.

9:30 p.m.
Had to discuss again with Jas what she is going to wear on Friday. She can go in the nuddy-pants for all I care.

Tainted love

Thursday October 1st

4:30 p.m.

For some reason I found myself outside Peter Dyer's house and knocking on his door. Ellen and Jas, Jools, Patty, Sarah and Mabs were all hiding behind the hedge at the bottom of the garden. What is the matter with me? I am DESPERATE – that's what the matter is.

I didn't know whether to wear lipstick or not. I don't know what the point would be if it was just going to come off... What am I saying?

4:31 p.m.

Peter opened the door. He's about seventeen and blond, sort of sleepy-looking, not unattractive in a sort of Boyzone way. I notice he is chewing gum. I hope he takes it out, otherwise

I might choke to death. There is muffled giggling from behind the hedge. Peter hears it but doesn't seem fazed.

"Do you want to come in – er – what's your name?"

I say, "Georgia," (damn, I meant to say a false name) and we go into his house.

He has tight blue jeans on and there are those tinkly things that the Japanese have outside the doors. (Not on his jeans, obviously – on the door.) You know... wind chimes. Why do they do that? It's such an annoying noise and do you really need to know that the wind is blowing? We're doing Japan in geography and to annoy Hawkeye I have memorised the islands. Hokkaido, Honshu... er, well, I nearly have. I did it last year with Northern Ireland, and reciting the counties (you remember them by the mnemonic FAT LAD – Fermanagh, Antrim, Tyrone, Londonderry, Armagh, Down) can be very impressive to trot out when you are accused of not concentrating.

Oh-oh, we are going up the stairs to Peter's room. He hasn't said a word. His room is much tidier than mine. He has made his bed, for a start. On the walls are posters of Denise van Outen and Miss December, and so on. On my walls there's a poster of Reeves and Mortimer showing their bottoms and a group shot of the cast of *Dad's Army*. Is this the big difference between girls and boys? Is this... oh-oh, Peter is sitting on his bed.

"Do you want to sit down?" he says, patting the bed.

I think, No thanks, I would rather put my head in a bag of eels, but I say, "OK," and sit down.

He puts his arm round me. I think of putting my arm round him like a hilarious Morecambe and Wise joke but I don't because I remember the stuffed olive incident. Then, with his other hand, Peter turns my face towards his. It's a good job he didn't try that yesterday when I had rigor mortis of the head. Then he says, "Close your eyes and relax."

9:00 p.m.
Phew, I suppose I am a woman now. Libby doesn't seem to realise as she has made me wear her deely-boppers to bed. She is insisting I am a huge bee. If I say, "Look, it's your bedtime now," she just goes, "Bzzzz bzzz," and looks cross.

I have to say, "Bz bz bzzy buzz buzz," and point at her bed with my feelers before she will go.

When I got home neither Mum nor Dad seemed to notice the change in me. Mind you, I'd have to walk in with my head under my arm before Dad would get out of his chair. He's getting very chunky. I may mention it in a caring way. Anyway, as I said, phew.

When I closed my eyes Peter said, "We're going to do an ordinary kiss first." Then he kissed me. We started off with number one kissing, which is just lips, not moving. He said I was a natural, not too "firm" or toothy, which is apparently very common.

He told me how to know which side to go to (you sort of watch where the boy is going and then you fit in). Then we did a bit of movement and he told me what to do with my hands (waist is safest).

Oh, we got through a lot in half an hour. We did a bit of tongues, which was the bit I was most scared of, but actually it wasn't too bad, a bit like a little lizard tongue darting about. Cute really, in a bizarre way. The main thing to do is to strike a happy balance between "yielding" and "giving". Peter says you can take a horse to water but you can't make it kiss properly.

At the end of the session (he had a little alarm clock) he shook my hand and saw me to the door. I passed Mabs on the way out – it was her turn. I was glad that I had gone first. Jools and Ellen and Jas tried to pump me on the way home but I said, in a dignified sort of way, "I think I'd just like to think about this for a while, if you don't mind. *Bòn soir.*"

10:45 p.m.
Hahahahahahahaha. I'm a natural.

Friday October 2nd
4:00 p.m.
Party time!!! I don't know why I'm so excited as SG is not even going to be there. But maybe I'll be able to try out my new snogging skills.

Jackie Mathews has got a huge lovebite on her neck. She's put about six centimetres of concealer on it and is wearing a scarf... how inconspicuoso!! It's HUGE! What has she been snogging with – a calf? I think it is so common. Why would you let someone bite you?

The day dragged by. I really am going to complain about

Miss Stamp – she should be working in a prison. I'm sure she has done before. Even though it was icy outside she insisted that in our games period we ran round the hockey pitch. You could see your breath. She found Jackie and Alison hiding in the showers having a fag and made them change into their sports knickers and do the circuit twice. Which is almost a reason to have her as a teacher. It was hilarious! Jackie might look OK when she's all dolled up in some dark nightclub, but you should see her from behind in big navy knickers!!

4:15 p.m.
Only three hours to get ready and made up before I meet Jas, Jools and Ellen and the gang at the clock tower. We're going to arrive together. Dad is insisting on picking me up at midnight. It's useless arguing with him, he'll only say, "You're lucky, in my day... blah blah blah," and then we'll be back in the Middle Ages or the seventies as he calls it.

7:30 p.m.
Meet the gang. We look like a group of funeral directors going out for a drink. Black is our new black. Katie

Steadman's house is quite posh – she has her own room as well as a bedroom. Shagpile carpets all rolled up round the walls, for dancing.

When we arrived there were about thirty people there already, including Tom. Cue Jas going all dithery and daft. He was in a group but he came over to talk to us straight away. I left Jas to it and circulated. It was good fun. I had a mad dancing phase for about an hour. I suppose I was vaguely looking for substitute snoggers for SG, but all the boys seemed a bit on the nice but goofy side. There were one or two most unfortunate skin complaints. I feel lucky just getting the odd lurker – some people looked like they had mountain ranges of spots on their faces... and some down their backs too... *Au secours!!!!*

Then I saw Peter Dyer. I waved at him and he came over. He had been talking to Katie Steadman and she seemed a bit miffed when he came over to me. Peter said, "Hi!" and I said, "Hi... er... thanks for the other day. It was really... er... great. I learned a lot. Thanks."

He looked at me sideways and stood quite close. "There was something I didn't have time to show you, come with me." And he took hold of my hand and led me out of the room. We hadn't done hand-holding but I improvised... not too floppy but not too gripping. I don't think anyone besides Katie saw us go, they were too busy dancing stupidly to a Slade record.

We went outside into the garden and went behind a big tree just by the path. Peter started kissing me (he didn't seem to be a big talker).

There was a lot more tongue business. It was all right but it was making my jaw ache a bit. Peter seemed to like it quite a lot more than I did because he sort of moaned and pushed me against the tree. Then Peter started nuzzling my neck and I thought, Oh, we haven't done necks before, he's branching out a bit, and then I nearly choked to death trying not to laugh (up against a tree... branching out, do you get it?)... but I stopped myself. You have to keep reminding yourself about boys not liking a laugh. Then I heard a car door slam and people crunching up the drive towards us.

I stepped backwards but Peter was still attached to my neck. I tripped over a root and fell on to my bottom. Peter lost his balance and fell over on top of me and made us both go "Ooofff!". From upside down I found myself looking up at a tall blonde girl I recognised from the sixth form and, next to her... SG. He was all in black and looked really annoyed.

He said all tight-lipped, "Don't you think it's about time you two went inside to the party?" I remembered the blonde's name, it was Lindsay, a notorious wet. She was looking at my legs. Probably envying them. I looked down, and noticed that my skirt had all ridden up and you could see my knickers. I wriggled it down in a "dignity at all times" sort of way, but she still smirked.

Peter said quite calmly, "Hi, Robbie, I thought you had a gig tonight."

Robbie said, "I have, but Tom forgot his key so I'm just dropping it off for him."

He didn't even glance at me or say goodbye or anything.

Midnight

I bloody hate him, big, full-of-himself type thing. Bugger bugger, double *ordure* and *merde*. What business is it of his what I do behind trees?

Tuesday October 6th
3:00 p.m.

Peter phoned me over the weekend. I don't know how he got the number because I just left in a hurry from the party. Gemma must have given it to him. Dad answered the phone, which is the end of life as we know it because HE WILL NOT LET IT LIE. He thinks it is funny and calls Peter "Your fancy man."

Peter wanted to know if I would go to the pictures next week. I said that would be great. So it looks like I have sort of got a boyfriend. Why do I feel so depressed then?

Jas is unbearable since the party. She sent me notes all through Maths.

Dear Gee-gee,

Tom is sooooo cool. He walked me home and then, when we got to the door, he gave me a really nice kiss on the cheek. His lips are really soft and he smells nice, not like my brother. He asked for my phone number – do you think he will call? What day do you think he will call?

It's Monday today and I saw him on Friday so

that is three days already. I'd call tonight if I was him, wouldn't you? Should I say yes to any day he says for a date? Or if he says Friday should I say, "Oh, sorry, I'm busy that night, and then when he says "What about Saturday?" I can say "Oh, yeah, Saturday would be cool." What do you think? Or do you think he might think I'm putting him off if I say I'm busy on Friday, so I should say yes to any day he says? Please reply quickly.
TTFN.

I've given her my worst look but she keeps sending things. I am not interested in any of the prat family Jennings.

4:00 p.m.

Sadly it makes no difference to Jas whether I am interested or not. All the way home she was telling me what Tom said or did. The more I hear about him the less I think Jas should have to do with him. All right, maybe I am being unfair and bitter, but she is my best friend and should do everything I say...

Tom wants to go into the fruit and veg business. Oh, how fascinating... Jas thinks it is.

"I think it's great that he's young but he knows where he is going."

I said brightly, "Yes, you'd never be short of potatoes."

Eventually even Jas noticed that I wasn't so keen. She looked a bit confused and said, "I thought you liked him."

I didn't say anything. All I could think of was his brother looking down at me and sort of sneering. Jas went on, "Don't you think I should go out with him?"

I still didn't say anything.

She said it again. "So you don't think I should go out with him?"

I was all enigmatic, which is not easy in a beret.

11:30 p.m.

I am a facsimile of a sham of a fax of a person. And I have a date with a professional snogger.

Midnight

Angus has eaten some of Mum's knickers. She says he'll have to go. Why can't she go, and Dad go? Or am I being unreasonable?

Thursday October 15th

Noon

Slim has put a ban on levitation. She made an announcement in assembly this morning. She was all shaky and jelly-like, her jowls were bouncing around like anything. Anyway, she said, "This school is like the back streets of Haiti. It must stop forthwith. Any girl found practising levitation will face the gravest consequences. I, for one, would not like to be in that girl's shoes."

I whispered to Ellen, "She wouldn't get in any girl's shoes. How much do you think each leg weighs? Imagine the size of her knickers... you could probably get two duvets out of them."

Then we got the eagle eye from Hawkeye for giggling.

2:00 p.m.

I feel like killing something. If I was that sort of person I'd scare a first former, as it is I will have to content myself with hiding Nauseating P. Green's pencil case.

3:00 p.m.

On my way to the science block I saw Lindsay. How wet can you be? She really is Mrs Wet. She has the wettest haircut known to humanity – all curled under at the bottom. I saw her legs in hockey and they are really spindly. Little spindly legs like she has been in a wheelchair and not been walking for years, and also when she is concentrating she wears big goggly glasses like Deirdre Barlow. I bet she keeps those well hidden when she goes out with Pratboy. Oh, hell's teeth, it's my "date" in four hours. The horrible thing is that I don't want to go. I just don't. There's nothing wrong with him or anything. I just can't be bothered somehow.

My bedroom
Midnight
I wish I'd never started this snogging business. I feel like I've been attacked by whelks. I can't see Peter any more. Why is he so keen on me, anyway? I haven't had a chance to say more than, "Er, what are you doing at GCSE...?" before I'm attacked by the whelks again. I can't go out with him any more. How can I tell him, though?

1:00 a.m.
I'll make Jas do it.

Friday October 16th
9:00 p.m.
What a week!

I got Jas to dump Peter for me. I said for her to let him down gently, so she told him that I had a personal problem. He asked what, and she said that I thought I was a lesbian. Cheers, Jas.

Monday October 19th
4:00 p.m.
It's all round school that I'm a lesbian. In games we were in the changing room and Miss Stamp came in to change out of her gear. Suddenly everyone had disappeared, leaving me on my own with her. She really has got a moustache. Does she not notice?

Friday October 23rd
8:00 p.m.
Tom phoned Jas and they're going on a "date" to watch Robbie's band. The band is called The Stiff Dylans. I bet it's crap. I bet it's *merde*. I bet it's double *merde*.

Mum and Dad were talking in the kitchen and when I

came in they stopped and looked all shifty. Don't get me wrong, I like it when they shut up when I come in, well I would like it if it had ever happened before. Mum said, "Have you ever thought you'd like to see a bit more of the world, Gee?" and I said, "If you're thinking of trying to persuade me to visit Auntie Kath in Blackpool for Christmas, you can forget it."

I can be hilariously cutting when I try.

10:00 p.m.
No matter from what angle you look at it, I do have a huge, squishy nose.

I wonder if Mum would pay for me to have plastic surgery...? If I went to the doctor and said it was psychologically damaging, to the extent that I couldn't go out or do my homework, I wonder if I could have it done on the NHS?

Then I remember to have a reality check... I don't have the George Clooney-type doctor from *ER* – the caring, incredibly good-looking face of medicine. I've got Dr Wallace, the incredibly fat, red, uncaring face of medicine. It's hard enough getting an aspirin out of him when you've got flu.

11:00 p.m.

Jas rang. She had a great time with Tom.

"Did he bring you a present, a bunch of leeks or something?" I asked meanly but Jas refused to come down from cloud nine.

She said, "No, but he's a brilliant dancer. The Stiff Dylans were ace. Robbie is a cool singer."

I had to ask in a masochistic way. "Was Lindsay there?"

Jas said, "Yes, she was, she's quite nice really, she had her hair up."

I was furious with Jas for being so disloyal and said, "Oh, it's nice that you've made new friends. I can't help thinking though, that as Lindsay's BEST friend you could advise her that people with massive ears should not wear their hair up."

I put the phone down on her.

Midnight
Qu-est ce que le point?

Monday October 26th
7:00 p.m.

I've been ignoring Jas. It's tiring, but someone has to do it.

Thursday October 29th

In Slim's office today for a bit of a talking-to. Honestly, she has no sense of humour whatsoever.

The main difficulty is that she imagines we are at school to learn stuff and we know we are at school to fill in the idle hours before we go home and hang around with our mates doing important things. Life skills, like make-up and playing records and trapping boys.

Anyway, it was just one more little, trivial thing.

We had to have our school photo taken, all of the fourth form and the teachers together. Even including Herr Kamyer, the rogue male. Ellen and Jas, Jools and Rosie Mees and me were all in the back row because we are the tallest. Well, we've started this new craze which is based around those old TV puppet shows *Stingray* and *Supercar*. Rosie has all the old videos which we watch. We know all the key phrases like "Fire retro rockets" and "Calling International Rescue". And we walk around all stiffly like we are being worked (badly) by puppeteers. At the moment we are concentrating on Marina Aquamarina. She was part of an underwater kingdom, well her dad was the king of it, but they were being threatened by these horrible fish people (no they didn't wear codpieces but it would have been excellent if they did).

Anyway, Marina Aquamarina floated around underwater with her blonde hair trailing behind her and her arms all flopping by her side. All the boys really liked her, especially because she was dumb – when anyone spoke to her she just blinked in an appealingly dumb way. So anyway, when we are being Marina Aquamarina, as well as floating around with our arms by our sides we are not allowed to speak, just shake our heads and blink. So, for instance, if a prefect said, "Where is your beret?" you could only blink and stare and then float off quickly.

But then there is phase two, which is pretending to be a little boy in *Supercar* called Jimmy. Jimmy has a very upturned nose with freckles on it. Obviously you could just put your finger on your nose and force the tip back to get the snub nose effect but a more sophisticated method is to use egg boxes. You take one of the bits that the egg fits in and paint some nostrils on it, and some freckles, and Bob's your uncle. Pop it on some elastic and put it over your own nose. *Voilà l'enfant Jimmy!!*

So when we had the school photo done, Rosie, Ellen, Julia, Jas and me all had our Jimmynoses on. When you see the photo you don't actually notice at first, but then, when you look closely, you can see that five girls at the back all have snub noses with freckles. Bloody funny in anyone's language. Not Slim's, though. She was all of a quiver.

"Do you know how costly it is to have these photographs done? No you do not, you silly girls. Do you know how ridiculous you make yourselves and the school seem? No, you seem not to know these obvious things."

Forty years later we got let out. Our punishment is that we have to pick up all the litter in the school grounds. That should please Mr Attwood, the school caretaker. Revenge on us because we call him Elvis. He's only about one hundred and nine and the most boring, bad-tempered man in the universe, apart from my dad. I really don't know what is the matter with him lately (my dad), he's always hanging around, looking at me. Oh well, incest seems to run in my family. (That's quite a good joke, actually.)

A bit of rough

Thursday November 5th
7:00 p.m.

I hate November the fifth. On the way to school it was a nightmare of jumping-jacks and bangers. Boys are obsessed with loud noises and frightening people. I saw Peter Dyer (whelk boy) but he ignored me and also said something to his mate. He's going out with Katie Steadman now – she's welcome. I wonder if he will be my first and last boyfriend? Jas and I are talking again, which is a shame because all she wants to do is talk about Tom. She's miffed because he has to work in the shop all weekend. I said, "Well, that's what happens in the fruit and veg trade, Jas, you will always be second fiddle to his *légumes*." For once, she didn't argue back.

7:30 p.m.

Angus loves Bonfire Night. The dog next door has to be locked in a padded cell it's so frightened, but Angus loves it. He chases the rockets – he probably thinks they are grouse on fire. There's a big bonfire out on the backfields, all the street is going. I'm not, though, because I know that firelight emphasises my nose. I could wear a hat, I suppose. Is that my life, then, going around wearing a hat? No, I'll just stay in my bedroom and watch other people having fun through the window.

10:00 p.m.

Brilliant bonfire!!! I love Bonfire Night. I had baked potatoes and got chatted up by a boy from up the street. He looks a bit like Mick Jagger (although not, of course, eighty). He said, "See you around," when I left to come home. I think he might go to the thick boys' school but, hey ho, he can be my bit of rough. Snigger snigger.

Angus is curled up on my bed, which means I can't straighten my legs, but I daren't move him. He's got a singed ear and his whiskers are burnt off but he's purring.

Wednesday November 11th
4:20 p.m.

Jas comes round for a bit of a "talk" after school. I make her my special milky coffee drink. She starts to moan on. "Tom is going to be working again this weekend."

I said, "Well, I told you, it's a family business." I felt like a very wise person and also I seemed to have turned into a Jewess. I've never said "family business" in my life. *Ay vay*.

Jas didn't seem to notice my sudden Jewishness, she just raved on, "I don't know, I mean, I really, really like him but I want to have fun... I don't want to have to be all serious and think about the future and never go out."

I'd really got into the swing of my new role now. "Look, Jas, you're intelligent (see what I mean? I could say these things without any hint of sarcasm), you're a good-looking young girl, the world is at your feet. Do you want to end up with a fruit and veg man? Stay with him and the next thing you know you'll have five children and be up at dawn arguing about cabbages. Look what happened to my mum," I said meaningfully.

Jas had been following me up until that point but then

she said, "What did happen to your mum?" and I said, "She got Dad."

Jas said, "I see what you mean."

Monday November 16th
4:10 p.m.

Jas has finished with Tom. She came in all ashen-faced and swollen-eyed this morning. I had to wait until break to talk to her.

We went to the tennis courts even though it was bloody freezing. I refuse to wear a vest, though. I'm going to persevere with my bra, even if it does bunch up. I think my breasts are definitely growing. Fondling is supposed to make them bigger. Melanie Griffiths must do nothing but fondle hers, they're gigantic. Anyway, Jas told me the whole thing about Tom and how she has now become a dumper.

(Verb to dump: I dump, you dump, he/she/it dumps etc.)

Jas said, "He was upset and angry at the same time. He said he thought we were good together."

Jas looked as if she was about to cry again so I put my arm round her. Then I took it away quickly – I don't want to start the lesbian rumour again. I said, "Jas, there's plenty of other boys. You deserve better than a greengrocer with a horrible bigger brother."

10:00 p.m.
Oh dear God, Jas on the phone again. Has she done the right thing? etc. etc. etc... I must get her interested in someone else.

Thursday November 19th
8:00 p.m.
Drama drama!!!

We had a substitute teacher today for biology. No, I don't mean substitute, I mean reserve, no, I don't mean that, I mean... oh anyway, a student teacher. She was very nervous and short-sighted and we'd all got that mad bug that you get some days and we couldn't stop laughing. The student teacher, Miss Idris, asked me to hand out pipettes or something and I tried to get up, only to find that Ellen and Jools had tied my Science overall tapes to the drawer handles.

They were helpless with laughter and so couldn't undo them. It took me ages to get free. Then Rosie wrote a note:

This is the plan – Operation Movio Deskio. Whenever Miss Idris writes on the board we all shift our desks back a couple of centimetres, really quietly.

By the end of the lesson when she looked round from the board we were all squashed up against the back wall and there was a three metre gap in front of her. We were speechless with laughing. She just blinked through her glasses and didn't say anything.

Then it happened. Jas and I got to the school gate and Robbie was there. For one moment I thought he had realised that it was ME ME ME he wanted and not old dumbo, but he gave me a HORRIBLE look as I passed by. I said to Jas, "Did you see that? What's he got against me? All right, he's seen my knickers, but it's not a hanging offence."

Jas went a bit red. I said, "Do you know something I don't?"

And she said nervously, in a rush, "Well, erm, maybe. I think he's a bit cross, because Tom's upset we're not going out and I said it was partly because I'd spoken to you and you had said I really shouldn't go out with someone in a fruit and veg shop because it was not really good enough for

♡ 103

me. Well, you did say that."

I got hold of her by her tie. "You said *what*????!!!"

She just blinked and went pink and white.

Midnight

I CANNOT BELIEVE IT. Stabbed in the back by my so-called best friend. It was never like this in the Famous Five books. No wonder Robbie is so moody and stroppy with me.

Monday November 23rd
4:15 p.m.

Terrible day. Jackie "suggested" that we do something to pass the time in German, whilst Herr Kamyer amused himself declining verbs on the blackboard. (What a stupid language German is, you have to wait until the end of the sentence to find out what the verb is. But my attitude by then is, Who cares?? I think I might start calling my father Vater and my mum Mutter just for a change. Vati and Mutti, for short.)

Anyway, Jackie said we should mark each other out of ten for physical attractiveness. The list was skin, hair, eyes, nose, figure, mouth, teeth. You had to write out the list and put your name on the top of the paper and then pass it round to everyone to give you a mark. It was Jackie, Alison, Jas, Rosie, Jules, Ellen and Beth Morgan. I didn't want to do it but you don't say no to Jackie. I more or less gave everyone near top marks for everything... even in the face of obvious evidence to the contrary. For instance, I gave Beth seven for her teeth – my logic was that they might be nice when the front ones grow back in, you never know. All the marks were given anonymously. Then we got our papers back with the marks listed.

My list was:

skin	7	8	8	7	8	8	7
hair	8	8	8	8	8	8	8
eyes	7	8	8	8	8	8	8
nose	4	3	3	0	4	4 1/4	4
figure	7	6	7	7	7	7 1/2	7
mouth	6	6	6	6	5	6 1/3	6
teeth	8	8	9	9	8	9	9

Someone gave me a nought for my nose!!! I got the lowest marks out of anyone. My best feature was my teeth! Jas had got mostly eights for all of her features and so she was in that really annoying mood when you've done quite well in an exam and it makes you sort of "kind" to people who haven't done as well. We compared marks on the way home.

"You've got more marks for your mouth than me, Jas. What's wrong with mine? Why is yours so much better? Did you give me six and a third? That looks like your handwriting."

She was squirming a bit by now. "Does it?... No, I don't think it is."

Then I had her. "Well, if it's not that one you must have given me even less than that."

She backed down. "Oh yes, actually, yes, that is my writing, yes."

I was livid. "What is wrong with my mouth?"

"Nothing, that's why I've given you six and a third."

"But that's only average."

"Well, I know I would have given you more, because I think that it's definitely seven or even an eight when it's closed."

"When it's closed," I said dangerously.

Jas was as red as two beetroots. "Well, I had to consider things overall. You see, it's your smile."

"What about my smile?"

"Well when you smile, because your mouth is so big..."

"Yes, do go on..."

"Well, it sort of splits your face in half and it, well, it spreads your nose out more."

7:00 p.m.

In my room in front of the mirror. Practising smiling without making my nose spread. It's impossible. I must never smile again.

8:00 p.m.

Phoned Jas.

"Jas, you only gave me seven and a half for my figure, and I gave you eight for yours."

"Well?"

"Well I only gave you eight because you are my friend."

"Well I only gave you seven and a half because you are my friend. I was going to give you seven."

Midnight

How dare Jas only give me – what was it? – eight for my eyes? I gave her eight for hers and she has got stupid brown eyes.

1:00 a.m.

That stupid Morgan can only have given me four, three or nought for my nose. I gave her six and a half for hers and I was being very bloody generous when I did.

What is the point of being a nice person?

Thursday November 26th
9:00 p.m.

Vati dropped a bombshell today – he is going on a trip to NEW ZEALAND because M and D are thinking of going to live there! I don't know why they bother to tell me. I don't really see what it has to do with me. It was just as I was on the dash to school and Vati said, "Georgia, I don't know if you have heard anything but there's been a lot of redundancies at my place."

I said, "Vati, don't tell me you are going to have to go on the dole with students, and so on. You could always sell your apron if we get too short of money."

Monday November 30th
4:20 p.m.

Jas still moping about Tom. We have to avoid "his" part of town now. I hope I'm not going mad but Rosie told me that she draws stuff on the roof of her mouth with her tongue. Like a heart or a little house. I said she was bonkers but now I've started doing it.

5:00 p.m.

Bumped into the boy up the street I met at Bonfire Night. We sat on our wall for a bit. It's funny, he's one of the only lads I don't feel like I should rush off and cover myself in make-up for. I don't even flick my hair so that it covers half my face (and therefore half my nose). Dad says if I keep doing it I will go blind in one eye, and also that it makes me look like a Pekinese, but what does he know? And anyway, it won't bother him in New Zealand.

Bonfire Boy is called Mark and I suppose the reason I'm not too self-conscious in front of him is that he has a HUGE mouth. I mean it, like Mick Jagger. He is about seventeen and he goes to Parkway, the rough school. He's mad about football and he and his mates go play on the park. I think

♡ 109

I've seen them when I've "accidentally" taken Angus for a walk up there. He's sort of quite attractive (Mark, not Angus), despite the mouth. He wants to be a footballer and has got a trial somewhere. When I left he said, "See you later." Oh no, here we go again, on the "See you later" trail.

9:00 p.m.
Saw Mark walking down the street with his mates. He looked round and up at my bedroom window so I had to bob down quickly. I hope he didn't see me because I had an avocado mask on and my hair Sellotaped down to keep my fringe straight. I wonder where he is going? He had trainers and joggerbums on.

10:30 p.m.
Heard Mutti and Vati arguing. Oh perfect, now they'll split up and they'll both want custody of me.

10:40 p.m.
If I go with Mum I will have access to make-up, clothes, and so on, and I can usually persuade her to let me stay out later.

She laughs at my jokes and goes out a lot. On the other hand, there is Vati.

10:42 p.m.
Ah well, bye bye, Vati...

The Stiff Dylans gig

Tuesday December 1st
11:00 a.m.

Mucho excitemondo! There is going to be a Christmas dance at Foxwood school. Slim announced it in assembly.

"Girls, there is to be a dance at Foxwood school, to celebrate Christmas, on December 12th, commencing at seven thirty."

It was like something out of *Four at Mallory Towers*. Me and Rosie and Jas and Ellen went "Oooohhhhhhhhhhhhhhh ooohhhhhhh!" for so long that Slim had to say "Settle, girls". At last she went on, "To add to the festivities there will be a... band." We started doing our "ooohhhhing" again but Hawkeye glared at us so viciously we stopped.

I had thought of shouting "Three cheers for the Headmaster of Foxwood, and three for Merry England!" but I didn't.

Slim still hadn't finished. "The band will be The Stiff Dylans."

Lunchtime
12:30 p.m.
Jas and me had a confab by the vending machine. Jas said, "Do you think we should go? I mean, Lindsay will be there, and Tom might... well, he might go with someone else and then we'd be like..."

"Two spare wotsits at a wedding?" I suggested.

4:00 p.m.
The most cringe-making thing in the Universe of Cringe-making Things happened this afternoon in RE. It was with Miss Wilson, who is not what you might call normal (still, who would be – teaching RE?). She is a very unfortunate person, with ginger hair in a sad bob, her tights are always wrinkly, plus she wears tragic cardigans, usually done up the wrong way. She is not blessed in the looks department, but worse than this, she has not got a personality – at all – none.

Mostly she just talks and we get on with writing notes to each other or filing our nails. Last summer Rosie was so relaxed that she started moisturising her legs during RE. It was so hot that we hadn't been wearing stockings and Rosie put her legs on the desk and started putting cream on them. Well, even Miss Wilson noticed that. I remember she said, "Rosie, you'd better buck up your ideas and buck them up fast." Which struck us as very funny indeed – we were still laughing hours later.

Anyway, this afternoon, for some reason, Miss Wilson got talking about personal hygiene. I swear I don't know how she got there from religious education, maybe people in ancient Hebrew times cast someone out for being a smelly leper. I don't know.

We just heard her say, "Yes, girls, I know how that person felt because when I was younger I had a BO problem myself and people used to avoid me. I never used to wash because I was an orphan and depressed... We just sat there staring at our desks whilst she went on and on about her body odour... it was AWFUL. I have never been so glad to get up and go to PE.

We all ran screaming into the showers and washed ourselves like loonies. Miss Stamp was amazed, she usually has to prod us and shout at us to get us to change at all in winter. She came and looked at us in the shower in amazement. Then we remembered she is a lesbian. So we ran screaming out of the shower.

It's a bloody nightmare of pervs, this school. You'd be safer in Borstal.

8:00 p.m.
Jas came over for the night. We yattered on about a plan for the school dance.

9:00 p.m.
Looking through my bedroom window to see if we could see into next door's bedroom window because I wanted to know what Mr Next Door wore to bed. Jas thought jimjams but I thought shortie nightshirt.

Then as we were looking we saw Mark (Bonfire Boy) coming up the street with a girl. They stopped under a lamppost but I couldn't see what she looked like as they were kissing. Not in the shadows or anything, but under the lamp. We couldn't stop watching and to get a better view we got up on to the window ledge. It was a tight squeeze but you could see everything. Then I heard tip tap tip tap and

Libby came in, carrying her blanket (or blankin' as she calls it – it's not actually a blanket, it's an old bra of Mum's but she likes it and won't let it go. It must have been white once but now it's a horrible grey colour).

She spotted us on the window ledge and said, "Libby see."

I said, "No, Libby, I'm coming down," but then she started saying, "No, no, bad boy, bad boy... me see," and hitting me with her blankin' so that I had to lift her up. Honestly, I'm bullied by a three-year-old and a Scottish wildcat.

I lifted her up and she snuggled down in between me and Jas. She spotted the couple under the lamppost. "Oohh, look! Manlady manlady!!! Hahahaha." It was a bit difficult knowing where Mark ended and the girl began but all was revealed when Mark stopped kissing and looked over her shoulder. Right up at my window. I don't know if he could see us in the dark but we got down from the window ledge so quickly we fell on to my bed. Libby said, "More bouncy now!!!"

Pray God Mark didn't see us spying.

Wednesday December 2nd

8:30 a.m.

Dashing out of the house, Jas and I almost fell into Mark, waiting by the corner. Jas (big pal) said she had to run to her house first and she would see me at school. I went a bit red and walked on with him walking beside me. He said, "Have you got a boyfriend?"

I was speechless. What is the right answer to that question? I tell you what the right answer is... a lie, that's the right answer. So I said, "I've just come out of a heavy thing and I'm giving myself a bit of space."

He looked at me. He really did have the biggest gob I have ever seen. "So is that no?"

And I just stood there and then this really weird thing happened... he touched my breast!!! I don't mean he ripped my blouse off, he just rested his hand on the front of my breast. Just for a second, before he turned and went off to school.

12:30 p.m.

What does it mean when a boy rests his hand on your breast? Does it mean he has the mega-horn? Or was his hand just tired?

4:30 p.m.

Why am I even thinking about this? No sign of Mark (the breast molester) when I got home, thank goodness.

4:45 p.m.

Still, you would think if a boy rests his hand on your breast he might bother to see you sometime.

5:00 p.m.

Up in my bedroom "doing my homework" when the doorbell rang. I put down my magazine and answered it. It was Mark. He said, "I've dumped Ella, do you want to go to The Stiff Dylans gig?"

I said, "Er, well, er, yes thanks."

He said, "OK, see you later."

6:00 p.m.

On the phone to Jas, telling her about Mark, I said, "So then I said, 'Er, yes,' and he said, 'OK, see you later.'"

Jas said, "See you later – what does that mean?"

I said, "I don't know – who does know?... See me later tonight, or at the gig, or what?"

Jas said, "Well, do you like him?"

I thought about it. "I don't really know. He makes me feel like a cobra, you know, all sort of funny and paralysed when the bloke starts playing the bugle thing."

Jas said, "What do you mean? Your head starts bobbing around when he plays his instrument?"

I said, "Don't start, Jas. Anyway, what do you think of him?"

Jas thought. "He's got a very big mouth."

I said, "Yes, I know," and then she said, "But then so have you."

Midnight

Oh-oh. What to do. Why is life so complicated? Do I like Mark? Why did I say yes? Why can't Robbie realise that Lindsay is a drippy git? Ohhhhhhh. *Quel dommage!!! Merde.* Poo.

Monday December 7th
5:00 p.m.

Mark sent a note, which is quite sweet, except that it is very badly written:

Dear Georgia,

Away training till Saturday. Meet you at 8 at clock tower on Saturday.

Mark.

That's it, then. I have no choice. I have to go with him.

9:00 p.m.

Mum comes into my room and says will I come down for a "talk"? I pray it's nothing to do with personal hygiene or her and Dad's relationship problems. Dad seems a bit nervous and he's growing a moustache, how ridiculous, it looks like some small animal is just having a bit of a sleep on his top lip. He says, "Look, Georgie, you're a young woman now (what was I before? a young horse?) and I don't think there should be any secrets in our house (on the contrary, Vati, you will never know about the hand on the breast scenario even if hell freezes over), which is why I need to tell you that as work is so hard to find here in England I am flying off to Auckland straight after Christmas. I'll be staying there for a month or two to get a feel for the place and to try a new job opening there. Then, when I get settled, your mum and you and Libbs can come out and see what you think."

I said, "I know what I think of New Zealand, I have seen *Neighbours*."

Mum said, "Well, that's set in Australia."

What is this, a family crisis or a geography test? I went on patiently, "My point is, Mutti and Vati, that it is very far away, I'm not from there, all my friends are here. Or to put it another way: I would rather let Noel Edmonds adopt me than set foot on New Zealand soil."

We argued for ages – even Libby came down and joined in. She had dressed Angus up in her pyjamas and he had a bonnet on and a dummy in. I don't know how she gets away with it; if I went anywhere near him with a bonnet he would have my hand off.

Midnight
So Vati is off to New Zealand. But that still doesn't solve what I am going to be wearing for The Stiff Dylans gig.

Friday December 11th
2:50 p.m.
Christmas fever has set in at school. We all wore silver

antlers in physics this afternoon. Herr Kamyer tried to join in with the joke by saying, "Oh *ja*, jingle bells, jingle bells." It's pathetic really. Also, why are his trousers so short? You can see acres of pale, hairy ankle between his trousers and his plaid socks. (Yes, I did say plaid socks, now that is not just sad, it's double sad.)

8:00 p.m.
Mutti and Vati strangely quiet and nice to each other. I saw Dad put his arms round Mum in the kitchen. Also Libby was singing, "Dingle balls, dingle balls, dingle on the way," and Dad got all sort of wet round the eyes. Honestly, I thought he was going to cry, which would have been horrific. He picked her up and hugged her really hard. Libby was furious, she called him "Bad, big uggy, bad," and stuck her finger in his eye which made him cry properly.

Saturday December 12th
The Stiff Dylans!
7:00 a.m.
Damn, I didn't mean to wake up so early. Still, it gives me lots of time to get ready for tonight. I thought first of all I

would do my yoga, which I haven't been able to fit into my busy schedule.

7:20 a.m.
Now I know why I don't bother with yoga – it's too hard, that's why. When I did "dog pose" I thought I'd never be able to get up again. I'll just have a lie down and relax with an uplifting book for a few minutes.

7:40 a.m.
I'm not reading the *Tibetan Book of Living and Dying* ever again. I'm not going to become a Buddhist if I might come back reincarnated as a stick insect.

7:50 a.m.
Cup of milky coffee and toast, yum yum yum. Mum has got a new *Cosmo*.

8:10 a.m.
Back in bed for a few minutes' read. Hmmm, "What men say and what they mean".

9:30 a.m.

If a boy says "See you later" it might mean, "Leave me alone, it was great while it lasted but I am not ready for anything more serious" or "See you later".

9:40 a.m.

I am going to become a writer for *Cosmo* – you don't have to make any sense at all. Or maybe I'll be a bloke – they don't have to make any sense either.

10:00 a.m.

I am going to wear my short black Lycra dress. Jas has already phoned five times and changed her mind about what to wear each time.

1:00 p.m.

Rosie has asked the foreign exchange guest student who is staying next door to come to The Stiff Dylans. I said, "Are you sure that's a good idea?" and she said, "He's called Sven," and I said, "Well, that's what I mean."

Rosie says he's a "laugh", whatever that means. She said, "He doesn't speak any English but he is very tall."

When I asked where he was from she said, "I don't know. Denmark, I think. He's blond."

Apparently she asked him to go to The Stiff Dylans by pointing at him, pointing at herself and doing a bit of a dance. She's bonkers. We arranged to go to Boots because we needed to have perfume for tonight and we can use the samples whilst we pretend we might buy them.

4:30 p.m.

Back home, covered in Palomo – I hope it wears off a bit as it's making my eyes water. Also, I've got some new lip gloss which is supposed to plump up your lips. I'm not sure that this is such a good idea in my case, especially going with Mark. I wonder if the same rule applies to lips as does to breasts? I mean, if you use them more, I wonder if they get bigger?

5:00 p.m.

If using your lips does make your lips bigger, what on earth has Mark been up to? Am I going to let him kiss me? What does the hand on the breast mean? Do I want him to be my boyfriend? I don't think he's very bright but he might turn out to be a brilliant footballer like Beckham and then I could marry him and be kept in luxury.

5:10 p.m.
But then I'd be in all the papers. I'd have to have my nose done. I would have to be careful not to smile... what if I forgot? What if I got caught by the paparazzi smiling and my nose spreading all over my face... in the *Daily Express*?

5:15 p.m.
I can't marry him, the pressure is just too much. I am losing my own self-esteem whilst he gets all the attention. I'll have to explain to him tonight that it is all over.

6:00 p.m.
I feel a bit sick. I've got a bit of hair that will NOT go right, in a minute I am going to cut it off. Also, I think I have got knobbly knees. Maybe when I am Mark's wife I could have fat injected into them (possibly taken from my nose, so it would be a two-in-one operation... smaller nose and fatter knees all in one swift plunge of the huge, hypodermic, fat-extractor needle... er, I really do feel sick...).

7:30 p.m.

I wish I had gone with Jas and Rosie, all in a big gang. Now it means I'll have to walk in with Mark and everyone will look at me and think he's my boyfriend.

Midnight

I cannot BELIEVE my life. Well, if you could call it a life... When I think about tonight I feel like staying in bed for the rest of it.

Mark was at the clock tower, smoking a fag... he looked sort of OK. When I got near him he grabbed me and gave me a kiss right on the mouth, no messing about. I was surprised and also a bit worried... maybe the hand would sneak up to the breast for a bit of a rest... but no.

Mark doesn't seem to say much – after the kiss he took my hand and we started walking to the gig. It was a bit awkward because I am actually bigger than him, so I had to sort of let my shoulder down on one side like Quasimodo.

As soon as we got there Mark went to say hello to a few of his mates. Rosie's Sven was a GIANT – about eight foot tall, with a crewcut. Jas was all moony and looked a bit pale.

She said, "I wanted that anorexic model look, like I've been up partying all night. I want Tom to think I've not been thinking about him."

The gig was packed, mostly boys on one side and girls on the other. Jas said, "Aren't you going to talk to your boyfriend?"

Which is when Tom and Robbie walked in. They saw us and Robbie caught my eye and he smiled... I'd forgotten what a Sex God he is. He's all muscly and dark and oohhhhh. I smiled back, a proper smile because I'd forgotten about my nose for the moment. Then from behind me came Lindsay and crossed over to Robbie. He had been smiling at her!!! My face was so red you could fry an egg on it. Robbie kissed Lindsay on the cheek. She had her hair up and was quite literally all ears. Yukko.

Robbie went up on stage and Tom was left by himself as wet Lindsay chatted to some of her stupid, sixth-form mates. Jas said, "Do you think I should go over and say something to him?"

I said, "Have some pride, Jas, he chose vegetables over you." At that moment a dark-haired girl came out of the loos and went over to Tom. She put her hand on his arm and they went off together.

And it got worse.

The Stiff Dylans started playing and Mark came across to me, got hold of my hand and pulled me on to the dance floor. His Mick Jagger impersonation did not stop at the lips. He was a lunatic on the dance floor, strutting around with his hands on his hips. I nearly died. Then Sven joined in, dragging Rosie with him. His style of dancing was more Cossack, a lot of going down into a squat position and kicking his legs out. Then he lifted Rosie up above his head!!! He was whirling her around, going, "Oh *ja*, oh *ja*," and Rosie was trying to keep people from seeing up her skirt.

And that is when I lost it. It was just too funny... Jas, Ellen and Jools and I were laughing like hyenas. I had a coughing fit and had to rush to the loos to try and recover. I'd just calm myself down and then poke my head round the door to see Sven dancing around and it started me off again.

Then Mark wanted to slow dance. I knew because he grabbed me and pulled me up against him. He was all lumpy, if you know what I mean, and had his mouth against my neck. It was even more difficult dancing with him than it was holding hands. I had to sort of bend my knees and sag a bit in order to "fit in". At one stage I found myself looking straight at Robbie. He looked so cool. Oh bloody *sacré bleu*. Even though I hate him and he is a pompous pratboy, I think I may love him.

Then the band stopped playing for a break but Mark yelled, "Play more." Some of his mates started joining in, then they sort of rushed the stage and Mark grabbed the microphone from Robbie. He was "singing" – I think it may have been "Jumpin' Jack Flash". Robbie put his hand on his shoulder and then a massive fight broke out. All Mark's thick friends got stuck into the band and then the band's mates got stuck into them. All us girls were screaming.

Sven lifted two boys up at once and tossed them outside into the street and that's when Ellen, Jas, Jools and I decided to do a runner.

So, a gorgeous night. I am tucked up in bed, my "boyfriend" is a hooligan, before him I had another "boyfriend" called whelk boy. The boy I like hates me and prefers a wet weed with sticky-out ears...

ps My so-called 'pet' spat at me when I walked in all upset.

pps I have found my sister's secret used nappy at the bottom of my bed.

Sunday December 13th
5:00 p.m.

No sign of Mark, thank goodness. I stayed in reading all day. Mum and Dad are having a night out – they suddenly want to do things together, it's so unnatural! – so I have to babysit Libby. I don't mind as I never want to go out again.

6:00 p.m.

Libby cheered me up by pretending to be Angus. She curled up in his basket and hid behind the curtains, growling. I had to stop her when she started eating his dinner.

6:15 p.m.

Jas on the phone. "I'll never get a boyfriend. I may become a vet."

6:20 p.m.

Jas phoned again. "Do you think I am really ugly?"

6:30 p.m.

Rosie phoned. "I managed to get Sven home before the

police arrived. He has given me a bit of holly."

I said, "Why?" and she said, "I don't know, maybe it's a Danish tradition."

7:15 p.m.
Jools phoned. "Someone said they noticed that Lindsay wears an engagement ring when she's at school."

8:00 p.m.
Perfect. The doorbell rang but I made Libby be really quiet and pretend we weren't in. No note or anything.

Fed up, depressed, hungry.

9:00 p.m.
Fed up, depressed, feel sick.

Had:

2 Mars bars,

toast,

milky coffee,

Ribena,

Coke,

toast,

cornflakes and
Pop-Tarts.

10:00 p.m.
Going to bed. Hope I never wake up.

Monday December 14th
8:30 a.m.
Nearly bumped into Mark on the way to school. Got round the corner just in time, thank goodness.

9:45 a.m.
Slim was livid about The Stiff Dylans gig; she was trembling like a loon.

"I sincerely hope none of my girls were in any way associated with the hooligans who behaved like animals at the dance..."

Rosie looked up at me and put her teeth in front of her bottom lip like a hamster. I don't know why but it really made me laugh so much I thought I would choke. I had to pretend to have a coughing fit and get my hankie out.

Jas wasn't in school. I wonder where she is. Maybe the

"painters are in", if you know what I mean. Rosie was full of Sven this and Sven that. I said, "Is he your boyfriend, then?" and she went a bit red and said, "Look, I don't think we're going out or anything. He's only given me a bit of holly." But as I said, that could mean anything in Denmark.

Oh bloody hell, Jackie and Alison, the Bummer twins, are back with a vengeance. They sent a note round saying they want us all to meet by the canteen on Thursday lunch for, as they call it, "the latest".

4:30 p.m.

Note from Mark when I got in from school: *Georgia, I looked for you after the other night. Meet me at 10 at the phone box tonight. Mark*

9:50 p.m.

If I don't go I'll only see him in the street anyway...

I shouted to M and D (spending time together AGAIN), "I'm just taking Angus out for a walk."

Dad yelled, "Don't let him near that poodle."

I had to drag Angus away from Next Door's, he wants to eat that poodle. He has about four cans of petfood a day as it is. If he gets any bigger Mum says she is going to give him to a zoo, as if they would want him.

10:00 p.m.

Mark smoking by the phone box. He didn't see me coming – hardly surprising as Angus had dragged me behind a hedge, chasing a cat. In the end I tied him to the gatepost. From behind the hedge I could see Mark, and you know when you have one of those moments when you know what you have to do? No, well neither do I... but I did think, I must come clean with Mark, it is not fair on him, I'm going to say, "Look, Mark, I like you and you mustn't think it's you, it's me really, I just think I could never make you happy, we're so different. I think it is best that we stop right here and now before anyone gets hurt."

So I went up to him. He was half in the shadows and he threw his cigarette down when he saw me. I opened my mouth to speak and he just kissed me right on the open mouth. What if I had been sucking a Polo mint? I could have choked to death!! Also, he put his tongue in my mouth, which was a bit of a surprise... but then he did it again!!! He put his hand on my breast! What was I supposed to do? I hadn't gone to breast classes. My arms were sort of hanging by my sides like an orang-utan when I remembered what whelk boy had said about putting your hands on someone's waist, so I did that. He had one hand on my breast and one on my bottom. But just when I was thinking, What next? in the hand department, he stopped kissing me.

Was this a good moment to say he was dumped?

He said, "Look, Georgia, this is not personal or anything, but er... I think you are too young for me. I'm going back out with Ella because she lets me do things to her. Sorry, see you later."

Midnight

See you later? Mark has had the cheek to dump me just as I was about to dump him! I'm never getting up again. Ella lets him do things to her... what things? Two hands on her breasts?

Wednesday December 16th

1:30 p.m.

Jas still not back. I'll visit her after school.

136

4:15 p.m.

No reply at Jas's house.

6:30 p.m.

Phoned Jas. Her mum said she couldn't get to the phone as she is not very well. I said, "Is it the flu?" and her mum said, "Well, I don't know, but she's not eating."

Not eating. Jas. Jas not eating. Things are bad. I said, "What, not even Pop-Tarts?" and her mum said, "No."

Things are much worse than I thought.

Thursday December 17th

10:00 a.m.

Still no Jas. This is getting ridiculous.

1:30 p.m.

Jackie and Alison's "latest thing" turns out to be so bonkers it is not even in the bonkers universe. We all had to go out into the freezing cold at the back of the tennis courts... I was surprised that Jackie knew where they were. I don't think she's ever been near the sports area before. Then Jackie told us what it was all about. "OK, this is what you do. You crouch down like this, then you start panting really hard and then you stand up and start running forward."

I said, "Why?" and she looked at me and lit a fag. Tarty or what? She had a huge spot on her chin, it looked like a second nose. I'm not surprised her skin is so bad, it's probably been covered in make-up since she was five.

She blew the smoke in my face and said, "When you run forward it makes you faint."

Even Rosie, who usually doesn't say much to Jackie, had to repeat this, "You faint?"

Jackie drew on her fag like she was dealing with the very, very stupid. She didn't say anything, so eventually Rosie said, "Then what?"

Jackie totally lost it, then. "Look, four-eyes, think about how useful it can be to just faint when you want to... in assembly – faint, get taken out. In physics, when you haven't done your homework – faint, get taken out... games... anything."

Rosie is nothing if not stupid, so she kept going on. "Don't you think someone might notice if we crouched down in assembly or physics and started panting and then ran forward?"

Jackie walked over to Rosie, and she is quite a big girl. Her breasts are sturdy-looking and she's got big arms.

11:00 p.m.

I still feel a bit odd. I'm not going to be doing anything that Jackie and Alison say ever again. That is it. This stupid fainting thing is it. That is it. I did the panting and then stood up and started running and I did feel very faint, but not as faint as when I ran into Mr Attwood coming out of his hut. I may have broken my shin. Sadly Elvis was OK.

Friday December 18th
7:30 p.m.

Jas off all week. I'm worried about her now, she won't even speak to me on the phone. Even when I pretended I was Santa Claus.

Friday December 25th
10:00 a.m.

Happy St Nicholas's Day, one and all!!!

My fun-filled day started at five fifteen a.m. when Libby came in to give me my present, something made out of

Playdough that had horrible, suspicious-looking brown bits in it. She said, "Tosser's baby... ahhh," and tucked it up into bed with me.

As we are "a bit strapped for cash" as Vati puts it (due to his inability to hold down a job in my opinion, but I didn't say in case I spoiled Christmas even more) we could not have expensive presents. Mum and Dad got me CDs and make-up and leggings and trainers and undies and perfume, and I made Dad a lovely moustache holder which I think he will treasure.

I made Mum some homemade cosmetics out of egg yolks and stuff. She tried on the face pack and it gave her a bit of a rash, but on the whole livened up her complexion.

I made Libby a fairy costume, which was a big mistake as she spent the rest of the day changing us into things by whacking us with her wand. I had to be a "nice porky piggy" for about an hour. I never want to see a sausage again.

Jas phoned, but still isn't venturing out – so no escaping "merry" Christmas with the family.

Angus looked nice in his tinsel crown until it annoyed him and he ate it. When we had our lunch Mum made him a special mouse-shaped lunch in his bowl out of Katto-meat.

He ate its head and then sat in it. Heaven knows what goes on in his cat brain.

I think I may become a New Age person next year and celebrate the winter solstice by leaving my family and going to Stonehenge to dance with Druids. It couldn't be more boring than watching my dad trying to make his new electric toothbrush work. However, there was a bright moment when he got it tangled up in his moustache.

Saturday December 26th
Noon

Quel dommage!! M and D have selfishly asked me to babysit Libby whilst they have "a last night out together". Dad leaves for Whangamata on the 29th... sob, sob... and so as a brilliant treat he is taking Mum... to the pub!! With Uncle Eddie!!

If I was Mum I would have faked an accident, or if necessary had a real accident. A broken ankle would be a small price to pay to avoid Uncle Eddie's version of "Agadoo".

11:30 p.m.

Mum and Dad came crashing in, giggling. They were drunk. I was in bed TRYING to sleep but they have no consideration. I could hear them dancing around to "The Birdy Song". They are sad.

Then they crept upstairs saying "Ssshhhh" really loudly. Mum gave a bit of a gasp when she came into my room because Libby was in bed with me but she had gone to sleep upside down so her feet were on the pillow next to me. Mum put her in her own bed, but then horror of horrors DAD RUFFLED MY HAIR. I pretended even harder to be asleep.

Sunday December 27th

11:00 a.m.

M and D still in bed. I will take their lovely young daughter Liberty in to them to chat.

2:00 p.m.

Going out. Dad's given me a fiver to look after Libby.

Tuesday December 29th

8:00 p.m.

Vati left today. I must say even I had a bit of a cry. He went off in Uncle Eddie's sidecar. We all waved him off. He says that he'll ring when he gets to Whangamata. It takes two days to fly there – imagine that. I suppose it is the other side of the world. Mum is all glum and snivelling, so I bought her some Milk Tray. That made her cry more, so I don't think I'll do it again. Libby got her Angus's bowl to cry into.

Exploding Knickers

Friday January 1st

11:00 a.m.

Resolutions:

    I will be a much nicer person, to people who deserve it.

    I will be interested in my future.

    I will speak nicely to Mr and Mrs Next Door.

    I will be less superficial and vain.

    I will concentrate on my positive and not my negative, e.g. I will think less about my nose and more about my quite attractive teeth.

Saturday January 2nd

11:30 a.m.

At last! News of Jas. It seems that she might have glandular fever. I'm wearing a scarf over my mouth and nose when I visit her, just in case. Apparently you get glandular fever from kissing. It's a nightmare, this kissing business – if it's not a mysterious hand on the breast it's huge swollen glands. Celibacy or a huge fat neck, that is the stark choice. I wonder if Slim has got big fat feet from too much kissing in the foot area? Uuurgghh, now I feel really sick. I'm far too ill to visit the sick. I must go home to bed.

No... Jas needs me. I'll just try not to breathe the same air as her.

4:00 p.m.
Jas has finally let me see her. She's all pale and thin, just lying in bed. Her bedroom is tidy, which is a bad sign and she has turned her mirror to the wall. She didn't even open her eyes when I came in. I sat on her bed.

"Jas, what are you doing? What's the matter? Come on, tell me, your best pal."

Silence.

"Come on, Jas, whatever it is, you can trust me."

Silence.

"I know what it is, you think that just because everyone else besides Nauseating P. Green and Hairy Kate the lezzo have got boyfriends – or have kissed someone properly –

there is something really wrong with you, don't you?"

Silence. I was getting a bit irritated. I was trying to help and I had problems of my own. I was practically an orphan, for instance... and a substitute parent. It was all, "Will you babysit Libby?" since Dad had selfishly gone to the other side of the world. What did Jas know of trouble? Had she taken her little sister to the swimming pool? No, she didn't even have a little sister. Had her little sister's swimming knickers exploded at the top of the toddlers' water slide? No. Is there ever any point in trying to tell Mum that Libby always has bottom trouble after baked beans? No, there is not. The swimming knickers could not contain Libby's poo explosion and it was all over the slide and nearby toddlers. Did Jas know what it was to see a pool being cleared of sobbing toddlers, dragged out by their water wings? No. Did she know what it was like to sluice her little sister down and then have to walk the gamut of shame past all the mothers and toddlers and swimming-pool attendants in masks with scrubbing brushes? I think not. I had to take it on the chin like a taking-it-on-the-chin person, so why couldn't Jas?

I didn't say any of this to Jas but I took a tough line.

"Come on, Jas, what can be so bad about swollen-up glands?"

Jas spoke in a quiet voice so I had to bend down to hear her. "I haven't got swollen-up glands. I don't think I'll ever get a boyfriend, no one asked me to dance even. Tom was my only chance and even he preferred his onions."

Aha, time for all that stuff I read in Mum's *Feel the Fear and Do it Anyway* book. I got Jas's mirror from the wall and held it in front of her face. "Look into that mirror, Jas, and love the person that you see. Say, I love you."

Jas looked in the mirror – she couldn't help it, it was about three centimetres away from her nose. She was almost sick. "Uuurggghhhh, I look hideous."

She wasn't really getting it. I said, "Jas, Jas, love yourself, love the beauty that is there, look at that lovely face, look at that lovely mouth. The mouth that your friend marked eight out of ten. Think of that, Jas. Think of all the poor people who only got six and a third... and you have an eight for a mouth..." (I can be like an elephant for remembering things that annoy me. Sadly I can remember nothing to do with French, history, maths or biology.)

Jas was definitely perking up. She was puckering her

mouth and trying for a half-smile. "Do you really think I have got a nice mouth?"

"Yes, yes, but look at the rest of you, look at those eyes, look at the spot-free skin..."

Jas sat up. "I know, it's good, isn't it? I've been drinking lemon and hot water first thing."

Monday January 4th
7:00 a.m.
Woke up and felt happy for a minute until I realised I had to go back to loony headquarters (school) today.

2:30 p.m.
Gym. Discovered Angus had stored his afternoon snack in my rucksack. There are hedgehog quills in my sports knickers.

Tuesday January 12th
Noon
Victory. Victory.

Madame Slack has been on my case about being lazy in French and I have just got eighty-five per cent in a test. Hahahaha. *Fermez la bouche*, Madame Slack. I did it by learning twenty-five words and then making sure I answered every question by using only those words. So to question one – "In French, what is your favourite food?" my answer was "*Lapin*" (rabbit).

For my essay, "What did you do on a sunny day?" I made sure I played with a rabbit.

Describe a favourite book – *Watership Down* – lots of *lapins* in that.

1:00 p.m.

In line with my new resolution to concentrate on school and not boys I went to do my yoga in the gym at lunchtime. My yoga routine is called The Sun Salute and you stretch up to welcome the sun and then you bend down as if to say "I am not worthy." Then you do cobra pose and dog pose… it's all very flowing and soothing.

1:15 p.m.

Miss Stamp came in just as I was doing dog post. She said, "Oh, don't let me disturb you. I'm glad you're taking an interest in yoga, it's one of the best exercises for the body. It will be really good for your tennis in summer. Don't mind me, I'm just getting ready for this afternoon." Well, I was upside down with my bottom sticking up in the air. Not something you want to do in front of a lesbian. So I quickly went into cobra but that made it look like I was sticking my breasts out at her. I think she may now be growing a beard as well as a moustache.

Honestly, there is no bloody peace in this place.

1:30 p.m.

I tried my yoga outside, even though it was hard to do it with my gloves and coat on. Again I'd just got into dog pose when Elvis appeared round the corner. He's a grumpy old nutcase. "What are you up to?" he shouted at me.

I said, from upside down, "Nnn doing nmy nyoga."

He pulled down his cap. "I don't care if you're doing nuclear physics, you're not doing it in my yard. Clear off before I report you."

As I went, I said, "Did you know that Elvis is dead?"

4:30 p.m.

Saw Mark on my way home. I smiled in a mature way at him. He just said, "All right?"

6:00 p.m.

Mum has gone mental in Vati's absence. When I asked Mum if she would pay for my nose reduction surgery she came out with the old "We can barely afford to feed Angus" line. As if he needs feeding anyway; there's never a day goes by that I don't find something decomposing in the airing cupboard. Anyway, she can't afford to invest in the happiness of her daughter but she can afford to have the lounge decorated, apparently, because the decorator is coming next week.

9:30 p.m.

Watching TV Mum said, "Do you miss your dad?" and I said, "Who?"

Monday January 18th
Biology
2:40 p.m.

I can do a great impression of a lockjaw germ. Rosie passed me a note: Dear G. You know we have a double free period on Thursday? Well, do you fancy bunking off and going down town? Rrrrrrrrxxxxx

4:30 p.m.

Walking home with Jas. I think she is well on the way to recovery. "What do you think of this lip gloss? Do you think it makes me look a bit like Claudia Schiffer? My mouth is the same shape, I think." I wish I hadn't started this. Still, if she wants to live in a fantasy wonderland and it cheers her up... We went to her house and up to her room. Oh, the bliss of a normal household, no mad mum, no strange sister, no wild animals. Jas's mum asked us if we would like some Ribena and sandwiches. Imagine my mum doing that?... Imagine my mum being in! I suppose she is a good role model... if you want to be a hospital administrator – but couldn't she make the odd sandwich as well?

In Jas's bedroom we did our vital statistics with her tape measure. I am thirty-two, twenty-three, thirty-two and Jas is thirty, twenty-three, thirty-three. I think she was breathing in for the twenty-three myself. Also my legs are two inches longer than hers. (I didn't mention it to Jas but one of my legs is two inches longer and the other one is only one and a half inches longer. How can you develop a limp at my age? It might be because I carry my bag on one shoulder and it's making that side longer. I must remember to swap sides. Nobody likes a lopsided girl.)

Thursday January 28th
3:30 p.m.
Rosie got up first and left the room. Miss Wilson came in as we were working, to "supervise", but we asked her who invented God and she left pretty quickly. We were busy making a list of all the qualities we want in a boyfriend – sense of humour, good dancer, good kisser, nice smile, six-pack, etc. Rosie sent her list and it just said, *HUGE.* I wrote back, Huge teeth, you mean? And she replied, *Yes.* Sven has begun to infect her with his Danishness, I think.

Anyway, Rosie, Jools and Ellen went out first, and then me and Jas. We met up in the ground floor loos and put our boots and skinny tops and make-up on. We made sure the coast was clear and then went out of the back doors. We had to crouch down beneath the science-block windows – Hawkeye was teaching in there and she could smell a girl at twenty paces. Once past the Science block it was a quick dash behind Elvis's hut. He was in there, reading his newspaper, and as we crept by we heard him fart loudly and say "Pardon". I started giggling and then everyone caught it. We had to run like mad. All afternoon if anyone did anything we'd say "Pardon".

Great in Boots. We tried all the testers, and this stuff that you put on your hair, like a wand and it puts a streak of colour into your own hair. I tried all of them but blonde looked really brilliant. Just a streak across the front, I knew it would look good. I'm going to get Mum to let me dye my hair blonde now that Vati's safely in Whangamata.

Midnight

Brilliant day!!! Jas and I sung "Respect" by Aretha Franklin on the way home.

Jas must die

Saturday February 6th
11:00 a.m.

The doorbell rang. Mum was in the loo debagging Libby; it was not a pretty sight. At the weekend Mum wears these awful dungarees that only lesbians or people on *Blue Peter* in the sixties wear. Libby was singing "Three bag bears, three bag bears, see how they run, see how they run..." ("Three Blind Mice" to other people). Libby was as happy as a mad sandbag but Mum was all flustered. "Will you answer that, Georgie? It will be this builder called Jem I phoned up to look at the lounge. Let him in and make a cup of coffee while I finish with this."

When I opened the door I got an impression of blond hair and denims but then there was this awful squealing from next door's garden. Mrs Next Door was screeching,

"Get him, get him! Oh oh oh!" She was dashing around the garden with a broom. I thought that Angus had got the poodle at last, but when I looked over the fence he had a little brown thing in his mouth.

Mrs Next Door yelled at me, "I'm going to call the police! It's my niece's guinea pig, we're looking after it. And now this, this... THING has got it."

Angus crouched down not very far away. I said, in my sternest voice, "Drop it, now drop it, Angus."

Due to my training he recognised my voice and let the guinea pig drop out of his mouth. I started to go over to get it and the guinea pig started scampering away. After it had got a few centimetres Angus put his huge paw out and just let it rest on the end of its bottom. It squiggled and squiggled and Angus yawned and took his paw off again. The guinea pig streaked off and Angus lumbered to his feet and ambled after it. He biffed it on to its back and then he sat on it and closed his eyes for a little doze. I said to Mrs Next Door, "Sorry, he can be very annoying, he's having a game with it." She was very unreasonable. I managed to lure Angus away from his little playmate with a kipper. Mrs ND says she is going to complain to someone official. I wonder who? Cat patrol, I suppose.

Jem had been watching from the doorstep. He had a nice, crinkly smile. He said, "He's big for a cat, isn't he?"

I sighed, "Come in, Mum's in the bathroom, she'll be out in a minute." Jem came into the front room and I gave him some of my coffee. He's quite good-looking for an older man.

Mum came rushing in in her dungarees. Then she saw Jem and went all weird and even redder. She said, "Nnnnghhhh!" and then just left the room.

I shrugged my shoulders at Jem. He said, "Are you doing your GCSEs?" (Good, he thought I was at least sixteen... hahahahaha)... I went "Nnngghhh" as well. Then Mum came back with LIPSTICK on and proper clothes. I left them to it.

Sunday February 7th
11:00 a.m.
Got dressed in a short skirt, then me and Jas walked up and down to the main road. We wanted to see how many cars with boys in them hooted at us. Ten!! (We had to walk up and down for four hours... still, ten is ten!!!)

Monday February 22nd
4:15 p.m.

Something really odd happened today when Jas and I left school. Robbie was at the school gate in his mini. He was leaning against it. I wish my legs didn't go all jelloid when I see him. How do you make yourself not like someone? I think you're supposed to concentrate on some of their bad points. Maybe he's got horrible hands? I looked at his hands... they are lovely – all strong-looking but quite artistic too. Like he could put up a shelf and also take you to a plateau of sensual pleasure at the same time. I bet he doesn't rest his hand on your breast... I wish he would. Shut up!!!!! Anyway, I was getting ready to put on my coolest look and he said, "Hello, Jas, how are you?"

Jas flushed and said, "Oh, hi, Robbie, yeah fine thanks, and you?"

He said, "Cool." Then he said, "Jas, could I have a... could I speak to you sometime? Maybe you would come for a coffee next Wednesday after school?"

And Jas went, "Er... well...er... yes. Fine. See you then."

I was quite literally speechless.

When we got to Jas's house I just walked in through the

gate, through the door and straight up the stairs into her bedroom. It was like I had a furball in my throat. I thought I was going to choke and explode and poo myself all at the same time.

Jas sat down on her bed and just went "Foof".

I said, "What do you mean by 'Foof'?"

And she said, "Just that... 'Foof'."

I said, "Well, what does he want to see you about?"

And she looked at her nails in a very annoying way. "I don't know."

I said, "Well, you won't go, will you?"

And she said, "He asked me to go for a coffee and I said I would."

I went on, "Yes, but you won't go, will you?"

She looked at me, "Why shouldn't I go? He said he wanted to talk to me."

I couldn't believe it. "But you know he's my sworn enemy."

Jas went all reasonable. "Yes, but he's not my sworn enemy, he seems to really like me."

I was beyond the Valley of the Livid. "Jas, if you are my friend you will not go and meet Robbie."

She just went silent and tight-lipped. I slammed out of her house.

Tuesday February 23rd
11:00 p.m.

I left the house ten minutes early today and walked on the other side of the road. Jas usually hangs about outside her gate between eight thirty-five and eight forty-five and then she walks on if I don't turn up. I ran like mad past her house, keeping to cover, and arrived ten minutes before assembly.

Hawkeye stopped me. "I've never seen you early for anything, what's going on? I'll be keeping my eye on you." Honestly, she's so suspicious. I don't suppose she's got anything else to do, no real life of her own. When I went into the assembly hall I didn't stand in my usual place, I went and talked to Rosie. Jas came in to where we stand together, she caught my eye and gave a half-smile but I gave her my worst look.

I didn't see her again until lunch when she came into the loos. I was sort of trapped because I was drying my fringe under the hand dryer. I'd slept on it funny and it was all sticking up. My head was upside down and she said, "Look, this is really silly, we can't fall out over some bloke."

I said, "Nyot snum bluk."

She said, "Pardon?"

I stood up and faced her. "Jas, you know what I've been through with Robbie, he is not just 'some bloke'."

She was being Mrs Reasonable Knickers. "What are you so bothered about? It's just coffee... at the moment."

I pounced on that like a rat on a biscuit. "What do you mean, 'at the moment'?"

She was putting chapstick on, pouting in the mirror... she really has snapped, she thinks she looks like Claudia Schiffer. "I'm just saying, it's only coffee at the moment, if anything else happens of course I will let you know first." That's when I kicked her on the shin. HOW DARE SHE? That is it!!! I'm never speaking to her again.

Saturday February 27th
10:00 a.m.

Mum up and humming in the kitchen like a happy person, whatever that is. I've made a list of my friends:

I have 12 "close casuals",

20 "social only" and

♡ 161

6 "inner circle" (you know, the kind of friends who would cry properly at your funeral).

Libby is too small to be a chum, although she's a better chum than some, if you know what I mean. Jas is not on my list.

10:30 a.m.

I wonder if I have got enough friends? I worry that if British Telecom asks me for ten friends and family for my list of cheap calls I would have to count the astrological phone line for Librans which I ring more often than not.

11:00 a.m.

Doorbell went. Mum shouted, "Will you get that?" It was Jem; he really is quite cool and fit-looking. He was wearing a T-shirt and you could see his muscly arms. I smiled at him. Maybe I need an older man to teach me the ways of love...

11:05 a.m.

Mum came rushing out of the bedroom with Libbs. "Take Libby for a walk, love, will you? Thanks. Now, Jem, would you like a cup of coffee?"

He said, "I wouldn't say no, I've got a bit of a hangover."

She giggled (yes, she giggled), and said, "Honestly, what are you like? Did you have a good time?"

They went off into the kitchen. He said, "Yeah, we went to this club, it's a laugh, you should come one night."

She giggled and said, "Be careful, I might take you up on that."

I couldn't hear what happened after that because Libby hit me with her monkey. "Out now," she said, so I had to go.

What next? My mum goes off with a builder whilst my vati is trying to build a new life for her in the Antipodes?

Actually, when put like that, it seems fair enough...

Vati sent a letter and some photos from Whangamata. In his letter he said, **The village has the most geothermal activity in the world. When I had lunch in the garden the other day, the table was heaving and lurching around... I could hardly eat my steak. The ground lurches and heaves around because underneath the earth's crust thousands of billions of tons of molten steam is trying to get out. The trees go backwards and forwards, the sheep go up and down...**

Oh, very good, Vati, I'll be over there on the next flight. Not. And he sent some photos of his New Zealand mates... They were all heavily bearded like the Rolf Harris quadruplets.

Still, he is my vati, I will have to have a word with Mum in order to save the family.

12:05 p.m.
Can't be bothered.

My dad has become Rolf Harris

Monday March 1st
10:30 a.m.

Still not speaking to Jas, but things have gone horribly wrong in that she is not speaking to me either. I don't know how this has happened as I was supposed to be in charge. It's bloody difficult coming to school because if she gets ahead of me I have to walk really, really slowly behind her because my legs are longer.

Wednesday March 3rd
9:00 a.m.

Today is the day that Jas is to meet Robbie after school for a "coffee". I wonder if Lindsay knows about this? I wonder if I have a duty to tell her?

3:00 p.m.

I can't help myself – I have been trailing Jas around all day. I notice she has her very short skirt on and she's done her hair. Perhaps I could leap on her as she comes out of the loo and duff her up, or I could pay Jackie and Alison to do it.

3:15 p.m.

Rosie, Ellen and Jools are not taking sides in this, which I hate... how dare they be so fair-minded? Rosie said, "He's only asked her for a coffee to talk... you don't know what about," and Jools said, "It's a free world, you know, you can't make people do anything."

How dim and thick can you be? I'd stop speaking to them but then I wouldn't have anyone to talk to at all.

4:05 p.m.

He's there in his mini!! Where is Lindsay? Perhaps there will be a fight at the gates. There was a fight once before but that was Mr Attwood and an ice-cream man. Elvis had gone to see him off. He went up to the van and said, "Clear off!" and the ice-cream man said, "Make me, short arse."

Elvis took off his glasses and his cap and said, "Come out of that van and I will."

So the ice-cream man did come out of his van and he was about twenty-five foot tall and Elvis said, "Right, well, I've told you. That's my final word... As soon as you have sold as many ice creams as you want, you must leave the school boundaries."

4:08 p.m.

No sign of Lindsay. I said to Rosie and Jools and Ellen, "Where is Lindsay?"

And Rosie said, "She's playing badminton." For heaven's sake, she is so wet – some snivelling, scheming snot takes her fiancée/boyfriend and all she can do is run around in sports knickers, hitting a ping-pong ball with some feathers stuck in it.

4:10 p.m.

Jas came out in boots. Suede boots, knee-length, with heels!! She'll get offered money if she hangs around in the streets looking like that.

4:12 p.m.

She has reached the gates. Robbie has opened the door of his mini and gone round the other side and driven off.

Home

4:38 p.m.

I'm going mad. What are they doing now?

5:00 p.m.

Ring Rosie. "Have you heard anything?"

Rosie: "No."

I said, "Well, call me if you do."

5:20 p.m.

I've called everyone and nobody has heard anything yet. It's like being in one of those crap plays we have to study. I'll be left lonely and looking out to sea at the end... possibly with a beard.

5:30 p.m.

I've just found I've got hairs growing out of my armpits. How did they get there? They weren't there yesterday.

5:40 p.m.

I've got some on my legs as well. I'd better distract myself by getting rid of them with Mum's razor.

6:00 p.m.

Oh God! Oh God! I'm haemorrhaging. My legs are running with blood – I had to staunch the flow with Mum's dressing-gown. She'll kill me if she finds out. I'd better wash it.

6:10 p.m.

Put it in the washing machine with some other stuff before she gets home.

6:30 p.m.

Phone rings. It's only Mum. She and Libby are round at Uncle Eddie's and won't be home until later and I've got to get my own tea. *Quelle surprise!*

Go to the fridge.

6:32 p.m.

I wonder what I'll have? Hmmm... oh, I know, I'll have this mouldy old tin of beans that is the only thing in there...

7:00 p.m.

Phone rings.

I fell over the cord getting to it, legs started bleeding again. It was Rosie. "Jas just phoned."

I almost screamed at her. "And???"

"Well, they had coffee, she says he really is fantastic-looking and also very funny."

"And?"

"Well, he wanted to talk to her about Tom."

I started laughing. "Hahahahahha... and she wore her boots. Hahaha."

Rosie went on, "Yes, he wanted to know if she still likes Tom because he still likes her."

I put the phone down. Tom. Who cares? Hahahaha.

Life is fabby fab fab fabbity fab fab.

7:30 p.m.

La lalalalalalala. Fabbity fab fab.

7:40 p.m.

Yum yum, beans. Lovely lovely beans.

10:00 p.m.

Oh dear, slight problem. Mum's dressing gown has shrunk to the size of a doll's dressing gown. It might fit Libby, I suppose.

Hmmm.

Still. Fabbity fab fab. I'll think about it tomorrow. For now I must just dance about a bit to a loud tune.

11:00 p.m.

Heard Mum come in but I pretended I was asleep. I've hidden the dressing gown at the bottom of my wardrobe.

Thursday March 4th

8:30 a.m.

Jas was waiting for me at her gate. I saw her and started walking really slowly and pretending to be looking through my bag for something. Then I acted like I'd forgotten something and had to go home for it. I walked back and waited behind a hedge for about four minutes and then walked back again. Hurrah, she was gone, my plan worked. But just as I passed her gate she popped up from behind her hedge. She walked alongside me and didn't say anything and neither did I. It's funny being silent – you have to be careful to not make any noise. You can't belch or anything or even clear your throat in case the other person thinks you are going to speak first. When we got to school she handed me a letter. I wouldn't take it at first but I quite wanted to read it so I did eventually put it in my bag.

1:00 p.m.
First opportunity I've had to read the letter because I didn't want Jas to know that I was keen to read any stupid thing she had to say.

The letter said,

Dear Georgie,

I am sorry that a boy has come between us, it will never happen again. I was stupid and didn't think of your feelings even though you are my best friend. If there is anything I can do to be your friend again, I will do it.

Jas

PS He isn't engaged to Lindsay.

1:15 p.m.

So Jas thinks she can just forget the whole sorry affair – drop it just like that. Well, it will take more than a note to make me change my mind about her.

1:20 p.m.

Jas found me by the vending machine and she was a bit nervous. Let her suffer.

1:21 p.m.

Jas went "Er..." and I said, "What do you mean he's not engaged to Lindsay?"

In my room
5:00 p.m.

Jas is helping me to stretch Mum's dressing gown. As a punishment for her appalling behaviour she has promised that she will say it was her who put it in the washing-machine. My mum won't get cross with Jas.

5:15 p.m.

The dressing gown is exactly the same doll size except that

now it has very long arms like an orang-utan.

5:25 p.m.
Apparently Robbie was very surprised that he was supposed to be engaged. When he asked Jas why she thought that, she had to pretend that someone had told her.

5:30 p.m.
Jas is plucking my eyebrows. She said, "So what do you think I should do about Tom? Robbie says he still likes me, and that the girl at the dance was his cousin."

I said, "Oh, does that mean he can't get a girlfriend, then?"

Jas said (mid-pluck), "Georgie, don't start again. Do you think I should give him another chance?"

I thought, What am I, an agony aunt? But I said, "Well, maybe, but I'd play a bit hard to get. Don't kiss him on your first date... well, unless he really wants to."

Midnight
Got away surprisingly easily with the "It was Jas – I'm innocent!" plan re the dressing gown. Mum seems even

more mad than ever. And how long can it take to decorate one room? Jem is taking for ever. I'm not really surprised – he spends most of his time sitting around giggling with Mum. Libby called him "Dad" the other day.

Ho hum.

1:00 a.m.

Looking up at the sky from my bed I can hear an owl hooting and all is well with the world. Robbie is not engaged!!! Thank you, Baby Jesus.

Tuesday March 16th

3:00 p.m.

Miss Stamp says I show "promise" at tennis. It is very nice slamming the ball across the court past people. Or not past them, in Rosie's case, when it hit her in the face this afternoon. Her glasses went all sideways like Eric Morecambe which I thought was very funny. I couldn't serve for ages because of laughing so much.

10:45 p.m.

Woke up from a dream of winning Wimbledon. I think I

may be becoming sexually active, as the dream only really got interesting in the dressing room. First there was the usual stuff – you know, the final ace, the crowd going mad, going up for my trophy. Princess Margaret handing it over and saying, "Absolutely first class, most thrilling. It made me wish I still played."

Me saying, "Hahaha, I find it hard to believe you've ever played anything, Ma'am – except gin rummy." Then a quick wave and into the dressing room.

Once in the privacy of the changing room I began to get undressed for a well-deserved shower. When I had got down to my (well-filled D-cup) bra and knickers I was startled to find someone had come in the room. It was Leo DiCaprio. He said, "I'm sorry, did I startle you?" Then he started covering my quivering (but extremely fit and tanned) body with kisses. Just then someone else came in. I pulled away from Leo but Leo said, "It's OK, it's only Brad," and Brad Pitt came and joined us.

Monday March 22nd
2:00 p.m.

It's almost embarrassing how friendly Jas is being. A few days without my hilarious and witty conversation has reminded her of how much she likes me. In a roundabout way I suggested this to her on the way to school.

"Jas, I suppose a few days without my hilarious and witty conversation has reminded you of how much you like me."

She said, "Hahahaha..." but then saw my face and said, "Oh yes, how true. That will be it."

Wednesday March 31st
Assembly
9:08 a.m.

I nearly passed out with laughing this morning. As we were praying Rosie whispered, "Have a look at Jackie's nose, pass it on..." so the word passed right along the line. I couldn't see anything at first because Jackie had her head down and her hair was hanging over her face.

Then, as people were shuffling around to start the hymn, I went, "Jackie! Pssstt!" She looked up and round at me. The end of her nose was completely black!!! She looked like a panda in a wig. I almost wet myself it was so funny. Our whole line was shaking.

Jackie looked daggers at us but that only made it worse. There's nothing funnier than a really cross panda!! We staggered into the loos and were bent over the sinks, crying with laughter. At last, when I could speak, I said, "What... what... happened?"

Ellen said, "You know that DJ she was raving about? Well, he got drunk with his mates, came to meet Jackie and thought it would be very funny to give her a lovebite on the end of her nose."

Happy days.

The snogging report

Tuesday April 6th
5:00 p.m.
Had a game of tennis against Lucy Doyle from the fifth form and I beat her!!! I am a genius!!!

6:30 p.m.
Practising tennis against our wall at home but it's hopeless. Angus gets the ball and then takes it a few feet away from me and guards it. I go to get it and he waits until I can nearly get it and then he walks off with it again. I managed to hit him on the head with my tennis racquet but he doesn't seem to feel pain.

7:00 p.m.
Phoned Jas.

It's quite relaxing not having Dad around. No one bellowing, "Get off that bloody phone!" I'm beginning not to remember what he looks like.

So there's a silver lining to every cloud.

Jas's mum answered the phone and I asked to speak to Jas. She came down from her bedroom.

"Jas, I've got a good plan."

"Oh no."

"No, you'll like it."

"Why?"

"Because it's brilliant and also because it allows you to pay back your debt to me."

"Go on, then."

"Well, you know you said Robbie didn't know he was engaged, but Lindsay goes round with an engagement ring on...?"

"Yes."

"Well, if she only wears it at school and then takes it off when she sees him, well, that means that she likes him more than he likes her."

"I suppose."

"Of course it does. He must be getting tired of her by now – what on earth does he see in her?"

"She's supposed to be quite clever. I think she is applying for Oxford."

"So, she's a swot, that's no reason to like her – anyway, learning stuff is not clever. Just because I can't remember the Plantagenet line doesn't make me not clever."

"Well, no, I suppose."

"Exactly."

"You have quite a lot of trouble with quadratic equations as well."

"Yes, all right, Jas—"

"And you can't do the pluperfect tense—"

"Yes, I know, but what I'm saying is—"

"You're hopeless at German – Herr Kamyer said he's never known anyone so bad at it in all his years of teaching."

"Look, Jas, can we just get back to the plan? What I think we should do is to stalk Lindsay."

"Stalk her?"

"Yes."

"What... follow her around and then phone her up and ask her what colour panties she has got on?"

"No, not that bit, just the bit where we keep her under observation."

"Why? What is the point?"

"The point is, I will then be able to tell whether Robbie likes her or not."

"Why do I have to be involved?"

"Because a) you are my friend and b) it looks less suspicious because we are always hanging around together and c) my mum is going away with Libby in a few weeks and you could come and stay the night and we could invite Tom."

"When do we start stalking?"

That's my girl.

Friday April 16th
Operation stalking Lindsay begins
Friday night
4:15 p.m.

We had to hang around at the back of the science block after the final bell. Old Swotty Knickers (Lindsay) was chatting to Hawkeye. We could see them laughing together – how sad – fancy having to laugh with a teacher! Then, whilst Lindsay got her coat, we crept along the narrow alleyway that runs between the science block and the main school building. It is disgusting down there, full of fag-ends from Jackie and co. But if you follow it right along you end up a bit beyond the main gate. The tricky part is getting past Elvis's hut. I'd already made myself public enemy number one with him by putting a plastic skeleton with his hat on – and a pipe in its mouth – in his chair in his hut. I don't know how he knew it was me, but he did. Anyway, we got to Elvis's hut and he wasn't about so we shot across and into the last bit of the alleyway. We were wearing all black and had hats on – it was very like the French Resistance. We got to the end just as Lindsay (the stalkee) passed by. She looked at her watch and you could clearly see the flash of her ring.

5:15 p.m.
Outside Lindsay's posh house. The Yews.

The house is all on one level, which means that Lindsay's bedroom would be on the ground floor, which means we might be able to see in through the window.

Teeheee.

First things first, though, time for a nourishing meal.

183

6:30 p.m.

Double chips and Coke. Yum yum.

6:45 p.m.

Stalkee spotted leaving the front room, did not reappear. We suspect she has gone to her room to start the long, desperate job of making herself look OK to go out with Robbie.

6:58 p.m.

We decide to risk going round the back of the house. I whispered to Jas, "I hope they haven't got a cat."

And she said, "Don't you mean a dog?"

And I said, "Have you met Angus?"

There was a side path and we went really carefully down it. We had nearly reached the back garden when a head popped up from behind next door's hedge. A really bald head, like Uncle Eddie's. Quick as a flash, Jas said, "Sshhh, we are giving Lindsay a big surprise..." She winked at the man and he disappeared. We crept on round the back of the house. Lindsay's bedroom faced on to the garden and she had her curtains half pulled back so you could see in.

Her bedroom was a nightmare of frilly white things, frilly

pillows, frilly bedspread... Teletubby hot-water bottle cover!!!

Lindsay put on a tape and Jas and I looked at one another – it was Genesis. Jas mimed being sick. We had to keep bobbing our heads down if she turned directly to face the window. She disappeared off through another door and we could hear sort of gurgling noises. I said, "She's got an ensuite bathroom – that's very bad feng shui."

Jas said, "Why?"

And I said, "I don't know but it's very bad, you'd have to have about fifty goldfish to make it OK again... Have you seen her alarm clock? It's got a sleepy face on it."

Lindsay emerged from the bathroom with her hair all scraped back from her face and wearing a bra and a thong. I don't understand thongs – what is the point of them? I tried one of Mum's that she uses for aerobics... well, she is supposed to use it for aerobics but she only went once. She said that she nearly knocked herself out during the running on the spot because her breasts got out of hand. Anyway, I tried her thong on and it felt ridiculous... they just go up your bum as far as I can tell. Then I saw something even more grotesque. Lindsay didn't have any hair on her womanly parts! What had she done with it? She couldn't have shaved it off, could she? I thought of the state of my legs the last time I had shaved them. I felt quite faint.

Lindsay was so skinny!! At least I filled my bra. Then, before our eyes, the stalkee did two things that were very significant and would have gone in our notebook had we had one:

1. She took off her ring and kissed it!!
2. She got some sort of pink rubber things and put them in her bra underneath her "breasts". The rubber things pushed up her "breasts" and made it look like she had a cleavage. What a swiz.

I said to Jas, "I bet you Robbie doesn't know about that..."

But I noticed that I did not have Jas's full attention, she was looking over my shoulder at Mr Baldy-man, who had reappeared, peering at us over his fence. What is it with neighbours, don't they have lives of their own? He seemed a bit suspicious. So I said as naturally as I could. "She's certainly playing her music very loudly – she hasn't heard us tapping on her window. Do it again, Jas." Jas looked a bit stunned but fortunately had the presence of mind to do some mime. She mimed tapping on the window, then she mimed waving at Lindsay (who fortunately had gone back into the ensuite) and then she mimed hysterical laughter.

It's very tiring, this stalking business, but we seemed to satisfy Mr Baldy-man because he disappeared again and we crept round to the front of the house and along to the big hedge next door. We hid just inside next door's driveway to wait for Lindsay to come out.

7:40 p.m.
Brrrr... bit chilly. At last the front door opened and Lindsay came out with her hair up (mistake) and in a black midi (mistake for long-streak-of-water type person). We huddled back into the shadows of the hedge as she passed and gave her a few minutes before we followed. When she got to the main street she stood under a streetlamp and got out a compact to look at herself. Instead of running screaming home, she snapped the compact shut and walked on.

Suddenly I had the feeling that we were doing something wrong. Up until now I had been caught up in my French Resistance fantasy but what if I found out something I didn't want to know? What if she met Robbie and it was quite obvious that he really liked her? Could I stand it? Did I want to see him kissing her? I said to Jas, "Maybe we should go now."

And Jas said, "What, after all this? No way. I want to see what happens next."

7:50 p.m.

Outside the Odeon Robbie was waiting. My heart went all wobbly, he looked so cool. Why wasn't he mine? Lindsay went up to him. The moment of truth. I wanted to yell out, "She has bits of pink rubber down her bra... and she wears a thong!!!"

I held my breath and Jas's hand. She whispered, "Get off, you lezzer." Then... Lindsay put her face forward and Robbie kissed her.

8:00 p.m.

Walking home, eating more chips, I said, "What sort of kiss do you think it was? Was there actual lip contact? Or was it lip to cheek, or lip to corner of mouth?"

"I think it was lip to corner of mouth, but maybe it was lip to cheek?"

"It wasn't full-frontal snogging though, was it?"

"No."

"I think she went for full-frontal and he converted it into lip to corner of mouth."

"Yes."

"He didn't seem keen though, did he?"

"No."

"Didn't you think so either?"

"No."

"No, neither did I."

Outside Jas's gate
8:40 p.m.

I said, "The facts are a) she doesn't wear her ring when she is out with him, so that makes it clear that she says they are engaged but they are not, and b) he doesn't really rate her because he didn't do full-frontal with her."

Jas undid her gate. "Yes. Right, see you tomorrow. Don't forget to fix the sleepover."

Midnight

So... the plot thickens. All I have to do is get rid of Lindsay, convince Robbie I am the woman of his dreams, stop Mum splitting up the home, grow bigger breasts and have plastic surgery on my nose and I have cracked it...

Thursday April 29th
6:30 p.m.
Phone rang and I answered it. A strange voice said, "G'day, is that Georgie?" I was a bit formal – it might be a dirty phone call. (I had had one of those from a phone box in Glasgow. This bloke with a Scottish accent kept saying, "What colour pa—?" and then the pips would go and I'd say, "I'm sorry, what did you say?" and then he'd start again. "What colour panties...?" pip pip pip. Eventually he managed to say, "What colour panties have you got on?" and then the line went dead. So you can't be too careful.)

This strange, echoey voice said, "It's your dad, I'm calling from Whangamata."

I was a bit surprised and I said, "Oh-er-hello-Dad."

He was all enthusiastic and keen. "How's school?"

"Oh, you know... school."

"Is everyone all right?"

"Yes. Angus got next door's guinea pig."

"Did he give it back?"

"He did when I hit him with my tennis racquet."

"And Libby?"

"She can say 'tosser' now."

"Who the hell taught her that?"

"I don't know."

"Well, you should take better care of her."

"She's not my bloody daughter."

"Don't swear at me."

"I only said bloody."

"That's swear— look, look, get your mum on the phone, this is costing me one pound a minute."

"She's not here."

"Where is she?"

"Oh, I don't know, she's always out."

"Well, tell her I called."

"OK."

There was a bit of silence then. His voice sounded even weirder when he spoke again. "I wish you were all here, I miss you."

I just went, "Hmmmpgh."

I wish parents wouldn't do that, you know, make you feel like crying and hitting them at the same time.

I use it to keep my balls still

Tuesday May 4th

8:10 a.m.

Felt a bit sort of down in the dumps when I woke up. I'd had a dream that my dad had grown a Rolf Harris beard but it wasn't a beard really, it was Angus clinging to his chin.

Assembly. Maths. Physics... there is not one part of today that is worth being alive for.

4:30 p.m.

Home, exhausted from laughing. My ribs hurt. Slim has made me be on cloakroom duty for the next term but I don't care, it was worth it.

Well... here is what happened. It was during double physics and it was just one of those afternoons when you can't stop laughing and you feel a bit hysterical. For most of the lesson I had been yelling, "*Jawohl*, Herr Kommandant!"

and clicking my heels together every time Herr Kamyer asked if we understood what he had been explaining. We were doing the molecular structure of atoms and how they vibrate.

Herr Kamyer was illustrating his point with the aid of some billiard balls on a tea towel on his desk. It was giving me the giggles anyway, and then I put my hand up because I had thought of a good joke. I put my hand up with the finger pointing forward, like in "Who ate all the pies?" and when Herr Kamyer said, "Yes?" I said, "Herr Kamyer, what part does the tea towel play in the molecular structure?"

That is when Herr Kamyer made his fateful mistake – he said, "Ach, no, I merely use the tea towel to keep my balls still." It was pandemonium. I could not stop laughing. You know when you really, really should stop laughing because you will get into dreadful trouble if you don't? But you still can't stop? Well, I had that. I had to be practically carried to Slim's office. Outside her office I did my best to get a grip and I thought I had just about stopped and was under control when I knocked on the door and she said, "Come."

In my head I was thinking, Please, please don't ask me anything about it. Just let it go. Please talk about something else, just don't ask me about it. Please please.

Slim was all trembly and jelloid. "Can you tell me, Georgia, what is quite so amusing about Herr Kamyer's experiment on the vibration of atoms?"

I tried. God knows, I tried. "Well, Miss Simpson, it's just that he used a tea towel... he used a tea towel..."

"Yes?"

"He used a tea towel to... keep his balls still." And then I was off again.

Midnight
Bloody funny, though.

Thursday May 27th
Tennis tournament
2:30 p.m.

Through to the semifinals. Beautiful sunny day. I think I will be a Wimbledon champion after all. White suits me. All the gang are cheering me on and this is very freaky deaky and karmic and weird but... if I win my semi against Kirsty Walsh (upper fifth) I will play Lindsay in the final. How weird is that? Pretty weird, that's what. Lindsay is such a boring player, I'm sure I could beat her. She plays by the book... baseline follow through to the net, but she hasn't met Mighty Lob (me) yet.

OK, if I beat her that must mean I am meant to have Robbie. Lindsay has white frilly knickers on under her tennis skirt. (Not the thong, thank goodness, otherwise Miss Stamp might have had an outburst of lesbian lust and put me off my game.) I think my shorts are much more stylish. They look like I've just remembered I'm playing in a tennis final and I've just grabbed something and thrown it on in an attractive way.

3:30 p.m.
I won the first set and now I'm serving for the second and the match.

I feel pretty good. I'm a bit hot but I feel confident about my serve. Rosie and Ellen and Jools and Jas and all of my year are going mental. Chanting my name and "Easy, easy." Hawkeye keeps telling them to be quiet. (She is the umpire, worse luck.)

But even she can't make me lose. Hahahaha. I am ruler of the universe. Robbie is mine for the plucking.

First serve – an ACE!!! Yes! Yes! Yesssss!! Hawkeye says, "Fifteen-love."

Second serve – a brief rally and then a cunning, slicing cross-court forehand from me. Hawkeye says, "Thirty-love."

Third service. Whizzzz. Oh yes, another ace!! Kirsty was nowhere. What a Slack Alice. C'mon if you think you're hard enough!!!!

Hawkeye says, "Forty-love."

The whole court is hushed as I serve for the match. I take my place behind the baseline. Jas is playing nervously with her fringe. I looked at her. She stops.

I throw the ball up and bring my racquet down, putting a bit of top spin on it. Kirsty doesn't even try to get it. ACE!!!!

Hawkeye announces through tight lips, "Game, set and match to Georgia Nicolson." Yesss!!!!! Victory!!!!!!

I fall to my knees like McEnroe and the crowd is going mad. Full of euphoria I fling my racquet high up into the air.

It curves and falls down and hits Hawkeye right on the head. She is knocked off her umpire chair, unconscious.

In bed
8:00 p.m.

I CAN'T BELIEVE IT. Hawkeye was only unconscious for about a minute but I was made to forfeit the match. Kirsty played Lindsay. I couldn't bear to watch – more to the point, I wasn't allowed to watch – I had to go and tidy all the gym mats.

Lindsay won the cup.

I don't know what this means karmically. I don't think I believe in God any more.

11:00 p.m.

The only way I will believe in God is if something really bloody great happens to me soon.

Pyjama party

Friday June 4th
The pyjama party sleepover
5:00 p.m.

Mum will not get going. Why is she so slow? Libby still has not got any knickers on. I offer to put them on her and Mum says, "Oh, would you, love? Thanks. I cannot find my eyebrow tweezers anywhere. You haven't seen them, have you?"

(I remember they are in my pencil case.) "Er... no, but I think I saw Libby with them."

"Damn, they could be anywhere."

Libby decided that "knickers on" was a game and I chased her around for ages before I could get hold of her. Then when I was putting her knick-knacks on she was stroking my hair, going, "Prrr prr. Nice pussycat. Do you want some milk, tosser?" I think she thinks "tosser" is like a name.

Once I got her dressed I raced upstairs and got the tweezers, then I put them in Angus's basket. (Fortunately he was out murdering birds or he would have eaten them.) Then I shouted to Mum, "Hey, Mum, guess where your tweezers are? Come and see!"

Mum came out of the bedroom and I pointed to the cat basket. She said, "Honestly!! Thanks, love. Right now, I think that's everything. We can get off now, Libby."

She grabbed Libby, who was struggling and licking her face. Libby said, "Bad, bad Mummy, stealing Libby."

As they went through the door Mum said, "You'll be OK, won't you? I'll be back late tomorrow – eat something sensible and don't stay up too late."

She went through the door and then came back a moment later. "Don't even think about doing anything to your hair."

6:00 p.m.

Rosie was the first to arrive. She said, "Sven is going to come at about eleven thirty, after his restaurant shift finishes."

I said, "What have you got up to with him?"

She said, "Er... six and a bit of seven..."

We had this scoring system for kissing and so on, from one to ten:

1. holding hands
2. arm around
3. goodnight kiss
4. kiss lasting over three minutes without a breath
5. open mouth kissing
6. tongues
7. upper body fondling – outdoors
8. upper body fondling – indoors (in bed)
9. below waist activity
10. the full monty

I said, "What is he like at it?"

Rosie said, "He's good, I think Danish boys are better at it than English ones. They change rhythm more."

I said, "What do you mean?"

"You know English boys get really excited and just sort of kiss with the same pressure? Well, he varies the pressure: sometimes it's gentle and sometimes hard and then middley."

I said, "Oh, I like that."

Rosie said, "I know, I do too. Apparently all girls do. We like variety whereas boys like the same."

I said, "How do you know that?" and she looked a bit smug. "It's in *Men are from Mars, Women are from Venus.*"

Jools, Ellen, Jas, Patty, Sarah and Mabs all turned up and we got out our jimjams. We watched *Grease* and kept stopping it and doing bits from it. I did "You're The One That I Want" on the sofa.

Then, at about eleven o'clock, the phone rang. I answered and it was Tom wanting to speak to Jas. So Jas went off into the hall and shut the door so we couldn't hear. When she came back her face was a bit pink. She sort of croaked, "He's coming round with his mate Leo... ohmyGodohmyGod ohmyGod!"

11:30 p.m.

Eating toast and Pop-Tarts when Leo and Tom arrived. They brought their pyjamas too and put them on. What a good laugh. Then Sven turned up – I'd forgotten how big he is... Rosie and he disappeared off and the rest of us watched

Grease again. This time the boys joined in. Tom is quite a laugh. I desperately tried not to mention Robbie.

1:00 a.m.
Still up and chatting about EVERYTHING!!!! Haven't seen Rosie and Sven for hours. Surely they must have got past seven by now???

1:30 a.m.
Tom and Jas disappeared off and Leo and Ellen went off "to get some air". Why they think there is no air in the lounge, I don't know. The rest of us Normans (Norman no mates) decided to dare each other. It started off with taking your knickers off and putting them on your head, and so on, and then I dared Sarah to go and stand on the garden wall and drop her pyjama trousers and knickers.

 She did.

2:00 a.m.
Patty and Mabs dared me to streak down to the bottom of the street. They said they would buy me a new lipstick if I did. The "couples" were still away so I thought I'd do it. We

went outside (us Normans), all in our jimjams. It was a nice summer night, and there were no houselights on in the streets except for ours. So I took my jimjams off and ran like mad in my nuddy-pants down to the bottom of the street and back. It made us die laughing – the others couldn't believe that I had done it!!!

We were all collapsed on the front doorstep when the "couples" came back. I hid behind the others whilst I scrambled into my pyjamas. Tom winked at me. "I should tell my brother what he's missing."

I went purple. "Don't you dare, Tom. Promise, promise me you won't!!"

Tom said, "Do you think that me and Jas should go out with each other again?"

I said, "Oh yes!! I think you are perfect for each other."

And he said, "I've always liked you because you are so sincere."

At about two thirty the lads went home and we cleared up the house. Please don't let Tom tell Robbie about the nuddy-pants incident.

All us girls snuggled up under duvets in the front room, chatting about everything – boys, make-up... lesbians.

Rosie said, "How do you get to become a lesbian?"

I said, "Why? Are you going to give it a go?"

Jas said, "You can't just give it a go. You can't just think, Oh, I'll give being a lesbian a go."

Ellen sat up. "A go at what?"

Jas went a bit red (which is a lot red in anyone else's language). "Well, have a go at, er, snogging a girl."

We all sat up then and went "Erlacck!"

Rosie said, "Is that what they do, then – snog each other?"

Jas (the lesbian spokesperson) said a bit smugly, "Of course they do. They have proper sexual wotsits."

Rosie said, "How can they have proper sexual wotsits when they haven't got... you know, any proper sexual wotsits."

I interrupted, "Jas, how come you know so much about it, anyway?"

She went ludicrously red. Rosie had got all interested now. "But, I mean, what do they do when they haven't got proper sexual wotsits?"

I said to Jas, "Go on, then, Miss Expert Knickers. What do they do in the privacy of their own lesbian love-nests?"

And Jas sort of mumbled something under her duvet. I

said, "You don't know, do you?" and she mumbled again, "Snnubbing."

I repeated, "Snubbing. They do snubbing? They snub each other?"

Jas sat up and said, "No, rubbing."

I said "Goodnight" really quickly and we all went to sleep.

Wednesday June 16th
6:00 p.m.

Got a note from Jackie today: *We are knocking off school this afternoon and going down town to "get a few things". We'll tell you all about the plan at lunch.*

I knew that "getting a few things" meant shoplifting in Jackiespeak. I tried to hide from her at lunchtime but she found me in the loos. I was reading my mag in one of the cubicles – I had my feet off the ground so you couldn't see there was anyone there but she went into the next-door cubicle and looked over the top of the loo wall.

She said, "What are you doing?"

I didn't look up, I just said, "I'm practising origami."

She said, "Are you ready to go? We've got lists of what to

get and where we will meet later."

Suddenly I snapped. I really was sick to death of her and Alison, they didn't make me laugh or anything, they just kept making me do things I didn't want to do. I was sick of it. I found myself saying, "I'm not coming and I don't think you should go either."

Jackie was amazed. "Have you become a Christian? I haven't seen your tambourine. Come on, get your coat and we'll go over the back fields."

I said, "No," and came out of the cubicle. She followed me and came up close – she is quite big.

She said, "I think you had better." Alison was just behind her.

Then this odd calm voice came out of me. I'd been watching *Xena, Warrior Princess* and for one stupid moment I thought I was her. I said, "Oh good, I didn't realise I'd be able to try out my new martial arts skills so soon. If I break anything I apologise in advance. I've only practised on bricks before."

Jackie looked a bit puzzled (who wouldn't?) but she kept coming nearer and suddenly with a yell I grabbed her arm and twisted it right up her back. I don't know how.

But I was doing it for the little people everywhere (I don't mean dwarfs – I just mean, you know, vulnerable people).

8:00 p.m.
Jas phoned. "Everyone is talking about you – it's brilliant!!"

8:30 p.m.
I am cock of the walk. (I don't know what the girl equivalent of "cock" is... surely it can't be "vagina". I am vagina of the walk doesn't have the same ring to it, somehow...)

Midnight
Yesssss!!!!!

Saturday June 19th
9:00 a.m.
The Stiff Dylans are playing at The Market Place. Tom and Jas are going, and all the gang. Shall I?

11:30 a.m.
Mum is being ridiculous – she refuses to let me dye my hair

 207

blonde. I said, "Where would Marilyn Monroe have been if Mrs Monroe had said, 'No, Marilyn, you'll ruin your hair'?"

Mum said, "Don't be ridiculous."

But I went on, "And what about Caprice?... Do you suppose Mrs Caprice said—"

Mum threw her slipper at me. Oh great, now she has turned to violence. I may yet ring Esther Rantzen's childline.

2:00 p.m.
Nngut naface-musk on, I cnt muv mi face.

2:30 p.m.
Blocked the sink with my egg-yolk mask.

4:00 p.m.
I'm going to start my make-up now.

4:30 p.m.
Double *merde*. I'll have to start all over again, I've stuck the mascara brush in my eye. It's all watery and red.

5:30 p.m.

Lying down with cucumber slices on my eyes to take down the swelling.

5:50 p.m.

Libby crept in and ate one of my cucumber slices. It gave me a terrible shock to see her face looming over me when I wasn't expecting it.

6:00 p.m.

Ellen rang, we are meeting outside The Market Place at eight thirty.

Midnight

What an unbelievably BRILLIANT night. Double cool with knobs. Robbie KISSED me. The Sex God has landed. It was so mega.

The Stiff Dylans played some great music and Jas, Tom, Leo, Ellen and me worked out these funny dance routines. Lindsay was there, all po-faced. Robbie was great in the band. I felt a bit self-conscious about dancing at first but then I began to enjoy myself. I showed Tom and Jas a little routine I had made up in my bedroom – and then it was like in a film because everyone – loads of people – started copying it and joining in.

I was a bit out of breath at the end and hot, so when the band took a break I went outside the back door. There was this sort of patio area. As I was standing there Robbie came out... I felt really awkward and was going to go back in when he put his arm on mine and said, "Can I just speak to you for a minute, Georgia?"

I said, "Yes, fine..." He looked a bit embarrassed so I said, "Look, if it's about Jas and Tom I'm sorry that you were angry with me... I think he's really nice and Jas likes him a lot."

Robbie said, "Well, I'm glad, but it's not that. I've just been meaning to give you this." Then he kissed me!!!! I went completely jelloid – it was like being part girl, part jellyfish. It was mega brilliant. Twenty out of ten type kissing. I got all that stuff you're supposed to have – fireworks whooshing in your head, bands playing, sea crashing in and out... I don't know how long it went on for, I was so faint.

Eventually he said, "I've wanted to do that for a long time, but I know it's wrong."

I could hardly speak, it came out all mad. "Ng ng –'s OK, not wrong, no wrong, ngng ng – I mean it's, I, what I, you and, always, even when I ng." He looked at me as if I was talking a foreign language. But I wasn't, I was just talking rubbish.

Then one of the lads in the band came out and Robbie sort of leaped away from me like a leaping thing. Then he went back in, saying to me, "OK, so Georgia, will you pass that on to Tom? See you later."

"See you later?" What does that mean? Here we go again!!!

I told Jas and she said, "What's going to happen now? Are you his bit on the side? What does he mean, 'See you later'? Does he mean see you later or see you later?" I had to stick my hand over her mouth to shut her up. When Robbie took the stage again I had to stop myself gazing at him like an idiot. He was so gorgeous and he had kissed me!!

When the gig was over Robbie passed by me and said, "I'll call you." Then he went over to Lindsay. She put her arms round his neck and I couldn't watch any more.

When will he call me?

Angus was in my bed when I got home, and Libby. I had

to sleep in a sort of S-shape with my feet hanging out of the bed. But I don't care!!!!

Tuesday June 22nd
5:10 p.m.
I don't know if it's me or the weather but I am so hot all the time.

No call for three days.

Wednesday June 23rd
11:00 p.m.
No call today.

Thursday June 24th
6:00 p.m.
Phoned Jas.

"He's not called yet."

Jas said, "Look, leave it with me. I'll try to find out something from Tom."

"Will you do it subtly though, Jas?"

She said, "What do you take me for? I know what's subtle."

And I said, "Well, I'm sorry, but I feel a bit sensitive and I don't want anyone to know about it until I know what is going on myself."

She said, "Look, relax, my middle name is 'cool'."

I said, "Is it? I thought it was Pollyanna."

She said, "Well, it is, my mum liked the film, but that's not what I mean – and anyway, you said you'd never mention that I told you that."

I said, "OK, but just remember to be subtle, all right?"

She said, "Of course. Hang on a minute." Then I heard her yelling up the stairs, "Mum, will you ask Tom to come down here!"

I heard a bit of faraway noise then Jas's mum yelling from upstairs, "Tom says what do you want? He has just set up the computer and can't come away at the moment."

Then I heard Jas yell back, "Well, will you say that Robbie kissed Georgia and said he would call her later and he hasn't called her yet. Does he know anything about it?"

I couldn't believe my ears and it got worse because Jas's mum joined in, "Robbie kissed Georgie – but he's going out with Lindsay, isn't he?"

Jas yelled back, "Yes, but he's confused."

Then I heard Tom yelling down, "What kind of kiss was it?"
And Jas said, "I think it was six."
I REALLY WANTED TO KILL HER.
"Jas, Jas, SHUT UP!!!"

Friday June 25th
1:00 p.m.
Lindsay came up to me at lunch break. She's so wet close up, she's got really blinky blue watery eyes like a blue-eyed bat. Anyway, old blinky said, "I've heard what happened on Saturday."

I went a bit pale. "You've heard what?" I played for time.

"I heard that you have been going after my boyfriend."

How dare she suggest that I would do such a thing!! I went red and said, "What idiot has been saying that?"

Lindsay glared at me. "Robbie told me." I couldn't take it in. She went on, "He told me how you followed him at the break and then you just flung yourself on him. He said he was sorry for you but also very embarrassed."

I spluttered, I couldn't speak. She went on, "So I'm giving you a warning – don't be so sad. You're a silly little girl, don't let it happen again." I couldn't help thinking of the Ancient

Egyptians – they used to put long-handled spoons up people's noses and scoop their brains out. Of course, the people were dead first but in Lindsay's case there was hardly any difference between alive and dead. I was going to get some spoons and poke them up her beastly, sticky-up nose.

6:00 p.m.

Jas is going to gang up on Lindsay with me. I said to her, "Do you think Robbie really said I was sad and I flung myself on him?"

Jas was a real pal. "No, no, of course not... er... you didn't, did you?"

6:30 p.m.

Oh why this? Why would he be such a pig as to say that? Oh I hate him, I hate him.

Midnight

I hate him, I hate him.

12:30 a.m.

Oh I love him, I love him.

The sex god has landed

Thursday July 1st
Canteen
1:00 p.m.

Lindsay put her coffee cup down while she went to get her bag and I spat in it (the coffee cup, not her bag – although I will spit in her bag if I get the chance). I hate her.

Jackie and Alison get on my nerves even more now they have decided to be my friends. Jackie bought me a bar of chocolate today. It will be an apple next. It's a pathetic world when twisting someone's arm up their back gets them buying you things.

4:00 p.m.

I'm so angry with Robbie. I want to tell him what I think about him but I have too much pride.

4:30 p.m.

Phoned Robbie at home (I got the number from Jas). He answered the phone but I just slammed down the receiver. (And I had done one-four-one as well, haha hahaha.)

4:45 p.m.

Phoned Robbie.

He answered and I said, "Robbie, it's Georgia."

He sort of breathed out and then he said, "Er... I can't really find that science paper you asked me about, Mike, can I call you later? Thanks. Bye."

4:50 p.m.

Phoned Jas. "What does he mean by calling me Mike?"

Jas said, "Well, I suppose Lindsay must have been there."

5:30 p.m.

In bed with the curtains closed.

5:45 p.m.

Mum came into my room.

She said, "Do you want to talk about anything?"

I said, "Yes, suicide."

She said, "It can't be as bad as that."

I said, "Well it is, it's worse. I don't want to be here any more. I hate school. I hate England."

She said, "Well, do you think that maybe a summer trip to New Zealand might cheer you up? We could go over to Disneyland on the way."

I said, "I don't care what I do."

6:30 p.m.

So this is what men are like. Well, that is it, then. I am going to be a lesbian.

7:00 p.m.

I got out some photos of Denise Van Outen and tried to imagine kissing her.

7:05 p.m.

I can't do it. And I can't help thinking about Miss Stamp's moustache. And the rubbing.

7:10 p.m.

I'll have to be a nun, then.

8:00 p.m.

It's no use, if I pull all my hair back like a nun, it makes my nose look huge. Still, I don't suppose that matters when you are only saving poor people and making soup for them, like nuns do.

9:00 p.m.

The phone rang for me. I said to Mum, "Who is it?" and she said, "I don't know, it's a boy."

9:30 p.m.

Robbie is going to meet me tomorrow after school at my house. He was in a phone box and said that he couldn't really explain, he'd talk tomorrow. If he thinks he can "explain" this away he's very much mistaken. I have got some pride. I've got a lot to say to him about his "explanation"!!!

9:45 p.m.

What shall I wear? Maybe I won't go to school tomorrow to give myself time to get made up in a natural way.

Friday July 2nd
8:05 a.m.

Said goodbye to Mum and Libbs and went as normal to Jas's. She was waiting for me on the corner. I said, "I'm not coming to school today, I'm meeting Robbie. Will you say that I have got the painters in very badly? Thanks."

Then I went back home. I waited until Mum and Libbs left and then I slipped back into the house.

Day plan:

1. Steam face.
2. Apply face pack.
3. Sort out clothes to wear.
4. Tidy bedroom (well, put everything on the floor and then under the bed).
5. Put some interesting books near my bed (hide comics and boy mags).
6. Remove nuddy-pants poster of Reeves and Mortimer.

7. Make sure Libby has not peed or pooed in any secret corner.

11:00 a.m.

In my room tidying when I heard the front door open. If it was a burglar I only had Mum's tweezers to defend myself with. Where was Angus when you needed him? I hadn't seen the mad furry thing for hours.

11:02 a.m.

Not burglars, it's something much worse... it's Mum. And she's not alone! She has Jem the decorator with her. Oh fabulous, my mum is having an affair with a builder. Also she is older than him – also I already have a dad, who is bad enough, but better the dad you know than the builder you don't.

They went into the lounge so I crept downstairs to see if I could hear what was going on. I put my ear against the door but I couldn't quite hear. I pressed my ear quite hard up against the keyhole. I heard Jem say, "This is the door that sticks. I'm going to—" and that's when he opened the door and I crashed into the room.

Noon

In bed. I had to pretend that I had fainted. I lay still on the floor until Mum put something disgusting (smelling salts) under my nose. I thought my head was going to come off. I sort of pretended that I was all confused and that I had felt ill on the way to school.

Mum made me come to bed with an aspirin. Soon after, I heard the door slam. Mum came up. "Er – I just took an hour off to discuss the final details about the lounge with Jem."

I said, "He's taken about a hundred years to decorate one room. Libby thinks he is our new dad."

Mum laughed. "Don't be so silly, why would you think she thought that?"

I said, "Because she calls him 'my new dad'."

Mum ignored that and went on, "Well, I must get back to work, are you sure you will be all right?"

I said, "Oh yes, I'll be all right – will YOU be all right?" (I said it really meaningfully but she didn't know what I meant.)

Minutes later she came back in the room and said, "Georgia, I know that you like a bit of drama, but I'm afraid that Jem and I are not having a passionate affair."

I said, "Oh, what is it then? A really lukewarm affair?"

She sat down on my bed. "It's not any kind of affair. Look, love, I really, really miss your dad." And it was horrible because her eyes were all leaky.

I said, "You can't miss his moustache."

She said, "No, I don't miss that. But I love him. Don't you?"

I said, "He's all right."

She kissed me. "I know you do love him, you're just moody and someone has to suffer, but never mind, we'll be seeing him soon."

Then she left. God, I can't stand this having to talk about grown-ups all the time! I do wish my dad was here, then I could forget all about him!

4:00 p.m.

Robbie will be here in half an hour. I'd better just go to the loo again. I've only been ten times in the last ten minutes. I hope I'm not incontinent, I'll have to wear big nappies... Robbie will never stand for that – if he gets famous he won't want a girlfriend who wears nappies.

223

6:30 p.m.

Robbie has just gone. I feel all hollow inside like a hollowed-out coconut. He looked gorgeous, all in black, and sort of sad. He gave me a brilliant smile when he saw me and then he just pulled me towards him (quite roughly, actually...). I remembered how cross I was though, so I only snogged him for half an hour before I said, "How could you tell Lindsay that I was sad and that I followed you outside and flung myself on you?"

He looked puzzled. "I didn't say that."

"Didn't you?"

"No, I didn't... I haven't said anything to anyone."

"Well, that's what Lindsay said to me."

He looked uncomfortable.

I went on, "And are you engaged to her or not?"

He looked really puzzled then. "Engaged to her? Why should you think that?"

"Well, because she wears an engagement ring at school that she tells people you gave her."

He sat down. "This is bad."

I tried to go on being cross but he looked so gorgey porgey that I couldn't keep it up. Then he looked right into my eyes. I tried not to blink because not blinking is supposed to be attractive. He said, "Look Georgie, I'm having real trouble with this. The truth is, I've been trying to find a way to end it with Lindsay but I don't want to hurt her feelings."

I said, "Yes, it's tricky, isn't it? Because she obviously likes you a lot. Still, I've got an idea..."

He looked hopeful. "What is it?"

"I'll tell her, in a nice way of course, that she is a wet weed and that she is dumped. That should do it."

He did actually laugh! He said, "You're mad. Anyway, it's my problem and I'll sort it out, but there is something else I have to tell you."

Here it comes, I was thinking (but not blinking). He's going to say, "You are the girl of my dreams, will you be my girlfriend? You are the most gorgeous girl I have ever—"

I'd just got to that bit in my head when he interrupted me. "I have to tell you, it wouldn't be fair to you not to... but well, I am attracted to you (I tried not to smirk or smile too much in case he had second thoughts when he saw my nose spreading all over my face) but I can't go out with you."

I said, "Why not?"

And he said, "Because you are too young. I'm nearly

eighteen – it would not be right, it would be like cradle-snatching."

I argued with him. I even said, "I'm not really fourteen, I'm actually fifteen and a half, it's just that I'm not very bright and they've kept me back a year."

He laughed, but in a sad way. Then he gave me a last kiss sort of thing and went.

Midnight
Too young for him. Oh *merde merde merde, double merde*.

I wonder where Angus is? I could do with something to cuddle even if I did get a savage biting.

Monday July 5th
11:30 a.m.
Mucho excitemondo!!! Robbie has dumped Lindsay!!! Hurrah!!! She came into school with her eyes all swollen up like little boiled sweets. I passed her in the corridor and she said, "I hope you're satisfied now, you horrid little girl." Horrid little girl, that's nice.

I could have said, "At least I don't wear bits of rubber down my bra and a piece of string up my bottom." But unfortunately I began to feel a bit sorry for her – after all, she would never get another boyfriend, whereas even if I had to wait a whole year I would one day be older and then I could get Robbie.

5:30 p.m.
I'm glum, though – a year seems a long, long time and what if he finds someone else before I get old enough?

6:30 p.m.
Still no sign of Angus. This is a bit unusual. He always comes back for his dindins.

7:00 p.m.
Looking round the street for Angus. I had a dead mouse and a chop to entice him.

7:15 p.m.
Just stumbled into Mark, snogging in his driveway with some girl... he's always at it!! If it's true that stimulation makes things bigger (breasts etc.), perhaps he had very tiny lips when he was born and he has just overstimulated

them by snogging all the time.

9:30 p.m.
No Angus. I hoped he might be at home lurking behind the curtain ready to attack my legs, but he's not.

11:00 p.m.
No phone calls, no Angus. Libby came into bed with me. "Where big pussy tosser?" she asked me. I almost cried. I really cuddled her but it made her too cross and she bit me on the chin.

Had a dream about Robbie. I had blonde hair in the dream.

Tuesday July 6th
7:30 p.m.
Eureka!!! I've got it!!! I know what my dream was trying to tell me. There is a way I can convince Robbie that I am more mature than my fourteen years... I have to dye a blonde streak in my hair. A blonde streak will add years to my appearance!!!

Still no sign of Angus. Mum said, "I don't want to upset

you, but you know that he stalks cars and attacks them – it may be that this time he's had a bit of an accident."

I can't bear to think of this.

Midnight

I think of all the animals in the world and all the sad things that happen to them. Little chickens whose parents go for a day's outing on the farmyard truck and never come back because they have gone to be on somebody's table. And all the little sheep who see their mummies and daddies loaded into vans... oh I cannot stand this. I'm never going to eat meat again.

1:00 a.m.

They say vegetables feel pain. What about the little baby potatoes all snug underground with their brother and sister potatoes and then a big hand comes and uproots them and... slices them up. Oh God, now I can never eat chips again.

2:30 a.m.

What can I eat, then?

4:00 a.m.

If I starved myself to death I wonder if Robbie would think I was grown-up enough?

Wednesday July 7th

8:00 a.m.

I'm shattered this morning, and upset. I miss Angus. Even Mum does. Mrs Next Door doesn't, though. When I asked her if she had seen him, she said, "No I haven't. And I know he hasn't been in my yard because nothing is dead or dug up and my dog is not a nervous wreck." I hate her – I hope her husband gets stuck in his greenhouse and then she will know what I feel like. She will know what true pain is.

And suffering.

2:30 p.m.

Ink fight in RE, which generally cheers me up, but I couldn't even flick properly I was so upset.

The gossip at school is that Lindsay is not eating and has got what's it – anorexia. I don't know how you would know, she's so skinny anyway.

Nearly the summer hols, so it will be the last I see of this hell-hole for a bit.

Friday July 9th
8:50 p.m.
I really think Angus must have been run over or something. I miss him, we've been through a lot of stuff, me and him. Stupid furry freak. But I love him. It seems I am destined to lose everything I love.

Sunday July 11th
2:00 p.m.
Jas and I looked in all the streets around her house, just in case Angus had followed me one day and then lost his way. We were just by her place when Robbie pulled up in his mini. He looked a bit ruffled but I was too down in the dumps to think about it much. He said, "Have you found Angus?"

I said, "No, we've looked everywhere."

Wednesday July 14th
3:30 p.m.
Every cloud has a bit of a silver lining. I was sitting against

the school wall in the shade, just thinking. The others were all sprawled out in their knickers sunbathing by the tennis courts. The bit of wall I was leaning against was just near Elvis's hut. I saw him put on his coat and get his shopping bag... what a wally he looked. He closed the hut door but he didn't lock it and then he went off. I'd nothing else to do so I thought I'd go and sit in his hut for a while, see what it would be like to be a school caretaker.

There was nothing much in the hut – a chair and a table and a little fridge and some magazines he's been reading. I sat down and flicked through them... and my jaw nearly dropped off. Because they were naughty magazines, if you know what I mean. Called *Fiesta* and *Big Girls*. One of them was called *Down Your Way*, and was all full of candid photos of readers and their wives in the privacy of their own bedrooms. Some of them were so fat!! I flicked through the pages to the centrefold. And the centrefold was ELVIS and MRS ELVIS!!!! In the NUDDY-PANTS!!!! I couldn't believe it. Elvis in the nuddy-pants. Elvis was standing by the kettle in the nuddy-pants, pretending to make a cup of tea and Mrs Elvis was doing the washing-up in the nuddy-pants!!!

I took the mag with me and passed it around the whole

class. We were laughing for the whole afternoon, someone only had to say, "Fancy a cup of tea, my dear?" and we'd be off again. Ooohhhhh, it made my stomach really hurt with laughing.

Elvis knows someone has got his mag but he can't say anything. If I see him I just let my eyes drift down to his trousers...

Saturday July 17th
12:00 p.m.

Joy joy, double bubble joy. Hadihahahaha. Robbie has just phoned me. He has found Angus!! Robbie had been out searching for him and he heard all these dogs barking so he went to see what they were barking at. And it was Angus, tied up. Some people had found him, he had a bad paw so they had bandaged it up and tied him up until they found his owners. They had put up notices but I hadn't seen them.

Robbie said the people were bloody glad to get rid of him as he had already eaten two doormats and a clothesline. They were lucky they got off so lightly.

Anyway, Robbie is going to bring him round to me at five o'clock.

1:00 p.m.

Mum's out and I am determined to make Robbie realise that I'm a great deal older than I was fifteen days ago. I haven't any money and Mum has selfishly taken her purse with her, but I HAVE A PLAN.

2:00 p.m.

There is some peroxide that Gran uses to clean her dentures when she comes to stay. It's kept in the bathroom cupboard and I'm going to use it to bleach a really sophisticated streak of blonde in my hair at the front.

2:30 p.m.

I've put it on, I wonder how long you have to leave it? It's stinging my scalp so that must be a good sign.

3:30 p.m.

It's gone a sort of orange colour! Oh bloody hell, I'll have to put some more on.

4:15 p.m.

Now it's gone sort of bright yellow. I look like a canary.

234

5:00 p.m.

Thank goodness it's gone white. I think it looks quite good. It feels a bit stiff, though. Oh well, it'll soften up in time. I think it makes me look at least four years older.

5:30 p.m.

Robbie here with Angus. I was so pleased to see him I tried to give him a cuddle but he lashed out at me and was hissing until I gave him a rabbit leg. Then he started purring. (Angus, not Robbie.)

Robbie noticed my hair when I stood up. He was obviously impressed because he said, "Er – you've got a white streak in your hair."

I said, "Oh yes, do you like it?"

There was a bit of a silence between us. I was thinking, Go on, kiss me, kiss me! But he said, "Look, this is not easy for me, I think I should go now."

I said, "Thank you for Angus."

He said, "Oh, that's OK, I knew you liked him and the scratches will heal in time and I should be able to replace the trousers."

As he was leaving I had one final go to make him see that

I was mature and sophisticated beyond my years. I flicked my hair back like they do in movies and then I made the mistake of running my fingers through my hair. The white streak snapped off in my hand. I was just left holding it there, in my hand. Robbie looked amazed. He looked at the hunk of hair in my hand and then he looked at me and then he started laughing. He said, "God you're weird," and then he kissed me. (I shoved the hunk of hair on the sofa and Angus pounced on it – he must have thought it was a hamster or something.)

After a bit of number six kissing Robbie said, "Well, look, let's take it easy and start seeing each other, shall we... see how it goes, maybe keep it a bit quiet from people at first?"

So all is well that ends well. I am now nearly Robbie's girlfriend, hahahaha. Summer love, summer love!!!

The end

9:00 p.m.

Mum came in. "Right, we're all set – I've got them!!"

I said (in a sort of romantic daze), "What have you got, Mutti?"

"I've got the tickets for us!"

"Tickets for what?"

"Tickets for New Zealand. When you said you wanted to go I went and booked them. Dad paid for them and we're off to Whangamata next week."

Sacré bloody *bleu* and *merde*!!!

Georgia's Glossary

airing cupboard · This is a cupboard over the top of the hot-water heater in a house. It is used for keeping towels and sheets warm on cold winter nights. Er, at least that's what it's used for in normal people's houses.

"Agadoo" · The worst song ever written. It won the Eurovision Song Contest, which is a competition for the worst songs ever written. That is all I have to say. Oh, and grown-ups think it is a "laugh" to sing it when they are drunk. It isn't. (It goes "Aga doo doo doo, Aga doo doo doo" for twenty hours.)

agony aunt · A woman in a magazine who gives you advice if you are a sad person with no one else to talk to. For instance, Jas might write, "Dear Agony Aunt, My friend Georgia is so much better-looking, cleverer and all-round more brilliant that I feel inadequate. What should I do?" And the agony aunt would write back, "Kill yourself." (Not really, that last bit is a joke.)

bangers · Firecrackers. Fireworks that just explode with a big bang. That's it. No pretty whooshing or stars or rocketing up into the sky. Bangers just bang. Boy fireworks. Boys are truly weird.

Borstal · A sort of young person's prison for naughty boys.

catsuit · An all-in-one suit thing with trousers and a zipper up the front. Usually evening wear. It is supposed to be sexy, and perhaps it is, but try getting out of one quickly if you have to pay an emergency lavatory call. Like a grown-up version of a romper suit.

Crazy Colour · Hair colour that you paint on your hair and that can be washed out.(Crazy because it is blue or purple or red or green.)

deely bopper · Like antenna things with tiny balls on the end that you wear on your head. Popular with five-year-olds.

Denise Van Outen · She is a blonde on TV who is a bit on the breasty side. Boys seem to like her, although I can't see the attraction myself as I am not (probably) a lesbian.

dole · What unemployed people get (i.e. money) to stop them starving to death. Welfare.

double cool with knobs · "Double" and "with knobs" are instead of saying "very" or "very, very, very, very". You'd feel silly saying, "He was very, very, very, very, very cool." Also everyone would fall asleep before you finished your sentence. So "double cool with knobs" is altogether snappier.

duffing up · Duffing up is the female equivalent of beating up. It is not so violent and usually involves a lot of pushing, with the occasional pinch.

first former · Kids of about eleven who have just started "big" school. They have shiny innocent faces – very tempting to slap.

fringe · Goofy short bit of hair that comes down to your eyebrows. Some one told me that American-type people call them "bangs", but this is so ridiculously strange that it's not worth thinking about. Some people can look very stylish with a fringe (i.e. me) while others look goofy (Jas). The Beatles started it (apparently). One of them had a German girlfriend and she cut their hair with a pudding bowl, and the rest is history.

Froggie and geoggers · Froggie is short for French; geoggers is short for geography. Ditto blodge (biology) and lunck (lunch).

full-frontal snogging · Kissing with all the trimmings: lip to lip, open mouth, tongues... everything. (Apart from dribble, which is never acceptable.)

gorgey · Gorgeous. Like fabby (fabulous) and marvy (marvellous).

"have the painters in" · An expression to indicate that a girl is... er... having her... you know what. Oh, come on, you do know. Having her... er... well, to put it plainly... her... well, that "the red flag is flying", that her "little friend has come to visit". Period. Menstruation. Woman trouble. Trouble at the mill. I can't go on with this; it is making me tired.

hols · Vacation. In olden days when bishops wanted a day off, they decided to have a Holy Day or, as it has become, a Hol-i-day. Shortened to hols for obvious reasons. (Life is too short to use long words.) Apart from the fact that Anne Boleyn, Henry VIII's wife, designed dresses with long sleeves because she had a sixth finger growing out of her little finger, this is the only thing I remember from history class.

"how's your father" · A boy's... er... penis (or penid as I thought it was until I was eleven). Well, you wanted to know.

jimjams · Pyjamas. Also pygmies or jammies.

joggerbums · Trousers that you jog in. Jogging trousers.

jumping-jacks · A hellish combination. This is about ten bangers all tied together. When a jumping-jack is lit, not only does it bang A LOT, but it leaps all over the place and chases you about. Banging. Boys think it is hilarious to light them and chuck them into a group of girls. As I have said, boys are weird.

naff · unbearably and embarrassingly out of fashion and nerdy. Naff things are: parents dancing to "modern" music, blue eyeshadow, blokes who wear socks with sandals, pigtails... You know what I mean.

nuddy-pants · Quite literally nude-coloured pants. And you know what nude-coloured pants are? They are no pants. So if you are in your nuddy-pants you are in your no pants (i.e. you are naked).

O-levels · "Ordinary" level exams that perfectly nice teenagers were made to take when they were about fifteen. Now called GCSEs. These exams are of course sadistically timed for the summer months by teachers, etc., who have no life and therefore want to spoil it for everyone else.

one-four-one · The code you dial before a number if you don't want the person you are calling to be able to trace your number. Like a secrecy code.

Paloma · Paloma is a perfume made up by Paloma Picasso, who is the daughter of the famous artist Picasso. Her dad used to paint people with eyes on their cheeks – he invented this. It is not bad art, apparently, but "abstract". Anyone could say that about anything that was really crap. They could say, "No, you are mistaken, this is not a really bad drawing of a cow that looks more like a monkey, it is abstract art." But perhaps I am cynical.

po-faced · a po is a sort of basin thing that goes under your bed, like a bedpan. In the old days very poor people would use a po instead of a lavatory. Then they poured the contents of the po out on to the streets on to innocent passersby. Ergo, "po-faced" means someone who has a face like a lavatory bowl.

poxy · From Olde Englishe. "The pox" was crumbly horrible spots that Olde Englishe people got from not having proper lavatories. Or maybe it was rats. I can't remember. Anyway, hence the expression "poxy", meaning horrible.

prat · A gormless oik. You make a prat of yourself by mistakenly putting both legs down one knicker leg or by playing air guitar at pop concerts.

PVC jacket · PVC is that shiny wet-look material that whatshername in *The Avengers* used to wear about a million years ago. PVC has come back into fashion again, but some things never will. Culottes, for instance, will never be fashionable again; they never were, apart from with Swiss people. I rest my case fashionwise.

Reeves and Mortimer · Reeves and Mortimer are a comedy double act. They are very mad indeed. But I like them.

romper-suit · All-in-one garment that some sadist designed for children. The legs and body and arms are all joined together, which makes it impossible to get on or off. (And in Libby's case, if she has an accidental poo attack in one, you can imagine the result.)

runner · An escape. Hence the saying, "to do a runner". To run away.

sandwich spread · Stuff in a jar that looks like throw-up that you spread on bread.

shirty · Flustered and twitchy and coming on all pompous.

stroppy · Stroppy is a very useful expression and is the state between having a nervy b (nervous breakdown) and a tantrum. For instance, you would get stroppy or "throw a strop" if your mum did not let you borrow her Chanel handbag, for no reason other than she says you would lose it. You would not quite have a nervy b because it is after all just a handbag. However, you are perfectly entitled to get stroppy if you can't have what you want.

swiz · An unfair thing. Another girl gets a boy you like, that is a swiz. One of your friends gets to pierce her navel and your boring vati won't let you. This is an obvious double swiz.

tosser · A special kind of prat.

TTFN · Ta ta for now. Ta ta means "goodbye". I think this is a World War II expression like "Chocks away" and

"Luftwaffe at 5 o'clock", but so much of life is a mystery to me, I can't be absolutely sure on this one.

wally · See "prat". A wally additionally has no clothes sense.

wet · Drippy, useless, nervy. Lindsay.

whelk · A horrible shellfish thing that only the truly mad (like my granded, for instance) eat. They are unbelievably slimy and mucuslike.

'It's OK, I'm wearing really big knickers!'

To my dear family: Mutti, Vati, Sophie, Libbs, Hons, Eduardo Delfonso Delgardo, John S, Apee, Francesbirginia and especially Kimbo. Thanks you all for not killing me yet.

Also dedicated to my mates: Salty Dog, Jools, Jedbox, Badger, Elton, Jimjams, Jenks, Phil, Bobbins, Lozzer, the Mogul, Fanny, Dear GeH. MSH, Porky, Morgan, Alan D, Liz G, Tony G, Psychic Sue, Roge the Doge and Barbara D and the Ace Crew from school, Kim and Cock of the North xxxxxx.

An especial thank you to John, the Pope. Where would I have been without your wise advice – "Stop making such a fuss and just get on with it, you silly girl!"?

Heartfelt thanks and sympathy to Brenda, Jude, Emma and all the very fab people at Piccadilly.

And of course to Gillon and Clare – HURRAH!!

The Sex God has landed...
and, er, taken off again

Sunday July 18th
My room
6:00 p.m.

Staring out of my bedroom window at other people having a nice life.

Who would have thought things could be so unbelievably pooey? I'm only fourteen and my life is over because of the selfishosity of so-called grown-ups. I said to Mum, "You are ruining my life. Just because yours is practically over there is no reason to take it out on me."

But as usual when I say something sensible and meaningful she just tutted and adjusted her bra like a Russian roulette player. (Or do I mean disco thrower? I don't know and, what's more, I don't care.) If I counted up the number of times I've been tutted at... I could open a tutting shop. It's just SO not fair... How can my parents take me away from my mates and make me go to New Zealand? Who goes to New Zealand?

In the end, when I pointed out how utterly useless as a mum she was, she lost her rag and SHOUTED at me.

"Go to your room right now!"

I said, "All right, I'll go to my ROOM!! I WILL go to my room!! And do you know what I'll be doing in my room? No you don't, so I'll tell you! I'll be just BEING in my room. That's all. Because there is nothing else to do!!!!!!"

Then I just slammed off. Left her there. To think about what she has done.

Unfortunately it means that I am in my bed and it is only six o'clock.

7:00 p.m.
Oh Robbie, where are you now? Well, I know where you are now actually, but is this any time to go away on a footie trip?

On the bright side I am now the girlfriend of a Sex God.

7:15 p.m.
On the dark side, the Sex God doesn't know his new

girlfriend is going to be forced to go to the other (useless) side of the universe in a week's time.

7:18 p.m.

I can't believe that after all the time it has taken to trap the SG, all the make-up I have had to buy, the trailing about, popping up unexpectedly when he was out anywhere... all the planning... all the dreaming – it's gone to waste. I finally get him to snog me (number six) and he says, "Let's see each other but keep it quiet for a bit." And at that moment, with classic poo timing, Mutti says, "We're off to New Zealand next week."

My eyes are all swollen up like mice eyes from crying. Even my nose is swollen. It's not small at the best of times, but now it looks like I've got three cheeks. Marvellous. Thank you, God.

9:00 p.m.

I'll never get over this.

9:10 p.m.

Time goes very slowly when you are suicidal.

I put sunglasses on to hide my tiny mincers. They are new ones that Mum bought me in a pathetic attempt to interest me in going to Kiwi-a-gogo land. They looked quite cool, actually. I looked a bit like one of those French actresses who smoke Gauloise and cry a lot in between snogging Gerard Depardieu. I tried a husky French accent in the mirror.

"And zen when I was, how you say? *Une teen-ager, mes parents, mes très, très horriblement parents*, take me to *Nouvelle Zelande*. Ahh *merde*!"

At which point I heard Mum coming up the stairs and had to leap into bed. She popped her head round the door and said, "Georgie... are you asleep?"

I didn't say anything. That would teach her.

As she left she said, "I wouldn't sleep in the sunglasses if I were you, they might get embedded in your head."

What kind of parenting was that? Mum's medical knowledge was about as good as Dad's DIY. And we had all seen his idea of a shed. Before it fell down on Uncle Eddie.

Eventually I was drifting off into a tragic snooze when I heard shouting coming from next door's garden. Mr and Mrs Next Door were out there, banging and shouting and throwing things about. Is this really the time for noisy gardening? They have no consideration for those who might want to sleep because they have tragedy in their life. I felt like opening the window and shouting, "Garden more quietly, you loons!"

But then I couldn't be bothered getting out of my snuggly bed of pain.

Police raid
Mucho excitemondo
12:10 a.m.

When the doorbell rang I shot out of bed and looked down the stairs. Mum had opened the door wearing a nightdress that you could quite easily see through! Even if you didn't want to. Which I didn't. She has no pride. There were a couple of policemen standing at the door. The bigger one was holding a sack up in front of him at arm's length and his trousers were shredded round the ankles.

"Is this your bloody cat?" he enquired, not very politely for a public servant.

Mum said, "Well, I... er."

I ran down the stairs and went to the door.

"Good evening, constable. This cat, is it about the size of a small Labrador?"

He said, "Yes."

I nodded encouragingly and went on. "And has it got tabby fur and a bit of its ear missing?"

PC Plod said, "Er... yes."

And I said, "No, it's not him then, sorry."

Which I thought was very funny indeed. The policeman didn't.

"This is a serious business, young lady."

Mum was doing her tutting thing again, and combining it with head shaking and basooma adjusting. Deeply unattractive. I thought the policeman might be distracted by her and say, "Go and put some clothes on, madam," but he didn't, he just kept going on at me.

"This thing has had your neighbours penned up in their greenhouse for an hour. They managed to dash into the house eventually but then it rounded up their poodles."

"Yes, he does that. He is half Scottish wildcat. He hears the call of the wilds sometimes and then he..."

"You should keep better control of it."

He went moaning on in a policemany way for hours

and hours. I said, as patiently as I could, although I had enough things to think about as it was, "Look, I'm being made to go to Whangamata by my parents. It is at the other, more useless, side of the universe. It is in New Zealand. Have you seen *Neighbours*? Is there nothing you can do for me?"

My mum gave me her worst look and said, "Don't start, Georgia, I'm not in the mood."

The policeman didn't seem "in the mood" either. He said, "This is a serious warning. You keep this thing under control otherwise we will be forced to take sterner measures."

Mum was hopeless as per usual. She started smiling and fiddling with her hair.

"I'm really sorry to have troubled you, inspector. Would you like to come in and have a nightcap or something?"

It was so EMBARRASSING. He probably thought we ran a brothel in our spare time. The "inspector" was all smiling and he said, "That's very kind of you, madam, but we have to get on. Protecting the public from vicious criminals, dangerous moggies, and so on."

I didn't say anything as I took the wiggling sack, I just looked ironically at his chewed trousers.

Mum went BERSERK about Angus. She said, "He'll have to go."

I said, "Oh yes, perfect, just take everything that I love and destroy it. Just think of your own self and make me go halfway round the universe and lose the only boy I love. You can't just leave Sex Gods, you know, they have to be kept under constant surveillance and..."

She had gone into her bedroom.

Angus strolled out of the bag and strutted around the kitchen looking for a snack. He was purring like two tanks. Libby wandered in all sleepy with her blankin'. Her night-time nappy was bulging round her knees. The last thing I needed was a poo explosion at this time of night so I said, "Go tell Mummy about your pooey nap-naps, Libby."

But she just said, "Shhh, bad boy," and went over to Angus. She kissed him on the nose and then sucked it before she dragged him off to bed.

I don't know why he lets her do anything she likes with him. He almost had my hand off the other day when I tried to take his plate away and he hadn't quite finished.

Monday July 19th
11:00 a.m.

I am feeling sheer desperadoes. It's a day and a half now since I snogged the Sex God. I think I have snog withdrawal. My lips keep puckering up.

I HAVE to find a way of not going to Kiwi-a-gogo land. I went on hunger-strike this morning. Well, apart from a Jammy Dodger.

2:00 p.m.

Phone rang.

Mum yelled up at me, "Gee, will you get that, love? I'm in the bath."

I yelled back, "You can wash the outside clean, but you can't wash the inside!"

She yelled again, "Georgia!!!"

Dragged myself up from my bed of pain and went all the way downstairs and picked up the phone.

"I said, "Hello, Heartbreak Hotel here," and all I could hear was just crackle, crackle, surf, swish, swish. So I shouted really loudly, "HELLO, HELLO, HELLO!!!!" and this faraway voice said, "Bloody hell!"

It was my father, or Vati as I call him. Phoning from New Zealand. He was, as usual, in a bad mood for no reason.

"Why did you shout down the phone? My ears are all ringing now."

I said, reasonably enough, "Because you didn't say anything."

"I did, I said hello."

"Well I didn't hear you."

"Well you can't have been listening properly."

"How can I not listen properly when I am answering the phone?"

"I don't know, but if anyone can manage it, you can."

Oh, play the old record again, it's always me that does things wrong. I said, "Mum's in the bath."

He said, "Just a minute, don't you want to know how I am?"

"Er, let me guess... funny moustache, bit bulky round the bottom department?"

"Don't be so bloody cheeky! Get your mum. I give up on you. I don't know what you learn at that school besides how to put on lipstick and be cheeky."

I put the phone down because he can grumble on like

that for centuries if you let him. I shouted, "Mutti, there is a man on the phone. He claims to be my dear vati but I don't think he is because he was quite surly with me."

Mum came out of the bathroom with her hair all wet and dripping and in just a bra and pants. She really has got the most gigantic basoomas, I'm surprised she doesn't topple over. Good Lord.

I said, "I am at a very impressionable age, you know."

She just gave me her worst look and grabbed the phone. As I went through the door I could hear her saying, "Hello, darling. What? I know. Oh I know. You needn't tell me that... I have her all the time. It's a nightmare."

That's nice talk, isn't it?

As I point out to anyone who will listen (i.e. no one), I didn't ask to be born. I am only here because she and Vati... urgh... anyway, I won't go down that road.

My room
2:10 p.m.
I could hear her rambling on to Dad, going, "Hmmm – well I know, Bob... I know... Uh huh... I KNOW... I know. Yes, I know..."

In the name of pantyhose, what are grown-ups like? I shouted down to her, "Break the news to him gently that I'm definitely not in a TRILLION years coming."

He must have heard me because even upstairs I could hear muffled shouting from down the other end of the phone. I wasn't amazed by the shouting as my vati is prone to violence. Once I poured aftershave into his lager and lime when he was out of the room. For a merry joke. But he didn't get the joke. When he stopped choking he went all ballisticisimus and shouted, "You complete IDIOT!!!" really loudly at me. It's the kind of thing that will cost me hundreds of pounds in therapy fees in later life. (Should I have a life, which I don't.)

2:30 p.m.
Playing sad songs in my bedroom, still in my jimjams.

Mutti came into my room and said, "Can I come in?"

I said, "No."

But that didn't put her off.

She came and sat on the edge of my bed and put her hand on my foot. I said, "Owww!!!"

She said, "Look, love, I know this is all a bit complicated, especially at your age, but this is a really big opportunity for us. Your dad thinks he has a real chance to make something of himself over in Whangamata."

I said, "what's wrong with the way he is now? Quite a few people like fat blokes with ridiculous moustaches. You do."

She came on all parenty then. "Georgia, don't think that rudeness is funny because it isn't."

"It can be."

"No it isn't."

"Well you laughed when Libby called Mr Next Door 'nice tosser'."

"Well Libby is only three and she thinks that tosser is like Bill or Dad or something. Can't you see this trip as an exciting adventure?"

"What, like when you are on your way to school and then suddenly you get run over by a bus and have to go to hospital, or something?"

"Yes, like when... NO!! Come on, Georgie, try to be a pal, just for me."

I didn't say anything.

"You know that your dad can't get a job here. What else is he supposed to do? He's only trying to look after us all."

After a bit she sighed and went out.

Life is *très merde* and double bum. Why doesn't Mutti understand I can't leave now? She can be ludicrously dim. It's not her that I get my intelligence from. It is certainly no thanks to her that I came top in... er... well anyway, it's nothing to do with her what I do. I am just the unfortunate recipient of some of her genes. The orang-utan eyebrow gene, for instance. She has to do a lot of plucking to keep her eyebrows apart and she has selfishly passed it on to me. Since I shaved mine off by mistake last term they seem to have gone even more haywire and akimbo. The shaving has encouraged them to grow about a metre a week. If I left them alone I'd be blind by October. Jas has got ordinary eyebrows, why can't I?

Also, while I am on the subject, the worst news of all is that I think I have inherited her breast genes. My basoomas are definitely growing. I am very worried that I may end up with huge breasts like hers. Everyone notices hers.

Once, when we were on the ferry to France, Dad said to Mum, "Don't stand too near to the edge, Connie, otherwise your chest might be declared a danger to shipping."

5:00 p.m.

I've just had a flash of whatsit!! It's so obvious, I am indeed a genius! Simple pimple. I'll just tell Mum that I'll stay behind and... LOOK AFTER THE HOUSE!! The house can't just be left empty for months because... er... squatters might come in and take it over. Anarchists who will paint everything black, including, probably, Mr and Mrs Next Door's poodles. They'll be begging for Angus to come back.

Excellent, brilliant fabulosa idea!! Mum will definitely see the sense of it.

I'll promise to be really mature and grown-up and responsible. I mainly want to stay in England because of the terrifically good education system. That is how I will sell it to Mutti.

"Mutti," I will say, "this is a crucial time in my schooldays. I think I may be picked for the hockey team."

Thank goodness I didn't bother Mum with my school report from last term. I saved her the trouble of reading it by signing it myself.

5:05 p.m.

You would think that Hawkeye could think of something more imaginative to write than, *Hopelessly childish attitude in class.* Just because she caught me doing my (excellent) impression of a lockjaw germ.

5:10 p.m.
I could have groovy parties that everyone would really want to come to. I'm going to make a list of all the people I will ask to the parties:

<u>First – Sex Gods</u>
Robbie... er, that's it.

<u>Second – the Ace Crew</u>
Rosie, Jools, Ellen and, I suppose, Jas if she pulls her pants up and makes a bit more effort with me. She has been a bit of a Slack Alice on the pal front since she got Tom.

<u>Third – close casuals</u>
Mabs, Sarah, Abbie, Phebes, Hattie, Bella... people I like for a laugh but wouldn't necessarily lend my mum's leather jacket to... then acquaintances and fanciable brothers.

5:20 p.m.

I may even allow crap dancers like Sven to come if they have pleasing or amusing personalities (and gifts).

5:23 p.m.

I tell you who I won't be asking – Nauseating P. Green, that's who. She is definitely banned. If I am made to sit next to her again next term I will definitely kill myself. Why is she so boring? She does it deliberately to annoy me. She breeds hamsters. What is the matter with her?

Who else will be on the exclusion list? Wet Lindsay, Robbie's ex. It would be cruel to invite her and let her see Robbie and me being so happy and snogging in front of her, etc. Also she would kill me and that would spoil the party atmosphere.

Who else? Oh, I know, Jackie and Alison, otherwise known as the Bummer Twins. They can't come because they are too common.

9:10 p.m.

Looking out of my window. I can see Mark, the boy with the biggest gob in the universe, going off to town with his mates. People are out there having fun. I hate that. I haven't

269

got any real friends – as soon as a boy comes along they just forget about me, it's pathetic.

I could never be that shallow.

I wonder if the Sex God is having second thoughts about me because of my nose?

9:15 p.m.
Jas phoned. Tearing herself away from Tom for a second. She said, "Have you told her you are not going, yet?"

"No, I try but she takes no notice. I told her that it is a very important time for me as I am fourteen and poised on the brink of womanhood."

"On the what?"

Jas can be like half girl, half turnip. I said, "Do you remember what our revered headmistress, Slim, said at the end of summer term? She said, 'Girls, you are poised on the brink of womanhood, which is why I want to see no more false freckles painted on noses. It is silly and it isn't funny or dignified.'"

"False freckles are funny."

"I know."

"Well why would Slim say they weren't?"

"Jas."

"What?"

"Shut up now."

9:30 p.m.

I've got Libby, her scuba-diving Barbie doll, which has arms like steel forks, and her Thomas the Tank Engine, all in my bed. It's like sleeping in a toy box only not so comfortable. Plus Libby has been making me play Eskimo kissing; it has made my nose really sore. I said, "Libby, that's enough Eskimo now," but she just said, "Kwigglkwoggleugug," which I suppose she thinks is Eskimo.

What is the matter with my life? Why is it so deeply unfab?

10:00 p.m.

Looking at the sky outside my window and all the stars. I thought of all the people in history and so on who have been sad and have asked God for help. I fell to my knees (which was a bit painful as I landed on a plate of jam sandwiches I had left by my bed). Through my tears I prayed, "Please, God, let the phone ring and let it be Robbie. I promise I will go to church all the time if he rings. Thank you."

Midnight

So much for Our Vati in Heaven. What on earth is the point of asking God for something if you don't get it?

Decided to buy a Buddha tomorrow.

1:00 a.m.

As time is short it might be all right to ask Buddha for something before I actually invest in a statue of him.

I don't really know how to speak to Buddha. I hope he understands English. I expect, like most deities, it's more a sort of reading your thoughts job.

1:30 a.m.

Because I haven't been a practising Buddhist for long (half an hour) I'll restrict my requests to the essentials.

Which are:

1. When I suggest to Mum that she leaves me behind to look after the house, she says, "Of course, my darling."
2. The SG rings.

1:35 a.m.

I'll just leave it at that. I won't go into the nose business (less of it and more sticky up) or breast reduction requests, otherwise I will be here all night and Buddha may think I am a cheeky new Buddhist and that I'm only believing to get things.

Tuesday July 20th
10:00 a.m.

My room... soon to be a shrine to Buddha. Unless God gets his act together. Birds tweeting like birds at a bird party. Lovely sunny day. For some. I can see the sunshine glancing off Mr Next Door's bald head. He's playing with his stupid yappy little squirt dogs. Just a minute, I've spotted Angus hanging about in the potting shed area. Uh-oh, he looks a bit on the peckish side, like he fancies a poodle sandwich. I'd better go waggle a sausage at him and thereby avert a police incident.

How in the name of Mr Next Door's gigantic shorts am I supposed to be a Buddhist with these constant interruptions? I bet the Dalai Lama hasn't got a cat. Or a dad in New Zealand. (I wonder if the Dalai Lama's father is called the Daddy Lama?... I amaze myself sometimes because even though my life is a facsimile of a sham I can still laugh and joke!!)

10:36 a.m.

What is the point? Mum just laughed when I told her about looking after the house and told me to go and pack.

Midday

Even though it is quite obvious I am really depressed and in bed Mum comes poking around being all efficient and acting as if life is not a tragedy of a sham (which it is). She made me get up and show her what I had packed for Whangamata. She went ballisticisimus. *"Men are from Mars, Women are from Venus*, eyelash curlers, two bikinis and a cardigan?!"

"Well I won't be going out anywhere as I don't like sheep and my heart is broken."

"But you might wear your bikini?"

"I've only packed that for health reasons."

"What health reasons?"

"Well, if I can't eat anything because of my heartache, the

sun's rays may keep me from getting rickets. We did it in biology."

"It's winter over there."

"Typical."

"You are being ridiculous."

That's when all the pain came raging out of me. "I'm being ridiculous!!??? I'm being ridiculous??? I'm not the one who is dragging someone off to the other side of the world for NO good reason!!"

She went all red. "No good reason?! It's to see your dad!"

"I rest my case."

"Georgia, you are being horrible!" And she stormed off.

I feel a bit like crying. It's not my fault if I am horrible. I am under pressure. Why can't Dad be here? Then I could be horrible to him without feeling so horrible. (And without having to go to the other side of the planet. Most teenagers only have to go into the sitting room to be horrible to their dads.)

It's not easy having an absent dad, that's what people don't realise. I am effectively (apart from my mum and grandparents and my crap cousin James, etc.) an orphan.

1:00 p.m.

Libby crept into my room carrying a saucer of milk really carefully. She was on her tippy toes and purring. I said, "You are nice, Libbs. Just put it down; Angus is out hunting."

She very slowly and on tippy toes brought the saucer over to me and put it on my desk. She put her little hands on my head and started stroking my hair. My eyes filled up with tears. I said, "If I can't be happy in my life I can try and see that you have a nice life, Libbs. I will give up all thoughts of happiness myself and be like your Buddhist nurse. For your sake I will wear flat shoes and those really horrible orange robes and..."

Then Libby started pushing my head quite roughly down towards the saucer of milk. "C'mon, Ginger, come on. Milky pops."

She'll make me sleep in a cat basket soon. Honestly, I think it's about time she started kindergarten and mixed with normal children.

It takes twenty-four hours to fly to New Zealand.

6:00 p.m.

Uncle Eddie roared up on his pre-war motorbike. He's come round to collect Angus. How can I live without the huge furry fool? How can he live without me? No one else knows his special little ways. Who else will know that he likes you to trail his sausages around on a string so that he can pounce on them from behind the curtains? Who else will know about mouse racing? Not Uncle Eddie, that's for sure. He truly does come from Planet Bonkers. He came in wearing his motorbike leathers, took off his helmet and said, "How're you diddling?"

What is the matter with him? Why Mum thinks anyone as bald and barmy as him could look after an animal I don't know. Anyway, it's irrelevant what anyone thinks as he will never in a zillion years catch Angus and get him in a basket.

6:30 p.m.

I don't think I could be more sad. We are going to be away for months. I will miss all my friends; I'll lose the SG. My hockey career will be in ruins. Everyone knows the Maoris don't play hockey. They play... er... anyway, we haven't done New Zealand in geoggers yet, so I don't know what they do. Who cares?

6:35 p.m.

Time ticking away. It's like waiting to be buried, I should think. Or being in RE.

Phoned Jas. I wanted to know if Tom had heard anything from his gorgeous older brother, the Sex God, but I didn't want to let Jas know that I wasn't interested in her life. So I asked her a few questions about her "boyfriend" first.

"Hi, Jas, how are you and Tom getting along?"

She went all girlish and giggly. "Well, do you know, we were just laughing so much because Tom said that he was in the shop the other day and—"

"Jas, did he mention anything, you know, interesting?"

"Oh yeah, loads."

There was a pause – she drives me INSANE!

I said, "Like what?"

"Well, he was thinking of suggesting that they start selling more dairy products in their shop, because—"

"No, no, Jas I said interesting – not really, really boring. Has he, for instance, mentioned his gorgey older brother?"

Jas was a bit huffy but she said, "Hang on a minute." Then I heard her shouting, "Tom! Have you spoken to Robbie?"

In the distance I heard Tom shouting, "No, he's gone away on a footie trip."

I said to Jas, "I know that."

Jas shouted again, "She knows that."

Tom shouted, "Who knows that?"

"Georgia."

Then I heard Jas's mum shouting from somewhere, "Why does Georgia want to know about Robbie? Isn't she off to New Zealand?"

Jas shouted, "Yes, she is. But she's desperate to see him before she goes."

I said to Jas urgently, "Jas, Jas, I wanted to find out when he's back, I didn't want to discuss it with your street."

Jas went all huffy. "I'm only trying to help."

"Well don't."

"Well I won't, then."

"Good."

There was a silence. "Jas?"

"What?"

"What are you doing?"

"I'm not helping."

I'm going to have to kill her.

"Ask Tom when Robbie is due back."

"Huh. I don't see why I should, but I will."

She shouted out again, "Tom, when is Robbie back?"

Jas's mum yelled, "I thought he was going out with Lindsay?"

Tom yelled back, "He was, but then Georgia and him got together instead."

Jas's mum said, "Well, Lindsay will be very upset."

This was UNBELIEVABLE.

Tom yelled back again, "Tell Georgia he's not back again until late Monday."

Next Monday! Next Monday. By that time I would be being bored half to death by Maoris. I tried to be brave so that I wouldn't upset Jas. "I know I can joke about it and everything, but I have fancied Robbie for so long. And it's not just because he is in The Stiff Dylans. You know that. It's a whole year since I started stalking him. It was so groovy when he kissed me, I thought I would go completely jelloid and start dribbling. Luckily I didn't. And I think he will forget about that chunk of my hair snapping off, don't you?"

There was this clanking noise and then Jas said, with her mouth full, "Hello? Hello? What were you saying? I just went and got myself a sandwich while Tom was shouting at you."

Qu'est ce que le point?

7:30 p.m.

I can't believe Jas. She is dead to me. Like in the *Bible*, when somebody goes off and becomes a prostitute or something. She is now the girl who has no name.

9:00 p.m.

Phone rang. I leaped downstairs.

It was Rosie, Ellen, Jools and She Who Has No Name (Jas) calling me from the phone box at the end of our road. Rosie said in a fake Chinese accent, "Bringey selfey to phone boxey."

I put on some mascara and lippy so that no one would know about my broken heart. Not that it made the slightest difference to Mutti and Uncle Eddie – they were too busy trying to trap Angus.

He's lurking on top of my wardrobe. I know he's got a few snacks with him because he dropped a piece of mackerel on my head when I passed. He'll be happy up there for hours. Serve them right if they can't find him. Catnappers!

I don't want to be rude to the afflicted but Uncle Eddie is bald in a way which is the baldest I have ever seen. He looks like a boiled egg in leather trousers. Once he came round and after he and Mum had had their usual vat of wine he fell asleep in the back garden face down. So I drew another face on the back of his head. Very, very funny indeed, especially as I did it in indelible pen. He got his own back, though, by turning up to a school dance on his pre-war motorbike and asking all my mates where I was because he was my new boyfriend.

Still, that is life for you... one minute you are snogging a Sex God and have got up to number six on the snogging scale without crashing teeth. The next minute you are made to go to the other side of the world and hand out with Kiwi-a-gogos. Whose idea of a great time is to sit in mud pools and eat toasted maggots. (This is very, very true as I have been reading a brochure about Kiwi-a-gogo land and it says it in there.) Oh pig's bum!! Or as our tiny French friends say, *Le gran* bum *de le* porker!!!

9:30 p.m.
When I got to the phone box the gang were all in there. They squeezed open the door and Jools said, "*Bonsoir, ma petite* nincompoop."

Once I was in we were all squashed up like sardines at a fish party. Rosie managed to get a hand free and give me one of those photobooth photographs.

"We brought you a present to remember us by."

It was a picture of her, Jools, Ellen and Jas (She Who Has No Name), only they had their noses stuck back at the tip with Sellotape so that it made them look like pigs with hair.

On the back it said, GRUNTINGS from your mates. STY in touch. This is a PIGTURE to remember us by.

It made me a bit tearful, but I put on a brave face. "Cheers, thanks a lot. Goodnight."

We had to get out of the telephone box because Mark (the boy from up the road with the enormous gob who I went out with for a fortnight but dumped me because this other girl Ella let him "do things to her") came to use the phone. He just looked at us as we all struggled out. He really has got the biggest mouth I have ever seen. I was lucky to escape from snogging him with my face still in one piece.

BG (Big Gob) said, "All right?" in a way which meant, "All right, you lesbians?"

What do I care, though? My life is over anyway.

We all walked back to my house arm in arm. I wouldn't link up with Jas though because she has annoyed me. Uncle Eddie must have eventually got Angus into the cat basket because the gardening gloves he was wearing were lying in the driveway with the thumbs torn off.

We all hugged and cried. It was awful. I'd nearly got to the door when Jas sort of threw herself at me. She couldn't speak because she was crying so much and she said, "Georgia, nothing will be the same without you... I... I love you. I'm sorry I ate my sandwich."

Wednesday July 21st
Dawn – well, 10:00 a.m.
Phoned my dearest friend Jas who loves me. Huh.

Now that she thinks she has got a "proper" boyfriend she acts like she is one hundred and eighty.

"Look, Gee-gee, I can't talk really because I am on the dash to meet Tom. Dig you later, though. *Ciao* for now."

...*Ciao* for now? I wonder if she has finally snapped? Nobody really cares about me. No one wants you when you are in trouble; no one is interested when you are not the life and soul of the party. I may have to try to make it up with God again at this rate.

2:30 p.m.

I don't care what happens. I am not going to New Zealand. Not. Definitely. They will have to carry me on to the plane. Or give me knock-out drugs.

That is it. I am not going.

3:00 p.m.

I am not speaking to Mum but as she has gone out shopping (again) she probably hasn't noticed.

3:19 p.m.

Sitting by the phone and using telepathy to make it ring. I've read about it a lot – it's where you use your willpower to make something happen. In my head I was saying, "Ring, phone!" and "The phone will ring and it will be Robbie... by the time I count to ten."

3:21 p.m.

"OK, the phone will ring and it will be Robbie by the time I count to a hundred..."

3:30 p.m.

"...in French. By the time I count to one hundred in French the phone will ring and it will be SG." (God, or whoever it is that deals with willpower, will respect that I am making a bloody huge effort by counting in a foreign language.)

Everything really is sheer desperadoes and in tins. In two days' time I will be on the other side of the world and the Sex God will be on this side of the world. And, what is more, I will be a day ahead of him. And upside down.

3:39 p.m.

I've got an appalling headache now.

While we are on the subject of French, why in the name of Louise the Fourteenth did Madame Slack (honestly – that is her name) make us learn a song called "*Mon Merle a Perdu une Plume*"?

My blackbird has lost a feather. That will be a great boon and help if I ever get to go to Paris. I won't be able to get a sandwich for love nor money but I will be able to chat to *le* French about my blackbird's feathers. Not that I have got a blackbird and, if I did have one, believe me it wouldn't be just the one feather it would lose with Angus around. Not that he is around.

I really miss him already. He is the best cat anyone ever had. I can still imagine his furry head snuggled up in my bed. Bits of feather round his mouth. The way he used to bring me little presents. A vole, or a bit of poodle ear or something.

3:41 p.m.
How do you say my blackbird has had its legs chewed off by my cat? *Mon merle a perdu les jambes...*

Phone rang
3:45 p.m.
Thank goodness, because I thought I was going to have to count up to a hundred in German and nobody wants that. (And besides, I can't.)

"It's me, Jas."

"Oh... What do YOU want?"

"I've just called to see how you are."

I said, "Dead actually, I died a few hours ago. Goodbye."

That will teach her. I'm not going to answer the phone if she rings back, either.

5:00 p.m.

She didn't ring back. Typical.

My room
In bed
10:30 p.m.

Mum and Libby came back in. When they popped their heads round my door I pretended to be asleep. Libby crept over quietly – well, her idea of creeping quietly, which is the loudest thing I have ever heard.

Mum whispered, "Give you big sister a kiss, Libbs, because she's upset."

Then I felt this wet thing sucking on the end of my nose. I shot up in bed. I said, "Does anyone else's sister kiss like that? Why is she so obsessed with my nose?"

11:15 p.m.

After the nose-sucking incident I am as awake as two awake things. Just gazing out of my bedroom window into the dark night. When you gaze at the stars it makes you feel really small. We have been discussing infinity in Physics: you know, how there is no end to the universe, and so on. Herr Kamyer said there might even be a parallel universe to the one we live on somewhere out there. There might be another Georgia Nicolson sitting in her bedroom, thinking, What on earth is the point?

11:17 p.m.
Another Georgia Nicolson who is being forced to leave a Sex God and all her mates (and this does not include Jas). To go to the other side of the world. Double *merde*.

11:29 p.m.
I've just had a horrible thought. If there is a parallel me, there will be a parallel Wet Lindsay. And a parallel Nauseating P. Green. And two pairs of Mr Next Door's shorts. Good grief.

Thursday July 22nd
Day before the last day of my life
Hunger protest
2:00 p.m.
Even though it is quite obvious even to the VERY dim that I am not eating, Mum hasn't noticed. She said, "Do you want some oven chips and beans?"

And I said, "I will never eat again."

She just said, "OK," and tucked in with Libbs.

I had to creep into the kitchen and finish off the chips she had left.

4:00 p.m.

In my room. Practising feeling lonely and friendless in preparation for the months ahead.

4:05 p.m.

I haven't heard from my so-called mates for days. Well, since this morning, anyway. I don't need to practise. I AM lonely and friendless.

4:10 p.m.

I went into the front room to watch TV. Libby was snoozing but woke up when I sat down. She stood up on her little fat legs and put her arms up to me.

"I love my Georgie, I lobe my Georgie."

She made it into a little song:

"Haha, I lobe my Georgie,

I love my little Girgie,

Gingie, Gingie.

Hahahaha. Ginger, I love Ginger... my Ginger."

In her tiny mad brain I am half cat, half sister. I picked her up and we snuggled down on the sofa together. At least I have someone who loves me in this family, even if she is bonkers.

Mum came in and said, "You look really sweet together. It only seems a little while ago that you were that size, Georgie. Dad and I used to take you to the park and you used to have a little hat with earflaps that were like cats' paws. You were such a sweet little girl."

Oh good Lord, here we go. It will be, "How did my little girl get so big...?"

Sure enough, Mum's eyes got all watery and she started stroking my hair (very annoying) and doing the "How did my little Georgie get so..." routine.

Fortunately (or unfortunately, depending on where you were sitting) Libby let off the smelliest, loudest fart known to humanity. It came out of her bum-oley with such force that she lifted off my knee – like a hovercraft. Even she looked surprised by what had come out of her.

I pushed her off my knee and leaped up. "Libby, that is disgusting!!!! I blame you, Mum, for the bean extravaganza.

It's not natural, the amount of stuff that comes out of such a little girl."

Phwoaar...

Grandad farted once when we were out in the street. Really loudly. When he looked around behind him there was a woman walking her dachshund dog. You know, those little sausage dog things. The woman heard Grandad's fart (who didn't?) and she said, "Well, really!!"

And Grandad said, "I'm terribly sorry, madam, I seem to have shot the legs off your dog." Which was possibly the last semi-sane thing he said. I'd still rather stay here with him than go to Kiwi-a-gogo.

I said to Mum, "Well, can I go and live with Grandad, then?"

And she said, "He lives in an old people's home."

And I said, "So?"

But she is so mad and unreasonable she wouldn't even discuss it.

11:30 p.m.

All my mates came and did a candlelit vigil underneath my bedroom window. Sven wore a paper hat. I don't know why.

Does it matter? It was just his Swedish way of saying goodbye. They all sang *"Mon Merle a Perdu une Plume"* as a tribute. Well, they sang the first verse before Mr and Mrs Next Door came and complained that they were frightening their dogs. Jas said, "I'm going to stay silently here all night."

But then Sven said, "Chips, now." And they all went off.

It was so sad.

Friday July 23rd
The day the world ends
Midday

Decided to have to be dragged out of bed by the police so that the world will know how I have been treated. I have tied myself to the bedhead with my dressing-gown sleeves. I can imagine the newspaper headlines: Promising hockey superstar teenager fights attempts to force her to Kiwi-a-gogo land. I've put on a hint of make-up just in case, for the photos.

12:10 p.m.

Mum surprised me by bursting into my room all flushed like a pancake.

"Guess what?!!!! We're not going to New Zealand because your dad is coming home!!!!!"

I said, "What?"

She was hugging me and didn't seem to notice I was like a rigid hamster in bed.

I was a bit dazed. "Vati, home, coming?"

Great news!!!!!!!!
1:00 p.m.

My dad has had his shoes blown off by a rogue bore!!!!! All this hot steam shot out of something he was fixing and he leaped off and broke his foot. Mum has put her foot down with a firm hand and said she will not take her children to a place where steam shoots out of the ground.

She said to me, "It's hard enough getting you to get out of bed as it is, I'm not giving you more excuses." Which is incredibly unfair, but I didn't say anything, because inside I was saying "Yessssss!!!!!!"

The only fly in the manger is that Vati is going to be coming home when his contract is finished. Still, if it is a choice of going to live in Kiwi-a-gogo land or having to put up with Vati snooping around my bedroom and telling me what it was like in the seventies, I suppose I will choose having the grumpy moustachioed one.

Mum is hideously happy. She won't stop hugging me. Which I think is on the hypocritical side but I didn't say anything. I just hugged her back and asked her quickly for a fiver. Which she gave me. Yesss!!!!

Beautiful English summer's day. Lovely, lovely drizzly rain!!! We don't have to go to Kiwi-a-gogo!!!

Thank you, God. I will always believe in you. I was only pretending to become a Buddhist.

3:00 p.m.
I put on some really loud music in my room and started to unpack my bikini. Lalalalala... fabbity fab fab. Marvy and double cool with knobs.

Uncle Eddie turned up with a bottle of champagne and Angus in a basket. I noticed Uncle Eddie had put a muzzle on him. What a week. Angus soon had it off and I could see him strolling around his domain. (The dustbins.) When I went downstairs Uncle Eddie had picked up Libby and was dancing around with her. She was singing, "Uncle Eggy, Uncle Eggy," which is quite funny when you think about it.

4:20 p.m.

My little room. I love you, my little room!!! Lalalalalalala.
Fabbity fab fab. Ho-di-hum. Everything is so lovely: my little
Reeves and Mortimer poster with them in the nuddy-pants,
my little desk, my little bed... my little window overlooking
next door's garden.

5:00 p.m.

Phoned the Ace Crew and they went mental. Just put the phone
down when there was a ring on the doorbell. It was Mr Next
Door. His glasses were on all sideways. He did not say, "I am so
glad you are not going, Georgia." In fact, he didn't say anything
but just handed over a sweeping brush and stomped off.

Attached to the bottom part of the brush was Angus. He
dragged the brush into the kitchen. There was the sound of
pots and pans and chairs crashing over. I called out, "Libbs,
Angus is back."

11:00 p.m.

Before I went up to bed I looked into the kitchen. Libbs was
feeding Angus cat food by hand. Aaahhh, this was more like
it!! Back to normal.

Saturday July 24th

Summer. Birds tweeting. Voles voleing. Poodles poodling. I notice that we have new neighbours across the road. I hope they are a bit more considerate than Mr and Mrs Mad who used to live there.

Oh, they've got a cat! It looks like one of those pedigree Burmese ones, all leaping around. In a sort of fenced enclosure. They are very expensive, pedigree Burmese cats. They are the Naomi Campbells of the cat world. Not that they do a lot of modelling. Too furry. And not tall enough. Although they would be really good on the catwalk!!! Hahahahaha. Lalalalala. I think I am a comedy genius. Now if only the SG would phone and say, "I'm coming round now, oh gorgeous one. I didn't realise how close I came to losing you. I am mesmerised by your beautosity." Life would be beyond fab and entering the marvy zone.

Midday

Met Jas and we went to the park. I've got a spot on my chin but I've made it look like a beauty spot with an eyebrow pencil. With my shades on I look a bit like an Italian person.

297

I think Jas was embarrassed about me not going to NZ after what she said. I am too considerate to mention it so I just said, "Do you really love me, Jas?"

She went all red.

As we strolled by the tennis courts we saw Melanie Griffiths sunbathing. I may have mentioned this before but she has got the largest breasts known to humanity. Some lads went by and went "Phwooar!". One of them pretended to be juggling. Sometimes I feel that boys will always remain a mystery to me. I've felt that particularly since BG from up the road rested his hand on my basooma for no particular reason. Mel saw us looking so I said, "Oh, hi Mel!" sincerely.

She said, "Hi!" but I don't think she meant it.

I said to Jas, "Where does she get her bras from? They must be made by those blokes who built the Forth Bridge, Ted and Mick Forth." I just made that up; I don't know what they were called.

We lay down on the grass to sunbathe and Jas said, "Do you think I should get a bra?"

I was thinking what I should wear when I saw Robbie again. I said, "Robbie hasn't phone yet, you know."

Jas was silent. I squinted round at her and she was sort of

wobbling her shoulders around. I said, "What in the name of pantyhose are you doing?"

She said, "I'm seeing if my basoomas wobble."

Jas can be spectacularly dim. I think that if I dressed Angus in her school uniform probably no one would notice for days. Unless they tried to take a snack away.

I said, "Do the pencil test. You put a pencil under a breast and if it falls out you are OK. If it stays there, sort of trapped by your basooma, you're not and you should get help and support in the bra department."

She was full-on, attention-wise, then. "Really?"

"Yeah. Sadly my mum can get a whole pencil case up there."

Jas was rummaging about. "I've got a pencil in my rucky, I'm going to try it."

"Jas, Tom hasn't said anything about Robbie, has he?"

As per usual Jas had gone off into the twilight world in her head. She was fiddling about with a pencil up her T-shirt. She said, "Hahahahaha, it fell out!!! I passed, I passed... you try it."

I wasn't interested. "Why would SG snog me and say 'see you later' if he didn't mean 'see you later'? Do you think he's worried about me being younger than him? Or do you think it's my nose?"

You might as well be talking to a duck. Jas was shoving the pencil at me. "Go on, go on... you're scared."

"Try it, then."

"No I'm not. I'm not frightened of a pencil."

"Oh for goodness' sake."

I grabbed the pencil from her and pulled up my top and put the pencil underneath my right basooma. Actually it stuck there, but I jiggled a bit. I said, "Yeah, it falls out."

Jas said, "You jiggled."

"I did not."

"You did. I saw you."

"I didn't. You're a mad biscuit."

"You did. Look, let me do it, I'll show you."

She grabbed the pencil and was trying to put it under my basooma when Jackie and Alison, the Bummer Twins, came round the corner of the tennis courts. Jackie removed the fag from her mouth long enough to say, "Well, well, well, our lezzo friends are out for an afternoon fondle."

Oh no, here we go again with the lesbian rumours. That will be something to look forward to next term.

Monday July 26th
2:00 p.m.

Phew, what a scorcher!!! Sun shining, birds tweeting. Mr and Mrs Next Door in their garden. They are wearing shorts – again. Mr Next Door's shorts really are gigantic in the bottom department. You'd think that out of courtesy to others he'd keep out of public view when he was wearing them. What if a very, very old person – even older than him – came along unexpectedly? And what if they weren't in peak medical condition? The sight of Mr Next Door in his shorts could bring on a dangerous spasm. Still, that is another example of the bottomless (oo-er!) selfishosity of so-called grown-ups for you.

Teatime
4:50 p.m.

Fabulous day... not. Grandad came round. Even he was wearing shorts. As I said to Mum, "There is really no need for that."

He is so bow-legged that Angus can walk in between his legs with a stick and Grandad doesn't even notice. Mind you he doesn't notice much as he lives in the twilight world of the elderly mad. After fiddling in his prehistoric shorts he gave me twenty pence and said, "There you are, don't spend it all at once." Then he laughed so much his false teeth shot out. He was wheezing away for so long I thought he'd choke to death and then I'd have to do the Heimlich manoeuvre. Miss Stamp (Sports Kommandant) made us learn it in First Aid. If someone swallows a boiled sweet or something and chokes, you grab them from behind and put your arms round below their breastbone. Then you squeeze them really hard until the sweet shoots out. Apparently some German bloke called Mr Heimlich made it up. Why Germans have to go round grabbing people innocently choking on sweets I don't know. But they do. That is the mystery of the German people.

8:00 p.m.
Well, that is it. No call from the SG. He must be back. I can't call him because I have pride. Well actually, I did phone him but there was no reply. I didn't leave a message. I don't understand boys. How could you do number six type snogging and then not call someone?

8:10 p.m.
Buddhism is the only way. I must meditate and be calm.

My room
8:20 p.m.

I found one of Mum's kaftans that she got when she went to India on the hippie trail. She has some very sad photos of her and Dad with hilarious haircuts in Katmandu. Dad looks like he has got a big nappy on. She gets the photos out when she is drunk, especially if you beg her not to.

I put on the kaftan and was listening to some dolphins on a meditation tape. It was called "Peaceful Universe". Squeak, squeak, squeak. On and on – it would go quiet for a bit and then squeak, squeak, squeak. If dolphins are so intelligent why don't they learn to speak properly? Instead of squeaking? It is fantastically irritating. I would turn it off but I am too depressed to get off the bed.

8:40 p.m.

Phone rings. Of course, everyone else is far too busy to answer it. So I'll tramp all the way downstairs and get it.

I yelled out, "Don't worry, Mum, I'll come all the way down and answer the phone which is probably for you. You try and get some rest!"

Mum shouted from the living room, "OK, thanks."

I picked up the receiver. "Yes?"

It was Robbie!!! Yes and treble fabuloso!! He's got such a lovely voice; quite deep – not quite as deep as Grandad's, but then he doesn't smoke forty cigarettes a minute. He said he'd been away.

I was thinking, I know you have, you great huge sexy hunk!!! My lips are stiff with puckering!!! But I didn't say that, I said, "Oh, have you?" which I thought was quite cool and alluring. Anyway, the short and short of it is that he's really, really glad that I didn't go to Kiwi-a-gogo and I'm going round to his place tomorrow!!! His parents have gone away.

Ooooooohhhhhh. I'm all shakey and nervous now. I'm like a cat on a hot tin roof. We did *Cat On a Hot Tin Roof* in English. There was no cat in it... or a tin roof... or... stop it, brain, stop it!!!!

8:45 p.m.
Phoned Jas.

"He called me!!"

"Who?"

It's like talking to a sock. "Jas. HE called me. HE – the one and only HE in the universe."

Jas came round to discuss what I should wear. We went up to my room. Unfortunately I forgot to warn Jas about the hammock that Libby had made for her dolls. She'd made it out of one of Mum's commodious bras and tied it across the landing. Jas grazed her shins quite badly when she fell over. She was going, "Ow, ow!", but I can't be bothered with minor injuries just now.

She hobbled into my room and we looked through my wardrobe. I held things up and Jas went, "No. No. Maybe. No, too tarty. No, no... er... maybe."

I was trying on a suede mini and she said, "Erlack!! The front of your legs are quite hairy but the backs of your legs are all baldy."

I had a look. She was right!!! Time for operation smoothy legs. I grumbled to her as we went down to the bathroom. "What is the point of evolution? Why bother giving us hairy front legs and baldy back legs? When can that ever have been useful in our fight for survival?"

Jas said, "Perhaps it was to frighten things off."

I said, "Oh yeah, that will be it. Stone Age girl would have said, 'Here comes a big dinosaur chasing me from behind. It thinks I am a push-over because of my baldy legs, but wait till I turn round! I'll scare off the big lug with my terrifying hairy front legs.' That will be the explanation."

Jas wasn't interested in my scientosity because she was looking through the bathroom cabinet. "Your mum has got loads of anti-ageing creams, hasn't she?"

"I know. It's sad. Why doesn't she save all that money and put it towards some new spectacles or a hat? Or a decent bra that can contain her gigantic basoomas."

9:30 p.m.

Mum's hair remover worked a treat; my legs were smoothy smooth. I was tempted to use a bit on my eyebrows but I remembered the last time I had shaved them and they had taken two weeks to grow back.

Clothes-wise we decided on a turtle-necked crop top (implies that I am mature for my years, on the brink of womanhood, etc... but doesn't go as far as saying "I am desperate for a snog"). In the leg department it was the tight Capri trousers.

Jas said, "Tom is going away on work experience this term. I will be on my own for weeks. I'll really miss him. Do you know, he said the other day that he..."

In a caring way I said, "Go home now, Jas, I have to get my beauty sleep."

11:00 p.m.
In bed nice and early. I've barricaded my door so that Angus and Libby can't get in.

Midnight
I am SO nervous... What if I have forgotten how to snog? What if all my snogging lessons go out of my mind at the last minute and we bump teeth?

1:00 a.m.
Or I lose my grip altogether and go to the same side with my head as he is going, and knock him out? Heeeeelp!!!!

What if I have one of those laughing fits that you can't stop? You know, when you remember something... like for instance when Herr Kamyer took us on a school trip and when we arrived at the railway station he said, "Ach yes, here ve are!" and then opened the door on the wrong side of the train and fell out of the carriage.

Hahahahahahahaha... hahahahaa. You see, I'm doing it

now. I'm laughing by myself in the middle of the night in my room.

OhmyGodohmyGodohmyGod. Hahahahahahahahaha.

Tuesday July 27th
SG Day
Setting off to his house.
7:00 p.m.

It's taken most of the day to achieve my natural make-up look. Just a subtle touch to enhance my natural beauty(!). I wanted the just-tumbled-out-of-bed look, so I only used undercover concealer, foundation, hint of bronzer, eye pencil, eight layers of mascara, lip liner, lippy and lip-gloss, and I left it at that.

7:20 p.m.

Jas phoned to wish me luck. She said, "Tell me all about it when you get home. Remember what number you get up to on the snogging scale. Are you wearing a bra? I think it would be wise because you don't want to wobble all over the place."

I said, "Goodbye, Jas."

I'm not wearing a bra; I thought I would go free and akimbo. I just won't make any sudden movements.

Walking down Arundel Street
7:30 p.m.

Brrr, not quite as warm and bright as it was earlier. A bit overcast, actually, and... oh no... it's starting to rain! It's too far to go back home for an umby... it will probably stop in a minute.

7:40 p.m.

Outside Robbie's gate. It really is raining quite hard now. I'm wet through and really cold. I think my trousers have shrunk; they are hugging my bottom in a vice-like grip. I wonder if I look all right?

I'll nip into the telephone box opposite his house and check my mirror.

In the telephone box
7:45 p.m.

My trousers have shrunk so tight around my bottom that I can't bend my legs. This is hopeless. Brrr. Why is everything going wrong? I can't go to see the Sex God looking like this. I'll have to phone him up and say I'm ill.

309

7:50 p.m.

SG answered the phone, "Hello."

Swoon swoon.

I said, "Roggie, nit's ne, Neorgia."

"What's wrong with your voice?"

"Der nl'd gat a trrible cold nd Im nin bed."

"Do they have beds in telephone boxes?"

"Dnno."

"Georgia, I can see you through the window."

When I looked across at his house, he waved at me. Oh GODDDDDD!!!!!!

He said, "Come over."

What can I do, what can I do? My top is all wet. And there are two bumpy things in it. Great! It looks like I've got two peas down the front of my top. Typical, the only thing Mum has ever ironed for me and she has ironed it wrong.

As I walked up to the door I tried to flatten out the bumpy bits. But it wasn't my top sticking up... it was ME!!! My nipples!!!!! What were they doing?!!! Why were they sticking out? I hadn't told them to do that. How could I get them back in again? I'd have to cross my arms in a casual way and hope he didn't offer me a cup of coffee.

7:55 p.m.

The back door opened and there he was!! The Sex God had landed. I went even more jelloid. He was so gorgey... so... oooooh and er and yum yum and scrumbos and yummy scrumbos. His hair was all floppy, he had on dark jeans and a white T-shirt and you could see his shoulders (one on each side). He's got really, really dark blue eyes and long dark eyelashes and a big mouth, sort of soft looking. He's not a girlie boy though, he's definitely a boyie boy, which I think is handy in a boy myself.

Midnight

I love him, I love him. I love you, Robbie, oh yes I do. When I'm not near you I'm blue... What else rhymes with Robbie? Gobbie? Snoggie? Knobbie?

12:30 a.m.

I can't sleep, life is too brilliant. I may never sleep again.

It was such a fab night. We talked for a bit – well, I said, "My dad had his shoes blown off by a rogue bore," and he said, "Does anything normal ever happen to you?" Which I took as a compliment.

He played me a song on his guitar. I didn't really know what to do when he did that. I just sat on the sofa next to him with an attractive half-smile on my face and my arms crossed). It was quite a long song and by the end of it my cheeks ached like billio. In fact, I think I might have cheek strain. I tried to keep my nose sucked in at the same time; I didn't want it wandering across my face.

He told me that he is going to go to university to do music properly. I said, "I'm going to be a vet." I don't know why as I'm not. I didn't seem to be able to make anything come out of my mouth that had anything to do with my brain. He looked into my eyes and went quiet, and I went quiet and looked back at him. I tried not to blink. That seemed to go on for about a million years. In the end I had a sort of nervy spasm and went and looked at a photograph of a dog that was on a table. He probably thinks I am obsessed with animals as I am a trainee vet (not).

He came over and put his arm round my shoulder. I had an overwhelming urge to start doing Cossack dancing as a very funny joke, but just in time I remembered that boys don't like girls for jokes. Then he kissed me. I think he may be the best snogger in the universe. Although I have only snogged two other boys so far, and one of those was part boy part whelk, so I can't be entirely sure. SG does that varying pressure thing that Rosie says foreign boys do. You know, soft and then hard and then medium and then hard again. I could have quite literally snogged until the cows came home. And when they came home I would have shouted, "WHAT HAVE YOU COWS COME HOME FOR? CAN'T YOU SEE I'M SNOGGING, YOU STUPID HERBIVORES???"

I think I may be a bit feverish.

1:30 a.m.

I am going to be nice to everyone from now on. Even Wet Lindsay, Robbie's ex. I won't say to her, "Yesssssss!!!!" I will be grown-up and nice.

The only fly in the landscape is that when he walked me to my gate and said goodnight he tweaked my nose. And he said, "I'll see you later."

1:35 a.m.

What does that mean? Not the "see you later" bit, because no one knows what that means. I mean the tweaking the nose business.

1:40 a.m.

Does it mean, "Hey, you adorable cute thing," or does it mean, "Cor, what a size that conk is, I wonder if I can get all of it in one hand?"

Wednesday July 28th
3:35 p.m.

I am a Sex God's girlfriend. But I will not let it spoil my naturalness.

Phoned Jas: "Even when I have loads of interesting and glamorous friends I would still want to be friends with you. Because we are proper friends. We should never let boys come between us."

Jas said, "Tom is going to buy me one of those stick-on transfer tattoos. I'm going to put it on my bottom while he is away and not wash it off until he gets back."

"Jas, can you leave your bottom out of this? Please."

Friday July 30th
5:00 p.m.

Made my dear mutti and sister a meal today. Mashed potatoes and sausages. I thought Mum was going to cry.

10:00 p.m.

Early to bed, early to rise, makes a girl... er... anyway, it gets a girl out of the way of her mutti who had a nervy b. when she saw the state of the kitchen.

10:15 p.m.

Why do I always get the blame for every little thing? Is it really my fault that a couple of pans caught fire? I put them out.

Still, I refuse to be upset. I will remain calm beneath my egg and olive oil face mask.

Saturday July 31st
7:55 p.m.

Dreamy dreamy, smiley smiley.

However no phone calley. Never mindey.

Snogging withdrawal

Sunday August 1st
8:00 a.m.
I've persuaded Jas to come to church with me to thank God for making Dad have his shoes blown off and also for giving me a Sex God as a plaything.

10:00 a.m.
When I got round to Jas's house she was sitting on her wall in the shortest skirt known to humanity. When I wear skirts like that my grandad says, "You can see what you had for your dinner." I don't know what on earth he is talking about but then neither does anyone else, except probably dogs.

Jas leaped off the wall. Her skirt was about four centimetres long.

I said, "Is it a long time since you went to church, Jas?" and she said, "It's OK, I'm wearing really big knickers."

Church
10:40 a.m.

Good grief. Now I know why I don't go to church much. It is not what is generally known as Fun City Arizona. I was forced to sing "All Things Bright and Beautiful" which is bad enough, but there was a further treat in store. The vicar, ("Call me Arnold") tries to be "modern". So to really get "with it" Call me Arnold had got some absolute saddos to play guitars as an accompaniment. One of the boys on guitar was called Norman and as if that is not cruel enough he had acne. And not just ordinary acne, he had acne of the entire head.

But as we left I remembered that I was supposed to be being grateful so I said, "Sorry about Spotty Norman, God, I will be nice to him next time I see him," (inwardly) and put a pound in the collection box.

Monday August 2nd

12:10 p.m.

Still no news from the SG. I've been going to bed really early to make the hours pass more quickly.

I tried snogging the back of my hand to stave off snogging withdrawal but it's no good.

3:30 p.m.

Cor phew... boiling again. The sun was shining like a great big fried egg. Jas and Jools and Ellen and me went sunbathing in the park. I took off my shades and got the shock of my life: in the sunshine my legs looked like Herr Kamyer's legs. They were all pale-looking. Not as hairy or German as his legs, obviously.

I said, "Ellen, why are your legs so brown?"

She said, "Oh, I used some of that Kool Tan stuff."

Maybe the SG noticed my Herr Kamyer legs? I must get some Kool Tan.

Tuesday August 3rd

10:30 p.m.

When Jas came round for us to practise hairstyles I made her let me kiss the back of her calf to see if she could feel any teeth. She leaped about, going, "Erlack, erlack, get off, get off, it feels disgusting, like a sort of sucky Spotty Norman." Which is not very reassuring.

She said Tom touched her basooma the other night. In revenge I said, "How would he know it wasn't your shoulder?" She honestly does think she is like Kate Moss. It is very, very sad.

Midnight
SG didn't touch my basooma. I wonder if that is bad? Mind you, I had my arms folded for a lot of the time because of the nipple emergency.

Wednesday August 4th
4:00 p.m.
Phoned Jas.

"I'm really worried now. It's been over a week. I wonder if it is my nose? Perhaps SG only likes little sticky-up noses like Wet Lindsay's?"

Jas said, "Maybe a headband would help. You should make more of your forehead and that would take the emphasis away from your nose."

"At least I've got a forehead, not like Wet Lindsay who has got a tiny little forehead. In fact, she is really just hair and then eyebrows. How could the SG go out with someone with no forehead?"

"She's got quite nice legs."

"What do you mean? Nice – not like mine? Shut up, Jas."

"OK, keep your hair on."

"Nauseating P. Green, on the other hand, has got the HUGEST forehead known to humanity. In fact, she is a walking forehead in a frock. I must get away from this forehead business, it's making me feel a bit mad."

4:30 p.m.

In the bathroom experimenting with a headband. Hmmm, headband seems to emphasise my nose. In fact, it's like wearing a big notice on my head that says, "Hey, everyone!!! Look at my incredibly big schnozzle!!"

4:40 p.m.

While I had been doing headband work I hadn't been paying much attention to Libbs. She had come into the bathroom and got up on the lavatory seat. Her hair was all sticking up like a mad earwig but she won't let you comb it. I said, "Libby, things will start nesting in it," and she said, "Aaahh nice." Then she started going, "Bzzz, bzzz, bzzy bzz, bzz," like a mad bee.

I was experimenting with sucking in my nose to see if it made it look any smaller when Mum came barging in. (Not bothering to knock or anything.) Anyway, she went even more bananas than usual. Libby had put all of the loo paper down her knickers because she wanted to be a bumble bee. I'd heard her buzzing but I didn't pay any attention. Mum was all red-faced.

"Georgia, all you think about is how you bloody look. The house could burn down around you before you would stop looking in that mirror."

I raised my eyebrows ironically. Talk about the pot calling the other pot a black kettle, er... well whatever. She really has got a volatile temper; she should go to anger management classes. I will suggest it to her. But not just now as she has got a brush in her hand.

4:50 p.m.
My violent, bad-tempered mother has gone out. Nothing in the fridge. Oh, I tell a lie, there is a half-eaten sausage. Yum yum.

4:55 p.m.

Grandad said that as you get older gravity pulls on your nose and makes it bigger and bigger.

5:00 p.m.

Why couldn't I come from a decent gene bank? Nice, well-formed parents, like Jas's mum and dad. Nice and compact, nothing too sticky-outy. Instead I get massive "danger to shippings" from Mum and a massive conk from my dad. If Robbie doesn't like me it is Vati's fault. If it is true about the gravity business then Dad will need a wheelbarrow to carry his nose around in soon. Good, serve him right for ruining my life.

7:00 p.m.

I'm so hot and restless. Oh Robbie, where are you? My nose feels tremendously heavy.

8:00 p.m.

I put on a really loud record and danced about to get rid of my excess snogosity.

8:05 p.m.

When I looked in the mirror I could see my basoomas bobbling about. Good grief and *sacré bleu*!! They look like they are doing their own dance!

In Mum's Vanity Fair it says that all the posh type ladies go to a special woman behind Harrod's to get their bras properly fitted.

8:15 p.m.

The Queen must go there, then. Apparently this woman who does the bras is such an expert that she can just look at someone and say what size bra they should have. No suggestion of pencil cases. I wish I could go to her.

8:30 p.m.

When the Queen goes, this woman must just look at her and yell to her assistant, "Get the Queen a bra in size forty-eight D." Or whatever size the Queen is.

9:00 p.m.

The Queen is about five foot high, so if she was a size sixty D that would make her like a five-foot ball.

9.30 p.m.

I wish I didn't have that in my head.

Midnight

Should I call him? Oh I don't know what to do. I don't know what to do.

Thursday August 5th
Still boiling
4:00 p.m.

Jools, Ellen, Rosie, Jas and me went to town to try on make-up in Boots and Miss Selfridge. I cheered up a bit, especially as we did this limping thing on the way home. You link up and all limp together. And you're not allowed to break arms no matter what happens. This tremendously old bloke got shirty with us because we accidentally stampeded his Labrador. After that we went into the park and sat on the swings for a rest. Rosie said, "Oh I fancy a fag."

I was shocked. I said, "I didn't know you smoked."

And she said, "It's just to relax."

Rosie put a cigarette in her mouth and got out her lighter. We were all looking. Unfortunately she must have set the flame too high because when she flicked it a flame shot up about twelve centimetres and set fire to her fringe. We beat it out but the hair was all singed and short. She went home with her hand over her fringe. After she had gone the rest of us swang backwards and forwards for a few minutes.

I said, "Rosie smokes quite a lot, doesn't she?"

And then we all got the helpless laughing. You know, that laughing that makes your tummy hurt and makes you cry and gulp and choke? And you've laughed for long enough and you want to stop but you can't. Then you do stop and you think it's all right but then someone starts again. I just couldn't stop. And that's when I saw HIM. The Sex God. With his mates from The Stiff Dylans. He looked like he was coming across to say hello. And you know when you really, really should stop laughing because otherwise it will be really bad and everyone will hate you? But you can't? Well I had that.

10:00 p.m.
Rang Robbie. His mum said he was at rehearsal. Still he likes a laugh himself, so it will be all right.

Midnight

On the other hand I wasn't by any means doing my attractive half-smiling when he saw me. I had a look at myself in the mirror doing proper, unadulterated laughing, the kind of laughing where you just let your nose and mouth go free and wild.

12:15 a.m.

That is it, my life is over; I must go to the ugly home immediately.

Friday August 6th

11:00 a.m.

A letter arrived for me. From Robbie. My hands were shaking when I opened it.

11:30 a.m.

Back in bed. I CANNOT believe my life. It is beyond pooiness. It has gone well beyond the Valley of the Poo and entered the Galaxy of *Merde*.

11:45 a.m.

I re-read the letter from Robbie again. It still says the same thing though.

> Dear Georgia,
>
> I have been thinking and thinking about this. And although I think you are great, and I really do like you, well, I saw you with your mates yesterday having a laugh and you seemed so young. The facts are that I am seventeen, nearly eighteen, and if anyone knew I was even thinking about going out with a fourteen-year-old I would never hear the end of it. Where would we go for our dates? Youth club or something? You see what I mean, don't you?
>
> I think it is best we stay away from each other for a year or so. You need to see someone more your own age. My brother has a really nice mate called Dave. He's a good laugh. You'd like him.
>
> I'm really sorry.
>
> Love Robbie xxxxxxxxx

Midday

On the phone to Jas. I was shaking with rage.

Jas said, "Well, erm... if he's a good laugh, maybe you should meet him."

"Jas, are you really saying that I should just stop liking one person and start liking another one, just like that? What if I said, 'Hey, Jas, forget about Tom, why not go out with Spotty Norman? He's got a really great shaped head underneath the acne'?"

Saturday August 7th
6:20 p.m.
I hate him. I hate him.

On the phone to Jas.

"How dare he find another boyfriend for me? I hate him!!!"

Sunday August 8th
3:50 p.m.
That is absolutely it for me now. He can't treat me like that. I have my pride. How dare he question my maturiosity?

On the phone to Jas. "Jas?"

"What?"

"You don't think I should just pop round to his house and sort of beg and plead, do you?"

Monday August 9th
11:40 a.m.

I will never get over this, never.

Mum says there are plenty more fish in the sea. Why is she so obsessed with fish? At a time like this! She doesn't care about my feelings anyway.

No one does.

Wednesday August 11th
2:49 p.m.

Took Angus for a long, moody walk. Part of me really hates the Sex God. Sadly it's only a little tiny part of me (near my knee), the rest of me really, really likes him!!!!

3:00 p.m.

Even my breasts like him. They want to break out of my T-shirt and yell, "I love you, I love you!!!"

3:32 p.m.

I hope I am not being driven to the brink of madness by grief. They say that some people never get over things, like whatshername, Kathy Thing. The one who wandered over the moors at night yelling, "Heathcliff, Heathcliff, it's me a-Kathy come home again." Was that Kathy Brontë, one of the Brontë sisters? Or was that Kate Bush? Anyway, whoever it was wandered off into the rain and died from heartbreak. That will be me. I feel a bit tired now. If I just lie down here in the grass I might never be found.

3:35 p.m.
Angus keeps tugging at his lead. It was murder getting it on him but at least it means he can't savage any small dogs that we see.

4:00 p.m.
Famous last words. Angus saw a Pekinese and dragged me to my feet and halfway across a field before I managed to get him under control. He's senselessly brave. There is something about small dogs that really irritates him.

4:30 p.m.
Angus can fetch sticks!!! I was just carrying a stick along, hitting things with it. Then my arm got tired so I flung it away. And Angus pounced on it and dragged it back!! Superdooper cat!!!

5:00 p.m.

I wonder if I could get him to carry a little flask of tea round his neck in case I fancied a cuppa when we were having our walk?

Friday August 13th
My bedroom
1:00 a.m.

Hot and stuffy. Big full moon. Sitting on the windowsill. (Me, not the moon.)

1:05 a.m.

I hate him.

1:06 a.m.

Oh I love him, I love him.

1:10 a.m.

I hate him, but he will not break me. I will make him regret the day he said, "I know a bloke called Dave. He's a good laugh."

She who laughs last laughs last.

2:00 a.m.

I am going to be a heartless babe magnet as revenge.

2:05 a.m.

Oh no, no, that's not what I mean. I don't want to be a babe magnet, that would mean I was a lesbian.

2:05 and 30 secs

Still, what is wrong with that? Each to their own, I say. After all, Mum must have kissed Dad (erlack).

2:06 a.m.

If anyone asked me to comment on sexuality, say in the *Mail on Sunday* or something, I would say that it is a matter of personal choice and nothing to do with nosey parkers. Or else I would say, "Don't ask me, I am on the rack of love."

Sunday August 15th
In bed
9:40 p.m.

In bed early, healing my broken heart in the "privacy" of my bedroom.

9:41 p.m.

How can I stop Libby hiding her pooey knickers in my bed?

Monday August 16th
9:00 a.m.

Up. Up at nine a.m. in the holidays. Nine a.m.!! This just proves how upset I am.

Mum hasn't even noticed, of course.

"Mum, shouldn't even you be able to potty-train Libby by now? At this rate she'll be a pensioner and still pooing all over the place. She'll never get a boyfriend... Still, that will make two of us."

Tuesday August 17th
8:30 a.m.

I think I've lost a lot of weight from my bottom. No one has noticed. Mum just wanders around in a dream. She has got a calendar up in the kitchen with the days marked off until Vati gets back and a heart drawn round the date. How sad is that at her age? I said, "Don't worry yourself about my breakfast, Mutti. I'll get it myself, you get on with your own very important life."

333

She was humming and slathering herself with creams and ignoring me. So I said even louder, "Something quite interesting happened last night; I slit my throat and my head fell off. Have you seen it anywhere?"

Mum called from the bathroom. "Has Libby got her shoes on?"

"I think Mr Next Door might be another transvestite like Vati."

She came out of the bathroom then. "Georgia, is it possible for you to help at all? Where is your sister?"

"Mum, have you noticed anything unusual about me? I am not happy... in fact, I am very unhappy."

"Why? Have you broken a nail?" And she laughed in a very unpleasant way. Then she called out, "Libbsy, where are you, pet? What are you doing?"

I could hear Libby's muffled voice from Mum's bedroom and a bit of miaowing. Libby called, "Nuffing."

Mum rushed in there, saying, "Oh God."

I heard bang bang, and Mum yelling, "Libby, that is Mummy's best lipstick!"

"It looks nice!!!!"

"No, it doesn't... Cats don't wear lipstick."

"Yes."

"No, they don't."

"Yes."

"Owww, don't kick Mummy."

"Bad Mummy!!!"

Hahahaha. She who laughs last laughs... er... the last.

Thursday August 19th
11:00 a.m.

Raining. In August. Typical. Squelching along on my way to meet Mrs Big Knickers, I was thinking... I could either give in and be a miserable, useless person, like Elvis Attwood, our barmy, sad old school caretaker. Or if I truly gave up I could be like Wet Lindsay. When Robbie dumped her she got all pale and even wetter than normal. She was like an anoraksick. (A person who is both very thin and wears tragic anoraks.) I just made that up as a joke. Even though I am very upset I can still think of a joke. I'll tell Jas when I see her. As I was saying, before I so rudely interrupted myself, I could be a sad old sadsack or I could gird my loins and be like in that song. The one where you have to search for the hero within yourself.

Jas was waiting for me at the bus stop. She said, "Why are you walking in that stiff way?"

"I'm girding my loins."

"Well, it looks painful, like you've got a stick up your bottom. You haven't, have you?"

"You really are sensationally mad, Jas. In olden days people would have thrown oranges at you."

As I said, I can sometimes surprise myself with my own wisdomosity. And humourosity. Even in adversosity.

Monday August 23rd
2:10 a.m.

In bed. Oh God, it's so boring being broken-hearted. I've spent so much time in bed I'll probably start growing a long white beard soon, like Rip van Thing.

2:15 a.m.

Or perhaps I could just grow my eyebrows and train them into a beard.

2:48 a.m.

I can't sleep. I've gone all feverish now. I'm going to creep downstairs and get Mum's *Men are from Mars* book and do some more research.

3:35 a.m.

God, it's too weird. Apparently boys might seem like they like you to be all interested in them, but really they want you to be like a glacier iceberg sort of girl. So you have to play hard to get. That's where I must have gone wrong. I have been too keen, I must do glacial.

Thursday August 26th
10:33 p.m.

Same bat time. Same bat place. Same scuba-diving Barbie digging me in the back.

According to the next bit in Mum's book, boys are like elastic bands. Good Lord!

It doesn't mean that boys are made of elastic, which is a plus because nobody wants a boyfriend made out of rubber. On the other hand, if they were made out of rubber you could save yourself a lot of time and effort and heartache by just rustling one up out of a car tyre. But that is not what the book means. Boys are different from girls. Girls like to be cosy all the time but boys don't. First of all they like to get all close to you like a coiled-up rubber band, but after a while they get fed up with being too coiled and need to stretch

♥ 337

away to their full stretchiness. Then, after a bit of on-their-own stretchy, they ping back to be close to you.

Hmmm. So in conclusion on the boy front, you have to play hard to get (the glacier bit), and also let them be elastic bands. *Sacré bleu!* They don't want much, do they?

Friday August 27th
4:20 p.m.
Round at Jas's house. Been to town. I bought myself some new lippy to cheer myself up and Jas got a new hot air brush thing that gives you bouncability. She was making her hair all turn under at the ends.

As she was tonging away at her hair she said, "I looked for a bra but I can't get one small enough. In fact, I don't need one, I'm more like Kate Moss. You have to wear one though, don't you?... Because of the pencil-case test thing."

"Just pencil... the case was my mum."

"Yeah, but the pencil stuck, didn't it? You said that if it did you had to have help and support."

"I know what I said."

When Jas really annoys me (i.e. all of the time) I notice that her fringe is more fringey than normal, if you know what I mean.

Fringey went on, "I'm only saying – there's no need to have a nervy b."

Jas was really, really beginning to annoy me. A lot. All her things are really neatly put away which is the sign of a very dull person in my opinion. When Jas and I stalked Wet Lindsay and looked through her bedroom window all her things were very tidy as well. Jas even puts all her knickers in the same drawer.

Besides it being VERY dull to do that it would also be useless at my house as Libby mostly uses my knickers as hats for her dolls. Or Angus eats them.

To change the subject I said, In a really caring way, "When does Tom go off to work experience?"

Jas stopped hot brushing her hair then and looked all mournful. Hahahahaha. She said, "Next Saturday – it's going to be really horrible. Do you think he'll meet someone else in Birmingham?"

I looked wise and oracle-like and like I was really thinking (which I wasn't). I said, "Well, he's a young bloke and we all know what young blokes are like."

"Do we?"

I laughed bitterly.

She said, "Just because Robbie went off doesn't mean all boys do."

"It does... in Mum's book *Men are from Mars* it tells you all about it."

She was interested then and came and sat next to me. "What does it say in the book? Does it say Tom is going to go off with someone else?"

I said, "Yes it does, Jas. It says in the worldwide number one bestseller written by some bloke in America who has never met Tom, it says in Chapter Two, 'Tom Jennings definitely goes off with someone else when he goes to do work experience in Birmingham for a month.'"

She looked a bit miffed. "Well, what do you mean, then?"

I waited for a bit. Teach her to go on and on about my breasty problem and the fact that SG had left me.

"Can I try your new shiny lippy?"

She wasn't interested, it was all just me, me, me with her. She just went on about her problems.

"Anyway, Gee, what do you mean about this book? Isn't it American?"

"Yeah."

"Well it will be about American boys, then, won't it?"

"No, it's about boykind."

"Oh."

I paused. She looked all goggly and attentive, it was quite a nice feeling. Perhaps I might reconsider my career and think about becoming an Agony Aunt rather than a backing singer. Especially since I can't sing. But I know all about agony.

Jas was as agog as two gogs. She said, "Go on."

I explained, "Boys are like elastic bands."

"What?"

"Boys are like elastic bands."

"What?"

"Jas, if you keep saying 'what?' every time I say something we may be here for some centuries."

"Well, what do you mean 'like elastic bands'?"

"They like to be all close and then after a bit of being close they have to stretch and get far away... and you have to let them and then they spring back."

"What?"

"You're doing it again and it really annoys me. In fact, I will have to kill you now because I have a lot of untamed energy because of the Sex God. I'm going to have to give you a bit of a duffing up." And I shoved her.

She said, "Don't be silly and childish."

I said, "I'm not."

She got up and started making her hair have more bouncability with the air brush thing again. I waited until she had got it just right (in her opinion), then I hit her over the head with a pillow. She started to say, "Look, this is not funn–" but before she could finish I hit her over the head again with the pillow. And every time she tried to talk I did it again. She got all red-faced, which in Jas's case is very red indeed. It made me feel much better. Violence may be the answer to the world's problems. I may write to the Dalai Lama and suggest he tries my new approach.

My room
Midnight

I've got a plan. It involves the two "isities". They are "maturiosity" and "glaciosity". Firstly I have to prove to SG that I am very sophis and grown-up. Not a laughing hyena in a school uniform as he thought the last time he saw me. (This is the maturiosity bit.) Secondly I must be distant and alluring and play hard to get. (This is the glaciosity bit.)

The conclusion of these two parts is that SG comes springing back like an elastic band.

Saturday August 28th

2:10 p.m.

Phoned Jas.

I said, "I've worked out a plan."

She said, "I can't talk, Tom and I are going to choose my tattoo."

Huh. Typico.

Well, old huge knickers always puts her boyfriend first. Just as well I am so popular.

10:00 p.m.

In bed listening to a tape. Sadly it is "the Teddy Bears' Picnic". Libby has made me listen to it five times. If I try to turn it off she has a nervy spaz and growls at me.

I phoned up my "mates" earlier to go out, but they were all busy.

11:00 p.m.

I wonder if I had an emergency, like appendicitis or something, would my mates be too "busy" to come to the hospital?

11:30 p.m.

I have got a pain in my side. It might be a grumbling appendix.

11:32 p.m.

In blodge we learned that rabbits have got some sort of shrub growing in their appendix. How normal is that?

Sunday August 29th
6:30 p.m.

Mutti and Libbs have gone to visit the elderly mad. (Grandad.) Mum asked me if I would like to go, but I just looked at her with pity. Sadly she didn't get it and asked me again. I explained politely that I would rather put my head in a pair of Elvis Attwood's old trousers. She said I was a "horrid, bad-tempered spoiled brat". Fat chance I'm spoiled. I'm lucky if I get one square meal a week. I'm getting really, really thin. Apart from my nose. And basoomas.

8:00 p.m.

Ellen, Rosie and Jools came round and we sat on the wall, looking at boys. There are, it has to be said, a lot of fit-looking boys, but they haven't got that certain Sex God factor for me.

Mark (BG) went by with his girlfriend Ella. She is practically a midget. I thought he was taking a toddler for a walk. Rosie said, "So what happened with you and Robbie?"

I said, "he sent me a note and said that I should go out with some loser called Dave the Laugh."

Rosie said, "That's sort of dumping by proxy, isn't it?"

I said, "Are you supposed to be cheering me up?"

"But I thought you got to number six and everything."

"Yeah, but he said his parents would go ballisticisimus because I am so young. They'd think I was jail thing."

The Ace Crew were all full-on, attention-wise. Ellen even took her chewing gum out.

Jools said, "What is jail thing?"

I didn't really know actually but I improvised (lied). "Er... it's when you are underage and you go to... er... number eight with a boy."

Rosie said, "What, if you let a boy touch you above the waist you have to go to jail?"

I said patiently, "No, he has to go to jail."

Rosie said, "Well, that's it for Sven, then."

I said, "Fair enough." But I don't know what I am talking

about really. I'm all upset and confused and still have Herr Kamyer legs, even though it's the end of August.

Monday August 30th
1:43 p.m.
Borrowed Ellen's Kool Tan. Soon my Herr Kamyer legs will turn into sun-kissed boy magnets. Hmmm, smooth it on smoothy smooth and leave for an hour.

2:00 p.m.
If I move my bed and open the window I can sort of sunbathe on my bedroom floor. SG is going to find it damn difficult to resist the new tanned me.

4:05 p.m.
Woke up to orange Herr Kamyer legs and a huge red nose!!

5:00 p.m.
I've just scrubbed my legs off. They are not quite so orange but my nose looks like one of those red clown noses. Brilliant.

Operation elastic band

Wednesday September 1st
7:00 p.m.

It's boiling having to wear stockings in this weather, but better than being blinded every time I look down at my still orangish legs.

Eight days till we go back to Stalag 14. I'm going to put my foot down with a firm hand this term and make sure I don't have to sit next to Nauseating P. Green.

Mum has gone out to Uncle Eddie's with Libbs. He is teaching Mum salsa dancing – can you imagine? How very sad. The tremendously old can be very embarrassing. Imagine my mum salsa dancing with Uncle Eddie the human boiled egg.

In public.

Or private.

7:05 p.m.

Jas called. Tom has gone off to work experience and she wants to come round. I am a substitute boyfriend. Well she can think again if she thinks I am going to be constantly available when Tom goes off to work experience. I am not so cheap.

7:08 p.m.

I may make her give me some expensive present that I choose from Boots. Oh no, hang on, I've got a better idea.

7:30 p.m.

Jas moaning on about Tom.

I listened sympathetically and said, "Shut up, now, Jas."

Then she looked at me. "Why have you got pink panstick on your nose?"

I said, "Shut up, now, Jas."

7:42 p.m.

I made my famous French toast for Jas. (Beat an egg and put bread in it and then fry it. The French bit comes in when you are eating the toast and you have to speak with a French accent.) As we were munching through the toast I said, "Jas, *ma petite*."

"*Quoi?*"

"I've got *le plan* to *impressez* the Sex God *avec* my maturiosity. It involves *vous*."

She almost choked on her toast. "*Non*."

"You will *aime* it."

"Oh *mon Dieu*."

The first part of my plan was that we got dressed up to look as old as we could and get on a bus and get full fares. As an experiment. She was grumbling as she got made up but at least she was on the move.

8:30 p.m.

Ready. I must say I think we looked v. Sophis. We'd got loads more make-up on than we normally wear, and darker lipstick. And we wore all black. Black is very ageing, as I continually tell Mum so I can get her black T-shirt and leather trousers. I said to Jas, "We'd better get back before she gets home because I have borrowed her Gucci handbag. She specifically said she would kill me if I ever borrowed it.

She is very, very mean with her things, which is why I have to borrow them in secret."

As we walked down the street I had another idea. "Let's keep pretending we are French as well."

"Why?"

"Don't you mean *pourquoi*?"

"No, I mean why?"

"Just *parce que, ma petite* pal."

Midnight

Oui!!! Très, très bon!! Merveilleux!!!! It was *très, très bon* plus *les grandes knobs.*

The bus driver was like a sort of mobile version of Elvis Attwood, our school caretaker – i.e. very old, mad and bad-tempered, but sitting in a bus rather than a hut. I said to Mobile Elvis, "*Bonsoir, mon très* old *garçon. Mon amie et moi désire deux billets pour* Deansgate, *s'il vous plaît.*"

He understood we wanted to go to Deansgate but unluckily, like all very old mad people, thought he could be funny and witty. He gave us the tickets (full fare! Yesss!!! Result!!!!). I handed over the money and he said, "*Merci* buckets." Then he laughed himself senseless (easy enough as he was mad in the first place). I thought he would choke to death because he was laughing so much, but sadly he didn't.

What is the matter with people?

12:20 a.m.

Snug in my bed. Maybe I should leave school as I look so old.

2:30 a.m.

I could go off and have sophisticated adventures instead of hanging around with very young people.

12:35 a.m.

I could go to India and visit the Dalai Lama, or is it Gandhi who lives there? I don't know. We haven't done India in geoggers yet. All I know is what Mum tells me about it, and that is mostly, "Oh it was just so... you know... great." Anyway, even if we had done India in geoggers Mrs Franks is so bad at explaining things that I wouldn't know any more than I do now. She called concentration camps "contraception camps" while we were doing world affairs.

1:00 a.m.

Now on to part two of the plan. The glaciosity bit. I must look for an opportunity to show SG how stand-offish I can be.

Saturday September 4th

5:50 p.m.

Five days to Stalag 14 (school) and counting. I got my uniform out of the back of the wardrobe. Angus must have been using it as his lair by the look of it. I bunged it in the washing machine and hoped the bits of feather would come off.

I did cheer myself up a bit because I thought of something funny to do with my beret. Which we are forced to wear by the Oberführer (Miss "Hawkeye" Heaton).

6:00 p.m.

Phoned Rosie.

"I've thought of something really cool to do with the beret this term."

Rosie said, "I thought we were going to do the rolling it up into the sausage and pinning it under our hair at the back routine again?"

"Yeah I know, but what about this... what about if we use it as combination beret and lunchbox?"

Rosie said, "How do you mean?"

I had to explain, patiently. It is not easy being the leader of the gang. I sympathise with Richard Branson on this one, although I still see no reason for his ridiculous beard.

Anyway, I said, "Pop your sandwiches or crisps or whatever into the beret, then tie it on to your head with your scarf. *Voilà*, beret and lunchpack all in one."

"Hawkeye would go mad."

"Exactamondo, *ma petite amie.'*

Rosie said, "You are a genius." She is not wrong.

Sunday September 5th
5:10 p.m.

Au secours and *sacré bleu*!! Just walking to the park to meet the gang when I saw Call me Arnold, the vicar. I ducked down behind a car to hide until he had gone by. But the car was his car. When he got in he saw me crouching down. I had to pretend I was looking at a really interesting pebble.

God will know that I was hiding from his maidservant.

353

Still, I don't know how I could possibly be made to suffer more than I am already.

5:45 p.m.
Now I know. Cousin James is coming round tomorrow.

Midnight
If he gets all weird like he has done in the past and attempt to kiss me or anything, I may go mad.

Monday September 6th
10:00 p.m.
Cousin James asked me if I wanted to play strip poker. I was so embarrassed, I just said, "I don't know how to play poker," and he said, "Well, let's play strip snap, then."

I pretended I could hear the phone ringing. When he left, five million years later, I noticed there was something lurking under his nose. I thought it was a bogey at first, but sadly I now think it was a sort of moustache. Erlack!

Wednesday September 8th

10:00 p.m.

Mum came in my bedroom and asked if I wanted a wake-up call for Stalag 14 tomorrow. I said, "Oh, hello Mum, what are you doing in?"

She patted me on the head and said, "Goodnight, my sweet-natured little elf."

Nothing seems to bother her now that Vati is coming home. She might have put his moustache out of her mind but I haven't. In fact, to remind her I have drawn a moustache on the heart she put in the calendar.

10:30 p.m.

Washed my hair but couldn't be bothered drying it. I know if I sleep on it while it is damp I will wake up with the "stupid hedgehog" look. There will be bits sticking up all over the place, so I am sleeping with my pillow tucked under my neck and my head sort of drooping over the other side.

This is how Japanese Buddhist people sleep – it's probably whatsit... zen. They probably do it because it lets their chi flow free. Chi is energy that is in your body it says in my Buddhist book. Heaven knows I need as much energy as I can get for working out my plan for SG retrieval.

I think all the blood may have drained into my head from my shoulders.

11:00 p.m.

What happens if you get too much extra blood in your head? If you were meant to have two shoulders and a neck's worth of extra blood in your head you would have a bigger head, surely?

Or inflatable ears that could accommodate the extra blood and so on. Do Japanese have big ears?

Perhaps that is why Wet Lindsay's ears are so huge – because she's got Japanese ancestors. I wouldn't be surprised.

That would explain her tiny legs.

But not her big goggly eyes.

Thursday September 9th
8:00 a.m.

Woke up all snuggled down under the covers. I must have dropped asleep and forgotten about my zen position. My awake mind said, "Ha-so, I am a Japanese zen person ha-sleep with head h-over end of bed." But my English subconscious took over when I was asleep and said, "Snuggle down, you know you want to..."

Bathroom
8:10 a.m.
OhmyGodohmyGod... my hair looks like I've been electrocuted. No time to wash it. I'll have to gel it down.

8:30 a.m.
Pant pant, rush rush. Jas waiting for me.

She said, "Why do you look like Elvis Presley?"

As we ran up the hill towards school, we could see Hawkeye standing like a ferret by the gates. Oh here we go again... the beret patrol!!!! I hadn't got mine on. No time for the "sausage" or the "lunchpack". Only one thing for it. I fished the beret out of my bag and pulled it right down over my ears. You could only just see my eyes.

When we ran past Hawkeye she shook herself like something nasty had made a nest in her knickers.

"Two minutes to assembly; don't start the term with a detention."

Oh very caring. "Hello, Georgia, welcome back," would have been nice.

As we dashed to the cloakroom I said to Jas, "Imagine her having a boyfriend! Erlack, no no, I must pull my mind away from that otherwise I'll start imagining her snogging or something. Urgh!!!! Urgh! I've done it now: I've let it in my brain!!! Hawkeye getting up to number seven on the snogging scale. Putting her tongue in someone's mouth. Maybe Herr Kamyer in his lederhosen. Urghhhh. Erlack. Get out, get out!!!"

I ripped off my beret and coat and went into the main hall.

Rosie, Ellen, Jools and Mabs – otherwise known as the Ace Crew – were all there. I gave them our special Klingon salute. They looked at me like they had never seen me before. Had they forgotten all we had shared after so little time? I felt a hand on my shoulder. It was Hawkeye. What fresh hell? She looked down her big beaky nose at me and hissed, "Take this, make yourself presentable and get back here as quickly as you can, you stupid girl."

I looked down and saw that she had given me a comb. When I went into the loos I saw my hair had gone the shape of my pulled-down beret because of the superdooper hair gel.

Sacré bleu! I feel like *un* nincompoop.

9:00 a.m.

Took my usual place next to Rosie and Jas. Our revered headmistress "Slim" Simpson (so called because she weighs about a ton) lumbered on to the stage. I whispered to Rosie, "Crikey, she has got chins on her chins."

Slim bored us half to death by telling us what fabulous treats were ahead of us this term. Exams (yippee!); the challenge of modern languages and physics with Herr Kamyer (superdooper!!!); a school trip to the escarpments of the Lake District (oh marvy!!!)...

As she said each thing Rosie and I were clapping our hands together in delight until Hawkeye gave us the evil eye. Good grief.

Break
11:00 a.m.

Jools, Ellen, Mabs, Rosie, Jas and I met behind the tennis courts for a confab. Elvis Attwood, the grumpiest caretaker in the universe, shouted at us as we passed his hut, "I've got my eye on you lot. Don't come sneaking into my hut otherwise there will be trouble."

He's beyond bonkerdom. He came to a school dance and did some exhibition twisting on stage until his back went and he had to be taken to casualty. That's when we started calling him Elvis.

I waved and shouted back, "Greetings, oh mad one."

We were grumbling and moaning as we sat down. As usual in this fascist hell-hole we have been split up in class and not allowed to sit together. I have my "pal" Nauseating P. Green next to me. She wears those glasses that look like they have been made out of jam jars, which is very unfortunate. She's got really bulgy eyes anyway. Rosie said, "I think there must be a touch of the goldfish in her family genes."

As we ate our snacks you could see right up Jas's skirt. I said, "Jas, do you always wear those huge knickers? A small dog could creep up a knicker leg and you wouldn't know."

"Well I like to be comfy."

"They're not very sexy, are they?"

"You said you thought little knickers were stupid. Remember Lindsay's thongs?"

"Shut up, don't upset me. You know how visual I am.

Now not only have I got Hawkeye snogging Herr Kamyer in my brain, I've also got Wet Lindsay's thongs."

Ellen said, "Anything happening with you and Robbie?"

I explained about my glaciosity and maturiosity plan. They all nodded wisely. We are a very wise group. Full of wisdomosity. I am almost certainly wiser than God, who doesn't seem able to grant the simplest of requests. Which is why I have turned to Lord Buddha.

Rosie spoilt the moment of wisdomosity by saying through a mouthful of cheesy snacks. "What in the name of pantyhose are you talking about?"

4:45 p.m.

At the end of my glorious day today Elvis made me pick up a sweet wrapper in the corridor. All because I did my VERY funny impression of him doing the twist and then his back going. If he doesn't want people to make jokes at his expense he should stay indoors. He's a barmy old fascist. I bet he goes round dropping sweet papers on purpose.

5:05 p.m.

Jas phoned, all breathless and excited.

"I've got two letters from Tom."

I said, "He's only gone to Birmingham."

"I know, but... well... you know."

No, I don't know.

5:15 p.m.

Libby and Mum came home. Libby has had her first day at kindergarten which I think is a good thing as it will make her less mad.

5:16 p.m.

Wrong. Libby has made me something to wear at kindergarten. She was ramming it on my head. I said, "Steady on, Libby, be gentle with my head. What is it you have made?"

"It's nice!!!"

"Yes. I know. But what is it?"

She looked at me like I was a halfwit and put her face nose to nose with mine. She said really slowly, "For... egg!!!"

"For my head?"

She hit me. "No, no, no, bad boy... for your EGG!"

Mum came in.

"Look, Georgie, she's made you an egg cosy."

"Well why is she trying to put it on my head?"

"She must have got mixed up. Maybe she thinks the teacher said 'head cosy'." And Mum started laughing like a drain. Libby joined in while I just sat there.

7:00 p.m.

What is there to laugh at? I am on the rack of love. Life is a sham and a facsimile and a farce.

7:15 p.m.

But at least I have an egg cosy.

8:00 p.m.

I am soothing myself by pampering my mind and body. I am pampering my mind by reading (an article about mascara) and I am pampering my body by eating a LOT of chocolate.

9:00 p.m.

Now I feel worried, fat, but very well informed about mascara. Which is a plus.

Wednesday September 15th

Assembly

9:00 a.m.

Does Slim go to a special evening class on how to be boring? She was going on about tiny people with small heads or the poor or something. I don't know, who cares? Well obviously someone cares, and maybe I will care again one day, but at the moment all my caringness is used up on myself.

RE

10:00 a.m.

Despite my tragedy I did cheer up a bit in RE. Honestly. Miss Wilson lives in the land of the very mad. Where does she get her stockings from? It can't be a normal shop. It must be a circus shop. They are all thick and wrinkly like an elephant has been wearing them. Perhaps they are Slim's cast-offs?

Rosie sent me a note: Dear Gee, Ask Miss Wilson if God has a penis.

Even in my tragedy it made me laugh and Miss Wilson said, "Georgia, what is funny? Perhaps you could share the joke with us all."

"Er... well, I was just wondering if God had..."

364

Rosie looked at me in amazement.

Miss Wilson was encouraging me in my religious curiosity. "You were wondering if God had...?"

"Yes, if God had a... beardy thing?"

Miss Wilson unfortunately did not realise how very funny I was being. She went on and on about the fact that he wasn't really a bloke with a beard in the sky but more of a spiritual entity. She didn't need to tell me that there is no big bloke in the sky. I know that. I've tried often enough to speak to him and get stuff. Hopeless. That is why if she had bothered to ask me I would have told her that I have become a zen Buddhist.

1:15 p.m.

What is it with Elvis? Jas and me were innocently moaning by the back of the science block and he comes along. Ears flapping in the wind. Raving on and on.

"What are you two up to?"

I said, "Nothing."

"Don't give me nothing. I know you two. You've probably been messing about in my hut."

What is the matter with him? And why does he always

365

wear a flat hat? I wonder if his head is flat underneath it? Probably. As we walked away I said to Jas, "He's obsessed with us going in his hut. He's ALWAYS saying we go in his hut. He goes on and on about it, like a budgie. Why does he go on and on about it?"

Jas was walking along. I said, "Why? On and on and on about us going in his poxy hut. Why us? Why keep accusing us of going in his hut? Why?"

Jas said, "Because we go in his hut."

"So?"

5:00 p.m.

Jas's room at her house. Jas has just popped down to the kitchen to make me some nutritious snack (Pop-Tarts) to cheer me up. I'm just not interested in anything, though.

5:03 p.m.

God her room is tidy. It's pathetically tidy. All her cuddly toys are neatly lined up in size order on her bed. I'm going to mix them up for a hilarious laugh. Ho hum, pig's bum. She's even got a box with "letters" written on it. I wonder if she's got a drawer that says "enormous pants" on it. There are some letters in the box. Probably private ones. It says PRIVATE on the top of them. Probably private, then. Probably letters that Tom has written to Jas. Very personal and private, I'd better put them away.

5:16 p.m.
She calls him HUNKY!!!! This is hilariously crap!! Absolutemento pathetico!!! HUNKY!!! Tom!!! Hahahahahaha.

5:18 p.m.
He calls her Po!!! Like in the Teletubbies. Good grief, that is sad.

5:19 p.m.
Po, for heaven's sake.

5:20 p.m.
My lips are sealed vis-à-vis Hunky and Po.

5:21 p.m.
Even though it is very very funny I must never mention Hunky or Po.

5:23 p.m.

Jas comes back in. I say, "How is Hunky?"

My bedroom
7:00 p.m.

Jas is not speaking to me because I happened to find some personal letters of hers... She's so touchy."

10:30 p.m.

And unreasonable.

Thursday September 16th
8:20 a.m.

On the way to school. When I got to our usual meeting place Jas had already set off, walking really fast ahead of me. I yelled, "Hang on a minute, Po!!" But she ignored me.

Honestly, people really take themselves seriously when they have got a so-called boyfriend.

In a sort of a way it was very funny walking behind Jas. She walked really fast for about five minutes but she is not in tiptop physical condition. In fact, the only exercise she gets is lifting Pop-Tarts and putting them in her mouth.

Anyway, she got tired and had to slow down so then I could catch her up. I walked about half a metre behind her: it was annoying her quite a lot but she couldn't say anything as she is not speaking to me.

By the time I got to the school gates I was walking about ten centimetres behind her. Her beret was practically sticking up my nose.

She tried to escape me in assembly by standing next to Rosie but I squeezed in between them and looked at her with my face really near hers. She was all red and furious. Even her ears were red. Tee hee.

11:00 a.m.

Followed Jas into the loos. I went into the next cubicle to her and talked to her through the walls.

"Jas, I love you."

"What are you doing? You're being stupid!"

"No. YOU'RE being stupid, Po."

"It was really mean of you to read my private letters."

"They were only from Hunky."

"You shouldn't read people's private things."

"How would I know anything if I didn't?"

369

There was a bit of a silence from the other side of the wall. Then she said, "What do you mean?"

I went on reasonably, "I wouldn't even know you were called Po if I hadn't read the letters."

She was on the edge of bamboozlement. "Yeah, but that's not the point... I..."

"You shouldn't have secrets from your very best pal."

"YOU have secrets."

"I don't – I even told you about my sticky-out nipples."

"Well, Tom says they stuck out because it was cold."

I couldn't believe it. The bell went for the end of break and I heard Jas flush the loo and go out. I rushed out of my loo and set off down the corridor, following her. "You told Tom... about my sticky-out nipples???"

I couldn't believe it. My nipples had been made a public mockery of a sham... I was so incensed I barely noticed Wet Lindsay talking to some unlucky fourth former. Although I did notice that she looked like an owl in a school uniform.

I was hissing at Jas. "You discussed my nipples with Hunky... I can't believe it!!!"

Then from behind me I heard Wet Lindsay's voice,

"Georgia, your skirt is tucked up in your knickers... I don't think it sets a very good example to the younger girls."

Then she went off, sniggering in a pathetic sniggering owl sort of way.

5:00 p.m.

In the bath. That is it. I am on the warpath. I am now a loner. I have no friends. My so-called best friend only likes stupid Hunky and discusses my private body parts with him. And then he probably goes and discusses it with his older brother. And he and the SG have a good laugh.

5:15 p.m.

Angus is sitting on the side of the bath. He is drinking the water even though it has got bubble bath in it. His whiskers are all soapy.

5:20 p.m.

Now Libby has wandered in. Come in, everybody, why don't you? I'm only having a bath. Naked. I'm surprised Mr and Mrs Next Door don't pop in for a bit of a look.

I said to Libby, "Libby don't push Angus like that, he'll—"

5:21 p.m.

Angus is soaking and furious. When I fished him out of the bath he savaged my hand. Libby couldn't stop laughing. What a life.

6:00 p.m.

Jas phoned. I said, "What do you want, nipple discusser?"

She said, "Look, can't we call it quits? I won't mention the Hunky business again if you forget about the nip nips incident."

I didn't want to give in because I was in too bad a mood so I just went, "Huh."

But then I was all agog attention-wise because she said, "Tom phoned and told me The Stiff Dylans are doing a gig at the Crazy Coconut club a week Wednesday. AND WHAT'S MORE Dave the Laugh is going to be there. AND WHAT'S MORE my mum is staying at my aunt's in Manchester."

6:02 p.m.
Thinking.

6:05 p.m.
Thinking and eating cornflakes. Hmmm.

6:07 p.m.

Obviously this is it!!! This is my chance to implement the elastic band theory. I have to go to The Stiff Dylans gig and get off with Dave the Laugh. In front of the SG. This will serve the twofold purpose of maturiosity (being at a nightclub) and glaciosity (getting off with another boy). SG will be very jealous. He will want to come pinging back (the elastic band theory).

11:00 p.m.

I must start softening Mum up so that she will not be suspicious when I say I am staying at Jas's on Wednesday night.

Saturday September 18th

Morning

10:00 a.m.

Mum nearly dropped Libby when I said, "Do you want me to get anything for you while I am in town this afternoon?"

She said, "Sorry, love, I thought for a moment you offered to do something for me. What did you really say?"

Even though I was irritated by her I kept a lovely smile on my face. "Oh Mutti... as if I never do anything for you!"

She said suspiciously, "Why are you smiling like that? What have you got on that is mine? If you have borrowed my gold necklace I'll go mad."

I snapped then. "Look, what is the matter with you? How can I ever be a nice person if you are so suspicious all the time? What are you, a mother or a police dog? Do you want to do a body search before I go out? Honestly!!!"

Then I remembered my Operation Elastic Band just in the knickers of time. I said nicely, "I just thought you might want me to bring something back for you. I know how busy you are, that's all."

In the end I think I convinced her, which is a bit of a drag as now I've got to lumber home with waterproof panties for Libbs. Hey ho. What sacrifices I make for the SG. I've almost forgotten what he looks like.

10:05 a.m.
I've remembered what he looks like. Yum yum yum.

1:00 p.m.

Miss Selfridge changing room. I tried on a size twelve T-shirt and I couldn't get it on. Jas (very loudly) said, "I think your breasts are definitely getting bigger, you know."

This was in the packed communal changing room and everyone looked round.

I said, "Er... Jas... I think there is someone in Australia who might not have heard you properly."

Rosie and Ellen met us in Luigi's coffee bar. I told them about The Stiff Dylans gig and my plan vis-à-vis Dave the Laugh. Rosie was eating the foam from her coffee with a spoon and slurping. So was Ellen. It was stereo foam slurping. After ten years had gone by Rosie said, with the spoon in her mouth which was very unattractive but I didn't say... anyway, she said, "So you're going to the gig so that you can get off with Dave the Laugh and that will make the SG into an elastic band?"

How difficult can life be? Very, very difficult, that's how. I said patiently (well, at least without hitting her), "Yes, yes, thrice yes!!!"

More slurping. She was obviously thinking about my masterplan (or mistressplan actually, as I had thought of it and I am a girlie). Then she said, "Can I borrow your brown leather boots?"

4:00 p.m.

Lugged home Libby's waterproof nick-nacks. All quiet on the home front when I got in. Where was everyone?

9:30 p.m.

Early to bed, early to rise, makes a... whatsit.

10:00 p.m.

I may wear some false eyelashes for the gig. I must be careful though, last time I tried them the glue tube burst and I couldn't get my eyes apart for twenty minutes.

Tuesday September 21st
4:15 p.m.

Boring day apart from when Wet Lindsay got her bag caught on her foot and fell up the science-block stairs.

11:00 p.m.

Libby in bed with me. I don't know why she can't sleep the right way up, her feet keep poking me in the eye.

11:10 p.m.

I wonder what Dave the Laugh looks like?

Friday September 24th
Morning break
11:00 a.m.

Ellen told me that her brother and his mates go out on "cat patrol".

I said, "Do they really like cats, then?"

She said, "No, him and his mates are the cat patrol and they go out looking for birds... you know, chicks... girls."

Good Lord.

Lunchtime
12:30 p.m.

Ellen says that her brother also calls breasts "nunga-nungas".

I know I shouldn't have asked but somehow I just had to.

Ellen said, "Well, he says that if you get hold of a breast and pull it out and then let it go... it goes nunga-nunga-nunga!"

I may be forced to become either a celibate or a lesbian.

Afternoon break
2:30 p.m.

Me and Ellen were sitting in the loos with our feet up against the back of the doors, so that the Hitler Youth (prefects) wouldn't know we were in there and send us into the torrential rain. The Hitler Youth call it a "slight shower". They'd still say that if the First Years were being swept to their deaths by tidal waves. Or if Elvis's hut was bobbing along with a sail up, or... anyway, who cares what they say?

I said to Ellen through the cubicle wall, "Is your brother a bit on the mad side?"

I could hear her crunching her crisps. She thought about it. "No, he's quite a laugh, really. He calls going to the loo 'going to the piddly-diddly department'."

I could hear her through the wall, laughing and choking. I just sat there staring at the loo door. After a bit she controlled herself and said, "If he's going to the loo to do number twos he says, 'I'm just off to the poo-parlour division'." And she was off, wheezing and choking again. *Sacré bleu*. I am surrounded by *les idiots*.

3:30 p.m.

If it's cold, Ellen's hilarious brother says it is "nippy noodles".

4:15 p.m.

Walked home. Thinking about the difference between girls and boys. For instance, when girls walk home we put on lippy and make-up. We chat. Sometimes we pretend to be hunchbacks. But that is it. Perfectly normal behaviour. When the Foxwood boys come out they hit each other, trip one another up and stuff leaves or caps down each other's trousers. Ellen told me that sometimes her brother sets fire to his farts.

On the way to my house we passed through the park. There is a park Elvis. He is supposed to be the park keeper but mainly he prods at things with a pointy stick. Oh and his second job is to yell, "I can see you!" at innocent snoggers in bushes.

We hung around on the swings for a bit just to annoy Park Elvis. Rosie (who by the way, since the flaming fringe incident is an ex-smoker) said she had made it up with Sven her Swedish boyfriend. She fell out with him because he said to her parents, "Thank you for your daughter, she is, how you say? *Jah...* a great SNOG."

I said, "How can you tell he's sorry? No one can usually understand a word he says."

And she said, "He knitted me a nose warmer."

It's really not worth asking.

Ellen said, "What about Dave the Laugh?"

I said, "What about him?"

"Well, do you really fancy him?"

"I don't know. I don't know what he looks like."

"Well, what is the point, then?"

"Well, he's like... erm... a red herring. In my elastic band strategy."

They all looked at me. It was no use them all looking at me like I know what I am talking about. I'll be the last one to know what I am talking about, believe me.

4:30 p.m.
My so-called private bedroom.

Angus was in my bed. I suspect not alone. I daren't lift the cover in case it's like in that film where there was a chopped-off horse's head in the bed.

6:07 p.m.

Lying on the floor on cushion but at least Angus is nice and comfy. In Mum's *Cosmo* it says, "Buddhism is the new optimism."

Okey-doky. That's what I'm going to do. Be a cheery Buddhist. Om hahaha om.

Monday September 27th
Sports
2:50 p.m.

It's windy and rainy. Naturally these two facts mean that Miss Stamp our games mistress (who is definitely Hitler reincarnated in a gym skirt... she even has the little black moustache)... Anyway, these two facts mean that Adolfa has decided that the best thing we can do is... play hockey outside!!! I'd write to the newspapers to complain but I'll probably drown out on the hockey pitch.

In bed
9:30 p.m.

Brrr. If I have pneumonia and die and never get to number ten on the snogging scale I'll blame Adolfa. Just because she doesn't have a life. Even now I'm only just getting feeling back in my bottom.

10:30 p.m.
When Mum said goodnight I took my opportunity and said, casually, "Mum, can I go and stay round at Jas's on Wednesday night? Her mum says it's OK if it's OK with you. We're doing a science project together... I mean me and Jas not me and Jas's mother – that would be stupid."

(Shut up, shut up now. Leave it! Don't babble on, she'll get suspicious and you will say something really stupid.)

Mum said, "You don't usually do your homework, Gee. This is a bit of a change of heart."

"Hahahaha – yeah right... I..." (Careful, careful, don't say anything stupid.) "...I... thought I might be a scientist." (Too late, she's bound to rumble me now!)

"A scientist – not a backing singer, then?"

"No."

"Hmmm."

"So can I?"

"Oh yes, I suppose so. Night-night."

Result!!!!!! Yesssss!!!!

Wednesday September 29th
Operation Elastic Band
Kitchen
8:00 a.m.

I grabbed a piece of toast and mumbled, "I'm off now, see you tomorrow night."

Mum didn't even look up from trying to fasten Libby into her dungarees. Libby had her porridge bowl on her head. Mum said, "OK, love, bye. Kiss your sister bye-bye."

I said, "Pass," I had kissed Libby before when she had been eating porridge and I didn't want the experience again. I blew her a kiss. "Byeeeeee!"

Phew. Now then, quickly out of the door. Victory!!!!! I've packed all my clubwear and make-up and so on in my rucky. Here we go with Operation Elastic Band.

Just at the end of the path when Mum came out of the house, shouting, "Georgie, what do you mean, 'See you tomorrow night'?"

OhmyGodohmyGodohmyGod.

I laughed casually (sounding a bit like a casual hyena). "Oh I knew you would forget, I'm staying at Jas's tonight – remember?"

She looked blank.

Inwardly I was shouting, "LET ME GO!! SHUT UP, SHUT UP!! I MUST HAVE THE SEX GOD. LET ME GO. LET ME GO. YOU HAVE HAD YOUR LIFE!!!!" Outwardly I said, "Mum, I have to go, I'll be late – see you tomorrow."

Yessss!!! I am cool as *le* cucumber. Or possibly *le* ice cube.

3:50 p.m.

Last bell. Jas and I ran down the hill. Only five hours to get ready.

I said to Jas as we ran, "Mutti was really suspicious this morning when I reminded her I was staying at your house. It was like she didn't believe me. You know, like I am bound to be lying."

"You are lying."

"Oh picky, picky, Jas."

Jas's house
5:00 p.m.

A nourishing meal to set us up for the evening: oven chips, mayonnaise and two fruit Pop-Tarts (for essential vitamin C). In Jas's room we put on some groovy music and started getting ready. Jas had a bit of a moony attack when she looked at Tom's photo by her bed. She started sighing and saying, "I just can't seem to get in the mood to go out."

I pointed at her with my mascara brush. "Jas, snap out of it, you know that Hunky would want you to go out. He phoned you up to tell you about it. He wouldn't want you moping about: he wouldn't want you to let your mates down by staying in. He wouldn't want to come home and find out that your mate had stabbed you with a mascara brush."

Jas was a bit huffy, but she got my nub. As she was putting her hair up she said, "What will you do with Dave the Laugh when you have got off with him?"

"How do you mean?"

I was stalling for time. I'd only really thought as far as getting my make-up on. The rest of it was a bit of a haze of a dream.

"Well, will you be... like his girlfriend then? Will you snog him?"

Luckily the phone rang. We both answered it. It was Rosie. She and Sven were calling from a phone box.

"We just rang to say we've made up this great new dance; it's called 'the phone box'."

She played a radio down the phone and in the background I could hear a lot of grunting and shuffling and Sven going, "Oh *jah*, Oh *jah*, hit it, lads!" or something in Swedish or whatever it is he speaks. Gibberish, normally. Not English, anyway. Then there was a bit of what sounded like tap-dancing. Rosie came back on the phone all breathless. "Brilliant, eh? See you in the next world... don't be late!" And she slammed the phone down.

9:15 p.m.

Left the house to catch the bus down town to the Crazy Coconut. I had so much make-up on I could hardly move my face, which is a plus really because it meant I wouldn't be tempted to go for full-on smiling. I was a vision in black leather. Prayed to God Mutti didn't go through her wardrobe before I could sneak things back in.

When the bus arrived and we got on I couldn't believe it. The driver was Mobile Elvis!! Sadly he remembered us and said "*Bonsoir*". And charged us full fare.

Crazy Coconut
9:30 p.m.

Rosie and Sven turned up. Sven was wearing silver flares. Good Lord. When he saw us he started twisting his hips, saying, "*Jah*, groovy. Let's go, babies!!!!"

The whole queue was looking.

I said to Rosie, "Does Sven always have to be so Svenish?"

Then the van with The Stiff Dylans in it arrived. Robbie got out. Oh bum, all my glaciosity turned to jelliosity.

He saw us and said, "Hi."

I went, "Nung." (I don't know what "nung" means, it just came out.)

The queue started to move and he sort of looked at me for what seemed ages, then he said, "Don't get into any trouble."

I was so mad. How dare he tell me not to get into any trouble? Now he had said that I was going to get into LOADS of trouble just to show him.

I'd show him how much maturiosity I had. At least I would if I managed to get in past the bouncers without them saying I was under age. I said quietly to Rosie and Jas and Sven, "Be really cool."

That's when Sven lifted me up under one of his huge Swedish type arms and shouted at the bouncers, "*Gut* evening, I have the bird in the hand and one in the bushes, thank you!" and strode in.

I don't know whether they let us in because we looked mature or whether they were so amazed by Sven they didn't notice us.

Anyway, Operation Elastic Band was underway.

ll:OO p.m.

Us girls went to the loos and did some emergency make-up repair work. It was quite dark and sort of red lightish in the loos. I was just thinking we looked like groovy chicks around town when the Bummer Twins walked in. I say walked but they waddled. Jackie was wearing a dress that was SO tight. Not a wise choice for a girl who is not small in the bottom department. She is so common. They were both smoking fags (*quelle surprise*). Jackie said, "Oh look, they must be having a sort of crèche here while the grown-ups are clubbing."

She went off into the loo. I could hear her weeing. It sounded like a carthorse. Alison was looking down her nose at us. I'm surprised she could see anything past the huge spot that was on it. She looked like she'd got two noses.

The club was amazing. It had loads of flights of stairs all leading down to a big dance floor, and a stage at one end. You had to go down the stairs from the loos to get to the dance floor. I hoped that no one could see up my skirt because I couldn't remember what knickers I had on. Jas would be all right with her biggest knickers known to humanity.

There were flashing lights and mirror balls and laser beams. The music was really loud and rocking. Rosie and Sven did their phone box dance. Sven was yelling "Whoop!" and "Hit it, lads!" They had loads of space to dance in because nobody wants to be flattened by a huge bloke in silver trousers.

Jas shouted in my earlug. "There's a gang of Tom's mates by the bar – can you see them? Over there. Dave the Laugh is probably one of them."

Jools said, "Yeah, but which one? There's ten of them to choose from."

I said, "Is anyone laughing?"

Jools looked at me. "Why?"

"Well, if he's called Dave the Laugh everyone will be laughing around him."

We looked across at the lads who were mostly looking around the room. Then I had another thought. "But what if he is called Dave the Laugh because HE laughs all the time?"

We looked again; now they were all laughing.

Jas for once in her life went all decisive and sensible (it was a bit scary, actually). She said, "I recognise one of them, he's called Rollo, he's been round to Tom's house. I could ask him who Dave the Laugh is."

I said, "Yeah, OK, but be really cool, Jas. Just find out which one is Dave the Laugh so we can look at him. But don't mention anything about anything."

Jas said, "I am not a fool, you know."

I didn't know that, actually.

Jas went over to the lads and I could see her going chat, chat, nod, nod, nod, wiggle, wiggle, wiggle, flickey fringe, flickey fringe... (Why does she do that? It is so annoying.)

I was acting really cool, doing a half-smile and sort of nodding along to the music. Sipping my drink, waving at people, even ones I didn't know. Then Jas came back. She was all breathless. She POINTED really obviously at a dark-haired boy in black combats. "That's him!"

Naturally he saw her pointing at him and he shrugged his

shoulders like he was asking a question. Jas then turned to me and POINTED again... AT ME, and nodded like one of those nodding dogs.

I couldn't believe it. It was unbelievable, that's why. My face was like a frozen fish finger. All rigid and pale. (But obviously not with breadcrumbs on it.)

I said out of the corner of my mouth, "Jas, I'm going to kill you. What in the name of your huge knickers have you said?"

Jas said huffily, "I just said, 'Who is Dave the Laugh?' and Rollo said, 'This is Dave the Laugh,' and Dave the Laugh said, 'Why?' and I just said, 'Because my mate Georgia really rates you'."

I was going to kill her and then eat her.

Out of the corner of my mouth – because Dave the Laugh was still looking – I said, "Jas! You told him I FANCIED him? I cannot believe it."

Jas said, "Well I think he's quite cute. If I didn't have Hunky I would..."

Just then SG walked by carrying his guitar. On his way to the stage to do the first set. He smiled as he passed. Even though in my heart I wanted to leap into his arms like a seal I ignored him. I looked through him as if he was just a floating guitar in midair.

Midnight

The Stiff Dylans were playing and I was dancing with Rosie and Sven and Jas. Jools and Ellen had gone off with some of Tom's mates. They were all quite fit-looking boys, actually, but... there is only one Sex God on the planet. SG looked sooooo cool; it's not fair that he is so good-looking. All the girls were looking at him and dancing in front of him. They had no style. Every time he came off stage there would be some girl talking to him. I tried not to look but I couldn't help it. What if he got off with someone in front of me? How could I bear it? There was a moment when our eyes met and he smiled. Ooohh, Blimey O'Reilly's trousers, he'd got everything... back, front, hair, teeth... I could feel my snogging muscles all puckering up but I thought NO! Think Elastic Band.

I made Jas go to the loos with me for a bit of a break from the tension. The Bummer Twins were still in there. I could hear them talking from one of the cubicles and a spiral of smoke coming under the loo door. Do they live in the lavatories? I said to Jas, "Perhaps the Bummer Twins have trouble in the poo-parlour department!!" and we both got the hysterical heebie-jeebies. I had to hit Jas on the back to stop her choking to death. And we had to reapply mascara twice.

On our way back to the dance floor Dave the laugh stopped me!! He said, "Hi."

I said, "Oh hi." (Brilliant.) And I half-smiled, remembering to keep my nose sucked in.

He said, "Are you Georgia?"

1:00 a.m.
Dave the Laugh is actually nice-looking in a sub SG way... and er... quite a good laugh.

2:00 a.m.
Dave the Laugh has been dancing with me a lot. He's a cool dancer. He even did a bit of mad dancing with Sven. I don't think he expected Sven to pick him up and kiss him on both cheeks, but he took it well. We all left the club together. I saw SG looking over at us as he cleared up his gear. There was some drippy blonde hanging about wanting his autograph or something (on yeah! Emphasis on the something). Time for a display of maturiosity and glaciosity. Dave the L. said, "Georgia, are you walking to the night bus stop?"

I made sure that SG was looking then I laughed like a loon on loon tablets. "Hahahahaha, the night bus! You make me die, Dave, you're such a laugh!!!!"

Dave looked a bit on the amazed side. He probably didn't think the night bus was his biggest joke. Me and Jas and Dave walked along. When we got to the bus stop there was a bit of an awkward pause. Jas was standing really close by like a goosegog. How was my plan vis-à-vis getting Dave the L. to go out with me going to happen if she just hung about like a goosegog? I kept raising my eyebrows at her but she said, "Have you got something in your eye? Let's have a look."

As Mrs Big but Stupid Knickers was prodding about at my eye Dave's bus came. He gave me a peck on the cheek and said, "Well, this is my bus. It was a great night; maybe see you later." He looked me in the eyes for a second, winked and then got on the bus.

As Mrs Loonyknickers Goosegoghead (Jas) and I walked home I was all confused.

"Does Dave the Laugh like me or not? He winked at me – what does that mean? SG definitely noticed us leaving, didn't he? And he saw me really laughing at what Dave the Laugh was saying."

Jas said, "That's when I thought Dave the Laugh might have gone off you, because he said, 'Are you catching the night bus?' and you nearly split your tights in half laughing. Your face went all weird and your nose sort of spread all over your—"

"Jas."

"What?"

"Shut up."

"Well, I was just saying."

"Well don't."

"Well I won't, then."

"Well don't."

"I won't."

"Well don't."

There was a bit of welcome silence for a bit then Jas said, "I won't."

She is so INCREDIBLY annoying.

3:00 a.m.

And she takes up loads of room in bed. I had to make a sort of barrier out of her cuddly toys to put down the middle of the bed. To keep her on her own side.

What does Dave the Laugh mean, "See you later"?

♡ 395

3:30 a.m.

Do I want to see him later even if he does mean "See you later"?

4:00 a.m.

If the Sex God was really jealous he would ring me up tomorrow and try to get me back.

Or maybe he is not fully extended elastic band-wise.

Thursday September 30th

3:00 p.m.

I fell asleep in German. Herr Kamyer is a very soothing teacher. I drifted off when he started telling some story about Gretchen and a dove in a dovecote. (Don't even ask, as I have mentioned before, the Germans are a mystery to me since I learned about the Heimlich manoeuvre.)

4:30 p.m.

On the way home we practised our new grasp of the German language.

I said to Jas, "What is 'a dove in a dovecote' in the German type language?"

Jas said, "Er... '*ein Duff in ein Duffcot*', I think."

"*Ach gut... so... Jas... Du bist ein Duff in Duffcot nicht wahr?*"

Jas said, "*Nein, ich nicht ein Duff in Duffcot.*"

I said, "*Jah.*"

Jas said, "*You have just said I am a dove in a dovecote.*"

"You are."

"You're bonkers."

I think I might be hysterical.

4:45 p.m.

So tired when I got in that I thought I would just have a little snooze.

5:00 p.m.

"Ginger, ginger, me home!!!"

Oh Lord, it was my dearly beloved sister. I heard her clattering up the stairs. Then a bit of deep breathing, and bumping, "Here we are, Ginger."

Then she and Angus got in bed with me. And they weren't alone. There was scuba-diving Barbie and Charlie Horse. And something really cold and slimy.

I shot up in bed and looked down at her. "Libbs, what is that?"

She gave me her idea of a lovely smile, which in her case

is terrifying. She scrunches up her nose and sticks her teeth out. I don't know why she thinks that is natural. She said, "It's nice."

I looked under the covers. "What is? Oh God."

Mum called up, "Libbs, where has your jelly rabbit gone?"

Giganticus pantibus

Monday October 4th
9:30 a.m.

No news from either SG or Dave the so-called Laugh.

Geoggers
10:00 a.m.

Brrr. It's only October and it's like Greenland here. Well, apart from the ice floes and Eskimos and polar bears. It is, as Ellen's amusing brother would say, very "nippy noodles" today. I didn't mean ever to start saying things like that, but it is really catching. What's more, just because I said it all the gang is saying it. It's like brain measles. In geoggers Rosie put up her hand and said to Mrs Franks (who is not what you would call "fun"), "Mrs Franks, could I just pop to the piddly-diddly department, please?"

Mrs Franks said, really frostily, "What is the piddly-diddly department, Rosemary?"

And Rosie said, "Well it's not the poo-parlour division."

We all laughed like stuffed animals. Mrs Franks didn't. In fact she said, "Grow up, Rosemary Barnes."

She let Rosie go though, and started to explain something indescribably boring about the wheat belt. Behind her Rosie started lolloping out of the door like an orang-utan. She was trailing her arms on the floor. It made me laugh A LOT. But silently, as no one really wants to do two hours' detention.

Break
11:00 a.m.

They are a bunch of sadists here. We get forced to go out into sub-Antarctic conditions. Even Elvis Attwood won't come out of his hut and he is half human, half walrus. Meanwhile the so-called prefects and staff get to hang around in the warm. Wet Lindsay, the Owlie One, said to me, "If you wore skirts that were a bit longer you might not be so chilly."

I said to Jas, "Did you hear a sort of hooting noise, Jas?"

Me and Jas sheltered out of the icy winds behind a wall but we were still cold, so we had an idea. We thought we would button our two coats together to make a kind of big sleeping bag. We fastened the buttons of Jas's coat into the buttonholes of mine. Then we buttoned the buttons of my coat into Jas's buttonholes. With us in the middle. All nice and snug. It did make it very difficult to walk and unfortunately we had buttoned ourselves up a bit far away from our bags. Our bags with our nutritious snacks in them (Mars Bars and cheesy snacks). We tried synchronised shuffling to get to them but Jas tripped and we fell over. We were laughing, but not for long, because the Bummer Twins arrived.

Jackie looked down at us all tied together in our coats and said, "Look, Ali, the little girls are playing a little game. Let's join in."

And then they sat on us.

And they are not small girls.

Alison said, "Fancy a fag, Jackie?"

We heard them light up. We were just trapped there.

Then Jackie said, "Oooh look, someone has left some cheesy snacks for us. Fancy one, Ali?"

Me and Jas were the Bummer Twins' armchair.

My bedroom
5:30 p.m.
No phonecalls.

Mutti came in.

I said, "Oh come in, Mum, the door is only closed for privacy." I said it in a meaningful way but she didn't know what I meant. She was all pink.

"Dad phoned again; he sends his love, he's really looking forward to seeing you. He's got you a present."

I said, "Oh goodie, what is it? Sheepskin shorts?"

She started that tutting thing.

I don't think she has asked me one thing about myself for about four centuries. What is the point of procrastinating... no I don't mean that, what do I mean? Oh yeah... procreating... What is the point of having children if you are not going to take any notice of them? You might as well get a hamster and ignore that.

5:35 p.m.
Oh yippee.

This is my gorgeous life:

1. I haven't been kissed for a month; my snogging skills will be gone soon.

2. I have a HUGE nose that means I have to live for ever in the Ugly Home. Address:
    Georgia Nicolson
    Ugly Home,
    Ugly Kingdom,
    Ugly Universe.
3. My Red Herring plan has failed.
4. I am the Bummer Twins' armchair.

6:00 p.m.

Mum called up. "I'm just taking Libbs to the doctors'; she needs her ears cleaning out."

Oh please. Save me from that thought.

6:30 p.m.

Phone rang. If it's Po moaning on about Hunky I'll go BERSERK!!

6:45 p.m.

I'm seeing Dave in the swing park after school on Friday. He got my phone number from Tom through Jas! Good grief. The Red Herring has landed. I'm quite excited, I think.

Am I?

He said it would be "groovy" to see me again.

He also said he hoped it wouldn't be too nippy noodles in the park. He made me laugh.

I am still only using him as a red herring, though.

8:00 p.m.

Mum came back with Libby. I was busily trying to save myself from starving to death by eating cornflakes.

I said, "The doctor didn't find my fishnet tights in Libby's lugholes, did he?"

Mum seemed to be in even more of a coma than normal. She said, "I borrowed them for salsa dancing with Uncle Eddie."

Charming. I'll have to boil them before I wear them again.

Mum said, "They've got a new doctor at the surgery."

Silence.

"He's very good."

Silence.

"He was so nice to Libby – even when she shouted down his stethoscope."

What is she going on about?

"He looked a bit like George Clooney."

9:40 p.m.

When I went up to bed she kissed me and said, "You haven't had your tetanus injection renewed, have you?"

What is she talking about?

Tuesday October 5th

10:30 a.m.

Rosie said she might go across to Sweden land with Sven in the Chrimbo hols. I said, "Are you sure? You're only fourteen and you've got your whole life ahead of you. Are you sure you want to go to the other side of the world with Sven?"

She said, "What?"

I said, "Going to the other side of the world with Sven – is it a good idea?"

She said, "You don't know where Sweden is, do you?"

"Don't be stupid."

And she said, "Where is it, then?"

I looked at her. Honestly. As if I don't know where Sweden is. I said, "It's up at the top."

"Top of what?"

"The map."

And she went, "Hahahahahahahaha."

I think she must be a bit hysterical.

I may forgive her. Because so am I.

Maths
10:35 a.m.

Oh good grief, welcome back to the land of the crap. The Bummer Twins sent round a note: *Meet in the Fourth Year classroom as 12.30 today. Everyone comes, and that means you, Georgia Nicolson and your lesbian mates.*

I wrote a note to Jas and the others.

Dear Fab Gang,

    This is it. Things have got sheer desperadoes. We have to put our feet down with firm hands. I for one am no longer prepared to be the Bummer Twins' armchair!!! Meet in the science block at 12.15. Or be square.

    Gee-gee

    xxxxxxx

12:32 p.m.

Hiding from the Bummer Twins in the science-block loos. Jas, Jules, Rosie, Ellen, Patty, Sarah, Mabs and me... all in one cubicle. We have to keep our feet off the floor so that no one will know we are in here. It's hard to keep your balance when there are eight of you standing on one loo seat.

Alert, alert!!!! Two people came into the loos. I recognised their voices. It was Wet Lindsay and one of her mates, Dismal Sandra.

Wet Lindsay said, "Honestly, some of the younger girls are so dim. One of them came to see me and asked me if she could get pregnant from sitting on a boy's knee."

Jas mouthed at me, "Can you?" Which I thought was quite funny but I couldn't laugh otherwise we would end up quite literally down the pan.

I wanted to look over the top of the cubicle so that Owlie would know I had seen her in the loo. Seen her removing her thong from her bum-oley!!!

Then Owlie's weedy mate Dismal Sandra said, "What's happening with Robbie?"

I was full-on, attention-wise.

Wet Lindsay said, "Well he says he doesn't want to get serious because of college and the band and everything."

I nearly yelled out, "It's not that, Owlie, it is because he DOESN'T like you..."

Dismal Sandra said, "So what will you do, then?"

Lindsay said, "Oh, I've got my ways, I'll charm him back in the end. He's not seeing anyone else, he says. I expect he's still upset about us splitting up."

Oh yeah, in your dreams, Owlie.

Physics
1:30 p.m.

Herr Kamyer was twitching about in his sad suit. It's sort of tight round the neck and short round the ankles. Do normal people wear tartan socks? Anyway, he was adjusting his spectacles and saying, "So zen, girls, ve haf the interesting question about ze physical world. Ver question is (twitch twitch), vich comes first... ze chicken or ze eggs?"

No one knows what he is talking about so we just carried on writing notes to each other or making shopping lists. Ellen was actually painting her toenails. You would think that Herr Kamyer would notice that she had her head underneath the desk, but he didn't seem to.

He really does jerk around. He sort of blinks his eyes and screws up his nose and flings his head round all at once. Someone said it was because he has had malaria. Once when he was walking across the playground and it was icy he had such a spasm that he slipped and crashed into the bike shed. Elvis had to restack sixty bikes. He grumbled for about forty years. You would think Elvis would have more sympathy for the afflicted. As he is so afflicted himself.

Suddenly about ten girls started sneezing really violently. Really violently, like their heads were going to blow off. Their eyes were streaming and they were stumbling for the door. Jackie Bummer managed to say, "Oh we must be... ATISHOO... ATISHOO... allergic to something in the science lab, Herr Kamyer. ATISHOO!"

They all got sent home in the end.

I found out later what the Bummer Twins' meeting was about. They had made everyone at the meeting put bath crystals up their noses in the middle of physics, and that had brought on the sneezing attacks. All because the Bummers wanted to go to some club in Manchester, and needed to be home early.

Good Lord. Three days to my date with the Herring.

♥ 409

5:00 p.m.

Jas made me go home with her. She is planning a special celebration for when Tom gets home.

"It will be one year since we first met on the day he gets back!"

I just looked at her.

"And look!" Before I could stop her, she pulled up her skirt and pulled down her voluminous pants to show me her stupid heart tattoo. "I've been washing round it!"

She went on and on about what she was planning to do. Even though I found some matchsticks and put them over my eyelids so it looked like they were holding my eyes open. Eventually I said, "Look, why don't you do a nice vegetable display for him?"

Midnight

Honestly, Jas is so mad and touchy. And violent.

Wednesday October 6th
4:30 p.m.

After swimming today Miss Stamp came into the showers to make sure we all went in. She says we pretend to have a shower and that we are unhygienic. That is why she must supervise us. But really it is because she is a lesbian.

She watched a few of us go through (twirling her moustache). She shouted, "Come on, you silly ninnies, get in and get out!"

I dashed in in the nuddy-pants and was soaping myself like a maniac in order to get out quickly because Miss Stamp is a lesbian and might... well might... er... look at me. As if that wasn't bad enough I had to be on even more red alert because Nauseating P. Green lumbered into the shower next to me. What if she accidentally touched me? It's a sodding nightmare this place, like the Village of the Damned. If P. Green fell against me I would be smickled with Nauseatingness. She really is a most unfortunate shape. What on earth does she eat? All the pies, that is for sure. In fact, she has no shape. You can only tell which way up she is because of her glasses.

As I was getting dried I did feel a bit sorry for her because the Bummers had hidden her glasses while she was in the shower. She blundered around in the elephantine nuddy-pants, looking for them. The Bummers (who had managed to get out of games by "having the painters in" AGAIN! How many periods can you have in a month?) were singing, "Nellie the elephant packed her bags and said goodbye to the circus." Then the bell went and the Bummers slouched off.

After they'd gone I gave P. Green her silly specs. She would have been in the shower rooms for the rest of her life otherwise. I hope she doesn't think that makes me her mate.

My bedroom
6:00 p.m.
No phonecall from SG. I wonder what Wet Lindsay means about using her charm on him? What kind of charm do owls have? Perhaps she will lay him an egg.

OhGodohGod. I'm getting the heebie-jeebies about my Red Herring extravaganza. How do I keep him as a herring without snogging him?

In *Bliss* in the letters page there's a letter from a girl called Sandy. She didn't really like a boy and was just using him to get off with someone else. Unfortunately the advice from Agony Jane was not "Carry on and good luck to you". The advice was "You are a really horrible girl, Sandy. You will never have a happy life, you cow." (Well, it didn't exactly say it in those words but that is what the gist and nub was.)

Decided to put the squeaking dolphins on and do some calming yoga. I used to be quite good at doing the sun salute last term until Miss Stamp surprised me in the gym with my bottom sticking up in the air.

Mmmmmm – much much better. All soothing and flowing. Lalalalala. Lift your arms up to worship the sun... breathe in... hhmmmmmm, then put your arms down to the floor like in "we are not worth" in football... aahhh, breathe out. Much calmer. Then swing to the right and swing to the left.

That's funny... if I turned to the right, then the left, a funny noise came out of me. Like a sort of wheezy noise. Could it be the dolphins? I didn't know they did wheezing.

Turned the tape off.

Now then, to the right, to the left. Oh no. Wheeze wheeze. If I went really fast from the right to the left I could hear wheeze wheeze wheeze. Which is not what you want.

It was really quite loud. Wheeze wheeze.

I'd probably caught TB from being made to do swimming in freezing conditions.

Mum came in with a cup of tea for me (without knocking, naturally) and caught me doing my wheezing movements. She said, "Are you dancing?" and I said, "No I'm not, I'm wheezing. I think I may have caught TB. It's not as if I'm in tiptop physical condition, with the kind of diet that we live on."

She said, "Don't be so silly, what is the matter?"

I didn't want her to listen to my wheezing but I had really freaked myself out. I let her listen. Side to side, wheeze wheeze.

She looked worried. (Probably thinking she would be chastised by the local press for child abuse and neglect.) She said, "Look, I think maybe we should pop up to the surgery and see George Cloon— er... the doctor. Get your coat."

Before I could protest she grabbed Libby and we were out of the door. As she started the car I said, "Look Mum, perhaps if I had a warm bath and you made me a nourishing stew..."

The next thing I knew I was in the doctors' waiting room. It was full of the elderly mad, all coughing. If I wasn't sick now I was soon going to be.

Libby got up on a table to do a little dance for everyone. It must have been something she had learned at kindergarten. It seemed to be sung to "Pop Goes the Weasel".

Libby sang (loudly and with a lot of actions), "Ha ha pag of trifle atishoo atishoo all fall down." The finale was her throwing up her dress and pulling down her panties.

Mum hadn't expected that bit. Who could? There was a lot of muttering from the very old. One woman said, "Disgusting!" which was a bit rich coming from someone wearing a balaclava.

Eventually we got to see the doc. Mum practically threw herself through the surgery door and I was left dragging Libby because she wanted to do an encore.

Mum said, "Oh, hello, it's us again!" in a really odd girlie voice. When I had got Libby's knickers back on I looked at the doctor. He was quite fit-looking actually, not at all the surly red-faced madman that normally treated us. There was a bit of the young George Clooney about this one.

He smiled (ummm) and said, "Yes, hello again, Connie. (Connie!) Hello, Libby." Libby gave him one of her very mad smiles.

Then he looked at me. I gave him my attractive half smile. (Curved lips but no teeth, nose snugly pulled in.)

He said, "And this must be Georgia. What can I do for you?"

Mum said, "Tell the doctor, Gee."

Reluctantly I said, "Well, when I do this..." (and I did the side to side thing), "...a wheezy noise comes out of me."

The doctor said, "Does it happen any other time?"

I said, "Er... no."

And he said, "Only when you go from side to side?"

And I said, "Yes."

And he said, "Well, I wouldn't go from side to side, then." And that was it.

Thanks a lot. All that money we (well, my parents) paid in taxes for his medical training not gone to waste, then!! He smiled at me, "When you move like that you force the air out of your lungs and it makes a sort of noise. That's all. They're just like bellows, really."

I felt like a fool. Two fools. It was Mum's fault for making me go. And she just hung around the doctor for AGES. Making conversation. Telling him she was learning salsa dancing. Did he like dancing? Etc. She kept saying, "Oh, I mustn't keep you," and then going on and on. It was only when the nurse knocked on the door and said one of the pensioners had fallen off their chair that Mum pulled herself together.

It was so embarrassing; Mum was practically dribbling.

She has zero pride. Now that my life was not in danger I noticed that even in the emergency of getting me to the doctor she had managed to squeeze herself into a tight top. You could see she was thrusting her "danger to shippings" at him. In a way, and I never thought I would say this, it will be quite a relief when Vati comes home.

In the car going home she said, "He's nice, isn't he?"

I said, "Mum, honestly, have a bit of dignity. You have made your life choice and the large Portly One is on his way home in a fortnight. It is not a good idea to risk your marriage, and also incidentally make yourself a laughing stock this late on in life."

She said, "Georgia, I really don't know what you are talking about."

She does though.

Do I have to worry about every bloody single thing round this place? When do I get a chance to be a selfish teenager? Jas's mum and dad have aprons and sheds, why do I have to have Mr and Mrs "We've Got Lives of Our Own" as parents?

Thursday October 7th
11:30 a.m.

The Bummer Twins have both got their knickers in a twist. They saw Nauseating P. Green coming out of a classroom, talking to Wet Lindsay. P. Green was probably telling her something about hamster feed. But the Bummers are saying she is a snitcher because they got done for knocking off school the other day. They call Nauseating P. Green "Snitcher the Elephant" now. They stole her *Hamsters Weekly*. I thought she was going to cry which would have been horrific.

Rosie sent me a note in Maths; it said, I am an equilateral triangle.

I wrote back and said, Does that mean all your angles are equal? and she wrote, I don't know, I'm a triangle.

I looked over at her and pushed my nose back like a pig. She did the same thing back. We could while away the hours much more amusingly if we could sit together.

I said that to Slim when she split us up last term. I said, "Miss Simpson, it is a well-known fact that if friends sit together they are encouraged to do more work." But she just shook in such a jelloid way I thought her chins would drop off.

She said, "The last time you two sat together, you set the locusts free in the Biology lab."

Oh honestly, not only has she got legs like an elephant, she has got a memory like one. How many times did we have to explain it was an accident? No one could have imagined they would eat Mr Attwood's spare overalls.

It is RE in a couple of hours so I will be able to have a decent chat to my mates instead of wasting time learning about stuff.

RE
1:30 p.m.

Rosie bunked off, she said she was going to the pictures with Sven. It must be nice to have a boyfriend, even if it was Sven. Oh well, ho hum, pig's bum. While Miss Wilson raved on and hitched up her sad tights I chatted to Jas. She wasn't officially speaking to me because of the veggie business, but I put my arm round her every time I went near her. In the end, to stop me and also to avoid more lezzie rumours, she forgave me (ish).

I said, "My vati is back on the nineteenth."

"Are you glad?"

"No, Jas, I said my vati is back on the nineteenth."

"I like my dad."

"Yes, but your dad is normal. He's got a shed. He does DIY. He fixed your bike. When my vati tried to fix my bike his hand got stuck in the spokes. We had to walk to casualty. I don't see why I had to go with him, everyone was calling out in the streets. And they weren't calling out 'What a brilliant dad you've got!'"

3:45 p.m.
I've managed not to think about meeting Dave all day. I am a bit nervous, though.

7:30 p.m.
In my bedroom. I've got my head under my pillow. This house is like a mental institution. In the front room Uncle Eddie and Mum are practising salsa. He turned up on his motorbike with a crate of wine. First of all he came snooping up to my room and opened my door (I don't know why we don't just take it off its hinges and leave it at that). I think he must have already had one crate of wine because he had a tennis racket he was pretending to play as a guitar and he said, "Georgia, this is a little song entitled, 'Get off the stove, Grandad, you're too old to ride the range'," then he laughed like King Loon and went off downstairs singing, "Agadoo doo dooo."

Honestly, what planet do these people live on? And why isn't it further away? Libby is in the airing cupboard with Angus. She says they are playing doctors and nurses.

11:00 p.m.

Does anyone care what happens to me?

I've got to meet Dave the L. tomorrow and somehow cover up the fact that I have a broken heart. I must be glittering and glamorous and brave.

I could hear Mum and Uncle Eddie giggling. I called down, "Mum... Libby is still in the airing cupboard if you were wondering, which I don't suppose you were as you are busy drinking and carrying on, and so on."

I wondered if I should confide in Uncle Eddie about Mum and George Clooney. Maybe he could have a word with her? Then I heard him coming upstairs again. He popped his very bald head round my door, the light glancing off it almost blinded me, and he said, "We can go and meet your dad on my motorbike if you like!!"

Yeah, in your dreams, oh mad bald one.

Friday October 8th
4:00 p.m.

The Fab Gang came round and we hung around in my room, listening to the Top 20. We were discussing Operation Red Herring. Well me and Mabs, Rosie, Jools and Ellen were, Jas wasn't there. Too busy waiting for her "boyfriend" to come home to worry about her very best pal in the world, who would never dream of putting boys first.

Ellen said, "OK, this is the plan. Say to the herring you have to be home by nine thirty because you are grounded for staying out too late."

I said, "Yes, that's good because it makes me seem sort of like dangerous and groovy but it also means I can get away if I need to. Good thinking, Batwoman."

Ellen went on, "And me and the rest of the gang will sort of be around the park any time things might be getting heavy."

I said, "Yeah. Because that is like double cool... almost with knobs. It means I have loads of mates that I just casually bump into at every whiff and woo AND it will stop any hanky panky in the snogging department."

Rosie said, "Exactamondo. Let's dance!"

And we did mad dancing to calm ourselves down.

422

7:00 p.m.

Met Dave the L. in the park. I went for casual glamour: leopard-skin top (fake, because otherwise Angus would have followed me thinking he'd made a new big mate) and jeans and leather jacket. It was a bit awkward at first. You know, like a first date. He is quite a good-looking bloke if you like red herrings. He said, "Hi, gorgeous," which I think is nice. I admire honesty.

He told me he wanted to be a stand-up comedian when he leaves school and I said, "You should have my life, that would give you lots of material."

He laughed. It was funny but I didn't feel nervous, not like with SG. I didn't say I wanted to be a vet or anything. I very nearly made sense.

As we walked along chatting our arms sort of brushed against each other a couple of times. I didn't mind and he's got a nice crinkly smile. But then he grabbed hold of my hand. Uh-oh. Hanky panky. Also he is slightly smaller than me and I had to do the bendy knee business so I could be more his height. I don't know what it is about boys these days but they seem on the small side. Or perhaps I am growing. Oh no. That might be it. I might only be half the size I am going to be. I might turn out to be a female Sven and that might be God's punishment for me turning Buddhist. Anyway, I lolloped along as best I could, trying not to be like an orang-utan. But, oh *sacré bleu* and *merde*, then Dave pulled me round to face him and took hold of my other hand. I had to lift up my shoulders so that I didn't have excess arm. I felt like that woman in *The Sound of Music*, you know, Julie Thing. Surely he wasn't going to start dancing round with me? Nooooo, he wasn't. He was going to kiss me!! Oh no, this wasn't in the Herring plan... Where were all my so-called mates???

As he looked at me and started to bring his face closer I said really quickly, "Have you noticed how when you go from side to side there is this sort of wheezing noise?"

But I only got to "Ha..." when he put his mouth on mine. I could have bitten through my tongue. I kept my eyes open because I thought that wouldn't be like a real kiss. But it made me go cross-eyed so I closed them. It was, in fact, quite a nice kiss. (But what do I know? I've only ever been with SG, a whelk boy and BG (Mark) who had such a huge gob that no experience with him can be counted normal. You've just got to be glad to escape without being eaten.)

My room
Thinking
11:00 p.m.

My so-called mates arrived at last. They gave us both a bit of a start, leaping out from behind a tree. Also if Rosie is thinking of taking up drama I would advise her against it. She said, "Oh hello, Georgia. It's YOU!!! What on EARTH are you doing here. I thought you were GROUNDED?" But she said it like somebody had hit her on the head with a mallet (which, incidentally, somebody should do).

11:30 p.m.

Hmmm. I am in a state of confusosity. I'd rate him as seven and a half as a kisser. Maybe even eight. He didn't do much varying pressure and his tongue work was a bit like a little snake. On the other hand he didn't do any sucking (like whelk boy) and there was no crashing of teeth. Or dribbling, which is never acceptable. He did nibble my lower lip a bit, which I must tell the gang about because it isn't on our list. It was quite nice. I might try doing it myself. When I retrap the SG.

Midnight

Also he didn't rest his hand on my basooma, which is a plus.

12:30 a.m.

Maybe he didn't rest his hand there because he thought he might never find it again? I wonder if my basoomas are still growing?

12:32 a.m.

Terrible news!! I can fit a pencil case underneath my basooma and it actually stays there for a second!!

I feel all hot and weird. Still, what else is new?

Saturday October 9th
11:50 a.m.

Angus is in love!!! Honestly. With Mr and Mrs Across the Road's Burmese pedigree cat Naomi. (I call her that, they call her Little-Brook-Running-up-a-Tree-With-a-Sausage-up-its-Bottom Sun Li the Third, or something foreign.) I saw Angus on their wall, giving Naomi a vole he'd killed. He was parading up and down sticking his bottom up in the air and waggling his tail about. Disgusting, really. Especially as he had a clinker hanging out of his bum-oley. Cats think that is attractive. So does Libbs.

Mr and Mrs Across the Road didn't seem too thrilled by his attentions. In fact, they threw stones at him. They are going to have to try a lot harder than that, he was brought up having bricks thrown at him. They should try a bazooka.

My room
2:30 p.m.

I must find some calm. I've got an instruction booklet on Buddhism from the library. Miss Wilson, who doubles as sad librarian, is beside herself with pleasure – she thinks I am taking religion seriously due to her excellent teaching. Sad really. She'll want me to go round for coffee at her house soon. I might go and ask her where she buys her tights. The book is called *Buddhism for the Stupid*. No, it's not really, but it should be.

Good grief. It's so boring. It's just all about world peace and so on, which is OK but you would think I could do that later. Once I was happy. And had got what I wanted.

4:00 p.m.

Jas turned up. She was really mopey like a cod.

"I got all ready for Tom to come home and then he called up from Birmingham and said he was going to stay on for a few more days. He says that he likes Birmingham and has got some great new mates."

I was thinking, Oh, good grief! As if I haven't got enough to worry about without having Hunky and Po in trouble. But I didn't say anything.

Jas moaned on: "He didn't used to like going out with mates, he used to like being with me."

I said wisely: "Remember he is a Jennings boy. He is the same as Robbie. Remember the elastic band thing, Jas... let him have his space. In fact, why don't you say you think you should have a break from each other for a bit? You know, to sort of find yourselves."

Jas said, "I know where he is, he is in Birmingham."

It's easier chatting to Angus. I kept on, though. "Don't be silly, Po! Anyway, I want to talk to you about Buddha. Do you know what Buddha says?"

"Didn't he say quite a lot?"

"Yes, but he said, 'When a crow finds a dying snake, it behaves as if it were an eagle. When I see myself as a victim I am hurt by trifling failures.'"

There was a silence and Jas started fiddling around with her fringe.

"Do you see?"

"Er... what has that got to do with Tom? He's not an eagle."

Honestly she is so dim. I explained, as patiently as I could, "It means, if you think your life is poo it will be."

"Well why didn't he say that?"

"Because a) he is Buddha and b) they do not have poo in Buddhaland."

5:30 p.m.

Phone rang. Mum yelled up, "Gee, it's for you... boyfriend."

Honestly, I could kill her. I went and answered the phone and sat down on a stool. It was Dave the Laugh. He said, "Hello, Gorge. I had a great time last night. I've just about recovered from meeting your mates. What are you up to?"

As I was chatting to him Libby came humming into the hall. She wanted to get up on to my knee.

I said, "Libbs, I'm on the phone, go find Angus to play with."

She gave me her frowniest look. "NO... UP!!! NOW!!!

BAD, BAD BOY." And she started spitting at me so I had to let her on my knee. Before I could stop her she was "talking" down the phone. "Hello, mister man. Grrrrrrr. Three bag pool, three bag pool."

Oh God. I struggled to get the phone off her and then she shouted, "Georgie has got a THERY big SPOT! Hahahahahaha."

I grabbed the phone back and put Libby on the floor. "Sorry about that, Dave, my little sister has... er... just learned to talk and, er she must have... er..."

Libby was singing, "Georgie's got a THERY big spot, lalalalala, THERY, THERY big spot... ON HER BOT... ON HER BOTTY."

6:00 p.m.
She's right, actually. How can you get spots on your bottom? I must have more vitamin C.

6:05 p.m.
Me and Jas chomping on bananas. Jas said, "Save the skins because they make really good face masks."

430

6:30 p.m.

As usual Jas is completely wrong. We washed off the banana on our faces; it felt disgusting.

I said, "I'm meeting Dave again tomorrow. He seems to really like me."

Jas was busy picking bits of banana out of her hair. "Does he? Why?"

"I don't know, he just does."

Bed
11:00 p.m.

Dave doesn't make my legs go jelloid and that is the point, isn't it? If a boy doesn't make you go jelloid you may as well be with your girlie mates... or boy mates that you are just mates with and no snogging involved.

11:30 p.m.

Oh, I don't know.

Midnight

Angus still on the wall looking down at Naomi the Burmese

sex kitten. She is rubbing herself against the wall, the little minx. I know what she feels like.

I wonder what the Sex God is doing now.

What shall I do about Dave?

1:00 a.m.

I really would truly prefer to put my head into a bag of eels than kiss Wet Lindsay.

1:15 a.m.

Sex God did take the bull by the nostrils and dump Wet Lindsay when he found true love (me). Even if he did then dump me.

1:30 a.m.

He was true to his feelings. Even though it upset Owlie he dumped her because it was the right thing to do (and it is always the right thing to do to dump Owlie).

Sunday October 10th
10:00 p.m.

Dave the L. turned up at my door earlier, wearing a false

moustache. He actually is quite a laugh. We went to the pictures and snogged again. He must be a bit surprised that my mates pop up every time we go anywhere. When Rosie put her head over the back of us in the pictures and said, "GEORGIA!!! HOW AMAZING!! What are you doing here?!!!" I thought he'd swallow his ice cream whole.

Monday October 11th
School
8:30 a.m.

I met Jas on the way to school. She was trailing her rucky along as we walked. I said, "Dave sent me a card today, it said, *Merry one week anniversary, gorgeous. Lots of love, D, kiss, kiss, kiss.*"

She didn't say anything. I said, "Jas, what are you doing?"

She was all pale, I noticed.

"I haven't heard from Tom and I tried to ring him and he was out."

"Ah yes, well."

"You said I should say, 'Have your own space, Tom'."

"Yes, well..."

433

"And now he's got loads of space."

"Ah yes."

"And so have I."

"Yes..."

"But I don't want it."

Oh good grief. I'm not going to be an agony aunt if all people do is moan on all the time.

Last bell
3:50 p.m.

Jas, Jools, Ellen, Rosie and me were lurking near the science block, hiding from the Gestapo (Hawkeye) who wants to ask me about the lunchbox beret idea. Everyone has been doing it. Slim told us not to be so silly; she said in assembly, "You are making a mockery of the school's good name in the community."

Anyway, we have taken her advice to heart and we are going to have a "blind day" instead. After last bell we went to the alleyway in between the Science block and main school, waiting for an opportunity to dash out of the gates when Hawkeye was not looking. We all had our lunchpack-berets on apart from old spoilsport knickers Jas.

Rosie said, "On the blind day next Wednesday the deal is we all shut our eyes for the whole morning and have to have minders that guide us around. From lesson to lesson."

I said, "Wait a minute, we have sports on Wednesday, it's hockey. That will be a laugh."

Jas said gloomily – she had been an unlaugh all day – "Hawkeye will stop us, with detention and so on."

Rosie said, "No, because we will explain that we are being sponsored and are doing it so that we will have a better understanding of the poorly-sighted."

That's when we saw something awful. The SG drove up to the school gates in his car and Wet Lindsay ran out and got in!

7:00 p.m.
In a way I feel free. If SG chooses Owlie over me then he is the loser. So be it. That is the Buddhist way. Omm. I will not be the crow finding the snake or whatever it found. Who cares? It's only a crow.

8:00 p.m.
I need a break from being a Buddhist for a minute. POOO!!! DOUBLE *MERDE*!!! Life really is a pooburger.

9:00 p.m.

Mum came in for a "chat".

"Dad's home in a week."

"Still time for a few serious medical complaints, then."

"What do you mean?"

"You and Doctor Clooney."

"Georgia, you're mad."

"Am I?"

"Look, all it is is that I think he's quite good-looking."

"Well that's because you are comparing him to Dad."

"Don't be rude."

"I'm not, I'm being factual."

"Anyway, you needn't worry, it's just innocent flirting."

"Yes it is for you but what if Doctor Clooney really likes you? And what about if he will be really upset if he finds out you are just toying with him? Like a toying person?"

She went off looking all worried. Good. That's two of us all worried and guilty. And confused.

9:30 p.m.

Dave phoned. He said, "I just called to say I really like you. Night-night."

Good grief.

I wonder if all heartless babe magnets feel guilty?

Tuesday October 12th
Hockey pitch
2:30 p.m.

Hockey match against boring old Hollingbury College. They really do think they are cool, but sadly they are about to find out that they are not.

I had a sneaky look in their changing room when I pretended to be fastening up my boots. It was a nightmare of thongs. I noticed Miss Stamp busily popping in and out, saying things like, "Don't mind me, I was just wondering if you had enough towels."

She was all red and keen. Running on the spot, and so on. Very alarming if you're not used to it. I noticed quite a few of the Hollingbury girls were rushing off into the loos when she came in. They were getting a bit jittery. So I used sporting tactics. I said, "Miss Stamp, I wonder if the

Hollingbury team would appreciate a bit of physio after the match. You know, if they had any little knocks or anything you could offer to... er... treat them yourself. Use those magic healing hands."

Adolfa was a bit suspicious. But she couldn't figure out my angle. I heard her go back into their changing room and say something about treatment. All of the Hollingbury girls shot out of the door and on to the pitch. Ah good, a nervous team, desperate not to get injured!! Result!!!

It's very nippy noodles. I've got three pairs of knickers on. I probably look like Nauseating P. Green from the back... or Slim. Still, better a fat bum than a numb bum. There is a little crowd supporting us, most of my mates actually. Although not Jas, she wasn't at school today. I hope she has not gone all weird because of Tom.

The slimiest wet weed who shall remain nameless (Lindsay) is captain of the team. Erlack... well I will not do anything that she says. In our pre-match talk she said, "So remember to watch me for instruction, and when you get into any kind of shooting position, watch for me to come and take on the shot."

Oh yeah, dream on, wet and weedy one. With a bit of

luck someone will knock her stick insect legs from under her. I am not saying I want her to be badly injured, just badly enough that she has to go away to a convalescent hospital somewhere (Mars) for a year or two. Thank you, Buddha. (You can see how I am not taking poo lying down.)

2:50 p.m.
Cracking match. I am playing a stormer, even if I say so myself. Zipping up and down the pitch, hitting the ball up to the forwards. Excellent passing!! I'm like David Beckham apart from the hockey stick and skirt and three pairs of huge knickers. Although who knows? Posh Spice may insist he wears sensible snug knickers in the winter time. She is a very caring person. But quite thin.

Half-time
No score
3:15 p.m.
Rosie, Ellen, Jools and Mabs are like cheerleaders. They have made up this song which goes, "One – two – three – four – go, Georgia, go!"

I said to them as I came off, "It doesn't rhyme," and Ellen said, "Well, it's too nippy noodles."

439

Brrr. She's right. I went into the loos to run my hands under the hot water tap. Oh no, the Bummer Twins had got Nauseating P. Green cornered in the changing rooms. She was blubbing. They didn't even look round when I came in. Jackie said, "So, Snitcher, what did you tell Lindsay about us knocking off school?"

Nauseating P. Green was trembling like a huge jelly elephant. "I... I... didn't say... anything..."

I thought I should shout at her, to help, "Tell them about your hamsters, P. Green, that will bore them to death and you can run off." But I looked at Jackie's big arms and thought I wouldn't bother.

As I was going out again the Bummers started shoving P. Green against the loo doors. Oh bum, bum.

Alison said, "We don't like snitchers... do we, Georgia?"

I said, "Oh, they're all right, I—"

Jackie shoved P. Green so hard that her glasses flew off. That did it. I could no longer be the Bummer Twins' armchair. I said, "Leave her alone now."

Jackie looked at me. "Oh yeah, big nose, what are you going to do about it?"

I said, "I'm going to appeal to your niceness."

She laughed and said, "Dream on, Ringo."

I said, "Yes, I thought that might not work, so this is plan two."

Actually there wasn't a plan two. I didn't know what I was doing. I was like a thing possessed. I leaped over to them and grabbed Jackie's fag packet out of her hand. Then I ran into the loos with it and held it over the toilet. I yelled, "Let her go or the fags get it!"

Jackie was truly worried then and had a sort of reflex action to save her packet of fags. Alison came towards me as well, leaving Nauseating P. Green trembling by herself. I shouted, "Run like the wind, P. Green!!!"

She picked up her glasses and just stood there, blinking like a porky rabbit caught in a car's headlights. Good grief! I tried to give her confidence. "Well, not like the wind, then, but shuffle off as fast as you can."

Eventually she went off and I was left to face the Bummers. I charged past them shouting, "Uurgghhhhgghhh!", that well-known Buddhist warrior chant. I chucked the fags out of the packet on to the floor. When I looked back as I dashed out of the door they were scrabbling around picking them up. I raced out on to the pitch for the second half to a big cheer from the

Ace Crew. I thought I may as well enjoy the game because the Bummers would be killing me immediately after it was over.

I noticed there were a few boys gathered at the opposite end of the pitch. One of them cheered when I ran on. Probably Foxwood lads. They sort of appeared any time there was the least hint of knicker flashing. Or nunga-nunga wobbling. I don't know how they knew, or had found out we were playing today. Probably Elvis Attwood got on the tom-toms in his hut and drummed out a message to let them know there was a match on. He was lurking around pretending to be busy, wheeling his wheelbarrow. There was never anything in it. Old Pervy Trousers. Anyway, let the lads look at my nunga-nungas if they wanted! Let my nostrils flare free. Let my waddly bottom waddle, what did I care??? I was going to be dead anyway when the Bummers got hold of me.

4:10 p.m.
Victory! Victory!!!!! We won one-nil.

It was a close match considering we were playing such a bunch of wets. One of their team blubbed when I accidentally hit her on the shin with my stick. I wonder if all the times I have been savaged by Angus have made me immune to p⌐

Anyway, it was a nil draw until the last few minutes. I raced up the wing and found myself in the opposition's penalty area. The Ace Crew were going, "Georgia Georgia!!" And then our so-called captain Wet Lindsay shouted from the left side, "Pass it to me, number eight!"

You know like in the movies when everything slows down and it's in slow motion? Well, I had that. I saw Owlie's face and her thin stupid legs and I thought, Hahahahahahaha! (Only really, really slowly.)

I kept the ball myself and raced for goal with it. I dribbled past one opposition player, then another. Tripped. Picked myself up, nipped the ball through someone's legs. The crowd were cheering me on. They were going BERSERK!! Then there was the goalkeeper. Good grief, she was a giant!!! But I feinted to one side of her and got past. Then there was just the open goal. I whacked the ball and scored!!!... just as Lindsay tackled me savagely from behind.

4:30 p.m.

Wet Lindsay tried to pretend that she had been "helping" me. Huh. Very likely... not.

ited Elvis to carry me to the sick bay but he
d war wound and brought his wheelbarrow
itch. He said, "Get in. One of your mates will
ha it because I hurt my back serving this country."

Oh yeah. I said to Jools, "His back has probably seized up
because he sits on his bottom all day."

Rosie wheeled me to the sick bay but I still couldn't walk
even after the sadistic Adolfa Stamp had strapped up my ankle.
While she was kneeling down in front of me bandaging it all
my so-called mates were behind her doing pretend snogging.
The Hollingbury girls didn't even bother to get changed, they
just shook hands really quickly and got on their coach.

I hopped about a bit after I was strapped up but it was
aggers. In the end Elvis said reluctantly that Rosie and Ellen
and Jools could push me home in the wheelbarrow. Cheers,
thanks a lot.

Elvis went grumbling back to his hut, saying, "Make sure
you bring it back tomorrow... it's my own private equipment
and shouldn't by rights be used for school business."

His own private wheelbarrow. How sad is that?
Sensationally sad, that's how.

We set off, wheeling along. It wasn't very comfortable in

the barrow and there was the suggestion of something brownish in one of the corners. But I was being all brave and heroic as I was the heroine of the hockey universe. And attractively modest. For a genius.

When we got to the school gates Dave the Laugh was there!!! He had been one of the lads at the match!!! He has seen my gigantic bottom bobbling around on the pitch. Closely following my gigantic schnozzle, bobbling around. OhmyGodohmyGodohmyGod.

He was laughing like a loon as we squeaked up to him in Elvis's wheelbarrow. Then he got down on his knees and was salaaming and chanting "We are not worthy" to me.

He said to Rosie and Ellen and Jools, "Let me push the genius home." And as he pushed me along he sang that really crap song by that band that Dad thinks he looks like the drummer from – Queen. The song was "We are the Champions". The Fab Gang joined in really loudly. Everyone was looking as us as we went down the High Street. I don't suppose shoppers often saw anyone in a wheelbarrow. They probably had very narrow lives and travelled around by car. Or moped.

Dave the L. kissed me when he left me at my gate! In

front of everyone! And he said, "Bye-bye, beautiful. See you soon. Let me know how the ankle is. I'll bring you pressies."

When he'd gone the girls went, "Aaaahhh."

Ellen said, "He really is quite cool-looking. Has he done that nibbling thing again? I quite fancy the sound of that."

But he is just a herring. We must not forget this.

6:15 p.m.

Mum was quite literally ecstatic about my ankle. She just left me in the wheelbarrow outside the front door and got on the blower immediately. I could hear her talking to the doctors' receptionist.

"Yes, it really does seem quite bad. No, no, she really can't walk at all. Yes, well thank you."

Libby came trailing out with scuba-diving Barbie and got in the wheelbarrow with me. She gave me a big kiss. Don't get me wrong, I love my sister, but I wish she would wipe her nose occasionally. When she kisses me she leaves green snot all over my cheek.

Mum came outside and said, "The doctor will pop round after surgery, Gee. Will you just lend me your mascara? I've run out."

I said, "Huh, it's just one-way traffic in this house... if it was me, if the shoe was on the other boot, if I said, 'Mum, can I just borrow...'"

She wasn't listening. She called from indoors, "Hurry up, love, just get me it."

I yelled, "I can't walk, Mum! That is why the doctor is coming to see me. That's why I came home in a wheelbarrow."

"You don't have to walk, just hop out of the barrow and up the stairs and get the mascara."

Hop hop, agony agony, hop hop.

Why was I hopping around getting things for my mother who only wanted them so that she could make a fool of my father? (The answer to that question is I didn't want her poking around in my room. She might come across a few things that weren't strictly mine, things that in a word were – er – hers.)

I hopped into her bedroom and said, "It is pathetic and sad. You are trying to get off with a young doctor and my poor vati is coming home to a – a – facsimile of a sham!"

She just tutted and went on primping. She said, "The trouble with you is that trivial things are really serious to you, and stuff you should care about that is serious, you don't."

I said, hobbling off, "Oh very wise. Is that why you are

stuffing yourself into things that are quite clearly made for people a) smaller than you and b) several centuries younger than you?"

She threw the hairbrush at me. That's nice behaviour, isn't it? Attacking a cripple.

7:00 p.m.
Doctor Home-wrecker arrived. He strapped up my ankle again and gave me painkillers. I said, "I suppose that is my hockey career over. Do you think that perhaps I have weak ankles because of my diet?"

He laughed. He had a good laugh, actually.

Mum said, "Can I get you a coffee, John?"

John? John? Where did that come from?

Mum went off into the kitchen and I heard her say, "Take Angus out of the fridge, Libbs."

"He likes it."

"He's eaten all the butter."

"Teehhheeeeeeheeee."

7:15 p.m.
I hobbled off to my room and played moody music really

loudly as a hint. It was ages before the door slammed. I looked out of my bedroom window. I could see John going off in his quite cool car.

7:45 p.m.
Lying on my bed of pain. Well, it would be if I could feel my ankle.

Mum popped her head round the door. She was all flushed. "How is the ankle?"

I said, "Fine if you like red-hot pokers being stabbed in you."

"That's my little soldier." She was humming.

Brilliant, a week before my dad gets back my mum starts a torrid affair with a doctor.

8:00 p.m.
Mind you, I would get tiptop medical priority.

8:30 p.m.
He might be able to get me a good deal on my nose job.

9:00 p.m.
I must get revenge on Wet Lindsay.

10:00 p.m.

I wonder how the Bummers will kill me?

10:10 p.m.

Why is the Herring so nice to me? What is wrong with him?

Wednesday October 13th
School
8:30 a.m.

Mum made me hobble to school. Unbelievable. She said a bad ankle didn't stop me learning things. I tried to explain to Mum that it would be just a question of hobbling in to be killed by the Bummer Twins, but she wasn't interested.

I made Jas wheel the wheelbarrow as I hopped along with a crutch. The Foxwood lads had a field day with us, shouting, "Where's your parrot?" and so on.

Jas had perked up enough to say, "I wonder how the Bummers will kill you?"

She sounded quite interested. She's only cheered up because Tom is coming home.

I managed to keep out of the Bummers' way for the

morning but eventually at lunchtime the fatal moment came. The Bummers cornered me in the loos. I tried to hobble off but they blocked the doorway. Here we go. Well at least death would solve the Dave the Laugh situation. Jackie just looked at me. She said, "Fancy a fag?"

What were they going to do, ritually set fire to me?

Jackie put a fag in my mouth and Alison lit it. Jackie said, "Cool," and Alison said, "Good call." And then they just went out.

What in the name of pantyhose did that mean? Why hadn't they duffed me up?

I hobbled over to the mirror to see what I looked like smoking. Quite cool, actually. I sucked my nose in. I definitely looked a bit Italian.

Out of the corner of my mouth I said, *"Ciao, bella."*

But sadly smoke went up my nose and I had a coughing extravaganza.

I can't believe life. As I was having my coughing fit Lindsay walked in and booked me for smoking in the loos. I saw the Bummer Twins sniggering in the corridor.

Great. Stacking gym mats for the rest of the term. Elvis passed by and saw me hobbling and heaving mats around. He laughed.

4:00 p.m.

Left school limping along next to Jas. I think it's quite attractive if you like Long John Silver. I said to Jas, "You know, I think I am going to give up on boys altogether – tell Dave the Laugh it's over, forget the Sex God and just concentrate on lessons and so on. I might ask Herr Kamyer to give me extra tuition."

"He'd have a spasm to end all spasms if you did."

I said, "I think I might be over the Sex God anyway. When I saw him pick up Owlie in his car, that did it for me. Anyone who can go out with Wet Lindsay, with her stupid no forehead and sticky insect legs, and... er..."

"Goggly eyes?"

"Yeah, goggly eyes. Anyone who can do that has got something very wrong with them. You know, if he asked me out now I would say n–ung."

I meant to say "no" but that was when I saw him leaning against his car. The Sex God. Oh don't tell me he was waiting for gorgeous (not) Wet Lindsay. Pathetic. *Très* pathetic and *très très* sad.

I hobbled past him. He wasn't so very gorgey. Well actually, yes, he was. He was a Sex God. Really. He looked me straight in the eyes and I went completely jelloid. In fact, my other leg nearly gave way. He half-smiled and I remembered what it was like to be attached to his mouth. Somehow I kept hobbling. We'd got past him and I was feeling all shaky when he called after us, "Georgia, can I talk to you for a minute?"

OhmyGodohmyGod. Was this an elastic band moment? Jas was just goosegogging at my side. I said, "You walk on, Jas, I'll catch you up."

She said, "Oh it's OK, I'm not in any hurry. Anyway, you might fall over and lie for ages with no one to help you. Like a tortoise on its back or—"

I opened my eyes really wide at Jas and raised my eyebrows. After about forty years she got it and walked on.

Robbie said, "Look, I know I'm probably the last person you want to talk to, but... well... I'd just like to tell you something... I'm really, really sorry about what happened between us... I handled it really badly, I know. She, you know, Lindsay, just was like, so upset, and you were so young and I couldn't... I didn't know what else to do. I thought I'd be going away soon and that would just sort things out... but then I was at the match..."

God, was there anyone in the universe who hadn't seen my huge wobbly bottom and enormous conk bobbling around the hockey pitch?

SG was going on in his really sexy voice, "...and I saw how Lindsay deliberately hurt you... and I... I'm sorry. I've caused a lot of trouble and you're a really nice kid... Look, I'll..."

Then I heard, "Robbie!!"

Wet Lindsay was walking over towards where we were and I just couldn't handle any more. I hobbled off.

5:00 p.m.
OhGodohGodohGod. I love him, I love him.

He thinks I am a kid.

It's all a facsimile of a sham.

And in tins.

And pants.

And pingy pongos.

And *merde*.

He was at the match. He saw my giganticus pantibus.

But he still spoke to me.

Perhaps Jas is not as mad as she seems. Perhaps big knickers are boy magnets?

Oh I don't know.

Why does he still make me go jelloid?

6:00 p.m.

Dave the Laugh had left me a card at home which said, *One-legged girls are a push-over. Love Dave xxxxxx* And some chocolates. Oh GODDDDDDD!!!!

Saturday October 16th

11:00 a.m.

I am a horrible person. I have dumped Dave. I had to. It was really double poo. I thought he was going to cry. He turned up at my house with some flowers because of my injury. He is so sweet and it didn't seem fair to lead him on. I explained that he had only really been a red herring.

2:30 p.m.

Phoned Jas.

"He said I was a user and, er... something else..."

"Was it 'selfish'?"

"No."

"The crappest person in humanity?"

"No."

"Really horrible and like a wormey..."

"Jas, shut up."

455

In bed
8:00 p.m.

Am I really horrible? Perhaps I am one of those people who don't really feel things properly, like Madonna.

10:00 p.m.

Personally I think I have shown great maturiosity and wisdomosity.

11:00 p.m.

Dave will some day thank me for this.

Midnight

Angus still on top of the wall across the road. Looking down at his beloved Naomi in her enclosure. He too is disappointed in love.

3:00 a.m.

Libby came in all sleepy. She said, "Move." And climbed in with the usual accoutrements – Barbie, Charlie Horse, etc. I've got about half a centimetre of bed. Marvellous. Bloody marvellous.

Monday October 18th
School
Break
2:15 p.m.

Well, at least life can't get any worse. Oh, I beg your pardon, yes it can. Raining again and cold and we have been forced outside by the Hitler Youth. I said to Wet Lindsay who was the prefect on duty, "It is against the Geneva Convention that we are forced outside in Arctic..." But she had locked the door and was sort of grinning through the window. She took off her cardigan as I was looking and wiped her forehead as if she was boiling. Oh *très amusant*, Owlie.

Jas and I wandered round to Elvis's hut to see if the old lunatic was in. If he wasn't we could sit in his hut for a bit and warm up. But oh no, there he was, reading his newspaper. Elvis had ear muffs on underneath his flat cap! Mrs Elvis must be very proud. I tapped on his little window so that I could say a friendly hello to him. But he couldn't hear because of the muffs.

I said to Jas, "As a hilarious joke I'll pretend to say something very urgent to him but I won't really be saying anything. I'll mime saying, 'Mr Attwood, my friend Jas is on fire!!!'"

♡ 457

So I went up to the hut door and I was mouthing, "Mr Attwood, my friend Jas is on fire!!!" and waving my arms wildly. In the end he took off his ear muffs, thinking that he couldn't hear me because of them. When he realised the joke he went ballisticisimus. He leaped up in a quite scary way for a one hundred and eighty-year-old man and came charging at us out of his hut. I hobbled off quite quickly. Unfortunately he didn't remember he had parked his personal wheelbarrow round the corner of his hut and did a spectacular comedy fall over it. I thought I would die laughing. Me and Jas went and bent over a wall at the back of the tennis courts.

I said to Jas, in between laughing and gasping for air. "Jas... Jas... he... he has got a flat head."

God it was funny. I had a real ache in my stomach from laughing too much.

French
3:00 p.m.

For a "treat" as it is Monday, Madame Slack taught us another French song. It was called "Sur le Pont D'Avignon". About some absolute saddos dancing about on a bridge. All I can say is that the French and me have a different idea of having a cracking good time. Also, if I do go to French land, although I will be able to tell my new French mates that my blackbird has lost a feather, and be able to dance on bridges, I will not be able to get a filled baguette for love nor money.

At the end of the lesson Wet Lindsay came into the classroom in her role as Oberführer assistant. She smiled in a not attractive or friendly way and said, "Georgia Nicolson, report to Miss Simpson's office... NOW."

3:30 p.m.
Outside Slim's office. Oh dear. *Quelle dommage. Zut alors* and *sacré bleu* even. Now what? Unfortunately Wet Lindsay was my guard and as I looked at her I was reminded of her thongs lurking under her skirt. Going up her bum-oley. And it started me off again.

The jelloid one called me in. I was like a red-faced loon trying not to laugh. She said, "Georgia Nicolson, this is an unforgivable offence. This time you have gone too far. Berets worn like lunchpacks, noses stuck up with Selllotape, false freckles painted on noses, all these childish pranks I have put up with... Last term there was the skeleton in Mr Attwood's uniform, the locusts..."

♥ 459

Slim raved on and on, shaking like a gigantic jelly. "...I was hoping that you had grown up a bit. But to lure an elderly man, not in peak condition..." Blah blah blah.

It was useless my trying to explain. Mr Attwood has dislocated his shoulder and I am being held responsible. Fab. Anyway, the short and short of it is that I'm suspended for a week and Jas is on cloakroom duty. Slim said she was going to write a stiff note home to my parents telling them the circumstances. I helpfully offered to take the stiff note home myself but Slim insisted on posting it.

Hobbling home with Jas and the gang. I was a bit depressed. Again. I couldn't even be bothered putting my lunchpack-beret on.

I said to Jas, "Slim is so ludicrously suspicious! What she implied was that I would not take the note home and would pretend that I am not suspended!!"

Jas said, "Hmmm... What were you going to tell your mum after you had destroyed the note?"

"You're as bad as everyone else, Jas."

"I know, but just for interest's sake, what were you going to say?"

"I thought I might try the mysterious stomach bug. I haven't used it since last year's maths test."

4:00 p.m.
Home. Great. Life is great. Just perfectamondo. Suspended. Suspended just in time for Vati to come home and kill me. In love with a Sex God who calls me a kid. Called a heartless whatsit by Dave the Laugh. And the spot on my bum is like a boil. I wonder what Buddha would do now?

4:30 p.m.
Waiting for Mum to come home so I can break the brilliant news.

5:00 p.m.
Phoned Jas. Her mum answered.

I said, "Hello, can I speak to Jas?"

I heard her shouting to Jas, "Jas, it's Georgia on the phone."

And I heard Jas shout back, "Can you tell her I'll talk to her later. Tom's showing me a new computer game."

A new computer game? Are they all mad?

If I had called down and said that a boy was showing me a computer game my bedroom would have been full of parents within seconds!!

Unless that boy was my cousin James, in which case I would have been left up there for years, because my family doesn't seem to mind incest.

6:30 p.m.

Mutti went ballisticisimus about the suspension. Even though I explained how it was not my fault and how provoked I was by Elvis.

When she calmed down she said, "Don't you think you might have a bit of a stomach bug?"

I said, "Here we go. Look, Mum, this is no time to be visiting Doctor Gorgeous. We should be thinking about Vati."

She said, "I AM thinking of Vati. And do you know what I'm thinking? I'm thinking that he'll go mad if he comes back and the first thing he hears is that his first born has been suspended. Now, are you feeling a bit poorly?"

462

My room
8:30 p.m.

Mum "suggested" I went to bed early and thought about the important things in life for once. She's right. I will think about the important things in life. Here goes:

My hair... quite nice in a mousey sort of way. I still think that a blonde streak is a good idea, even after the slight accident I had last time I tried it. The bit that snapped off has grown back now, but I notice Mum has hidden all the toilet cleaners and Grandad's stuff that he puts his false teeth in when he stays. She really is like a police dog.

Anyway, where was I? Oh yes, eyes... Nice, I think, sort of a yellow colour. Jas said I've got cats' eyes.

Nose... Yes well, it doesn't get any smaller. It's the squashiness I don't like. It doesn't seem to have any bone in it. I still can't forget what Grandad said about noses, that as you get older they get bigger and bigger as gravity pulls on them.

8:35 p.m.

You can make a sort of nose sling out of a pair of knickers! Like a sort of anti-gravity device. You put a leg hole over each

ear and the middly bit supports your nose. It's quite comfy.
I'm not saying that it looks very glamorous. I'm just saying
it's comfy.

8:40 p.m.
It's not something I would wear outside of the privacy of my
own bedroom.

8:45 p.m.
It's a good view from my windowsill. I can see Mr Next Door
with his stupid poodles. He's all happy now that Angus has
gone off poodle baiting in favour of the Burmese sex kitten.

8:46 p.m.
Oh hello, here comes BG, my ex, the breast fondler. At this
rate he will be the one and only fondler. I will die unfondled.
He must be coming home from football practice. I don't
know how I could ever have thought about snogging him, he
wears extremely tragic trousers. He is looking up at my
window. He has seen me. He's stopped walking and is
looking up at my window. Staring at me. Well, you know
what they say – once a boy magnet always a boy magnet. I'm

just going to stare back in a really cool way. All right, Mr Big Gob, Mr Dumper. I might be the dumpee but you still can't take your eyes away from me though, can you??? I still fascinate him. He's just looking up at me. Just staring and staring.

Mesmerised by me.

8:50 p.m.
Oh my God! I am still wearing my nose hammock made out of knickers.

8:56 p.m.
Mark will tell all his mates.

8:57 p.m.
He will now call me a knicker-sniffer as well as a lesbian.

Midnight
Oh for heaven's sake! What now? Woken by loud shouting and swearing. Surely Dad is not home already? Looked through the window. It was Mr and Mrs Across the Road. They were hitting things in their garden, shouting and

shining torches. What on earth is the matter with them? This is no time for a disco inferno.

2:00 a.m.

Woke up fighting for breath from a dream about my nose getting bigger and bigger and my breasts getting bigger and bigger. And someone laughing and laughing at me. I couldn't seem to move anything except my head. Paralysis for being so horrid to Dave the Laugh. Libby was laughing like a loony. (Which of course she is.) She pulled my hair, "Look, bad boy!!! Aaahhh."

The weight was Angus curled up on my chest. Purring. I couldn't move, he weighs a ton. Big fat furry thing. I'm going to cut down on his rations. He's like a small horse.

Hang on a minute. He's not alone. He's got Naomi with him, curled up on top of him!!! Oh Blimey O'Reilley's trousers!

I managed to get them off me and they slunk off into the night – not before Angus had bitten my hand for my trouble. Naomi is a bit forward for a pedigree cat; she had her head practically up Angus's bottom as they went off.

I'll think about it in the morning. I mustn't do anything hasty. Like tell Mr and Mrs Across the Road.

Tuesday October 19th
8:45 a.m.

All hell broke loose. Mr and Mrs Across the Road came round "asking" about the Burmese sex kitten. Mr Across the Road had a spade and the words "Skinned and made into slippers" were mentioned. As she shut the door Mum said, "Honestly, Angus gets the blame for any bloody thing that goes on round here."

I said, "Yes... he's a scapewhatsit like me."

She said, "Shut up and get the balloons out."

Balloon city.
4:00 p.m.

The house is covered in balloons. I even made a banner for the gate, it says VELCOME HOME, VATI.

Libby has made something disgusting out of Playdough and bits of hair. She is wearing ALL of her dressing-up things: her Little Red Riding Hood outfit, fairy wings, deely boppers and, on top, her Pocahontas costume. She can hardly walk about.

No sign of Angus and Naomi. They will have made a love nest somewhere. Pray God my knickers are not involved in any way.

♥ 467

First of the loons arrive.
5:00 p.m.

Grandad almost broke my ribs; he's surprisingly strong for someone who is two hundred and eight. He gave me a sweet (!) and said, "Don't send your granny down the mines, there's enough slack in her knickers!!"

What is he talking about? Mum gave him a sherry. Oh good grief. That means he will take his false teeth out soon and make them do a "hilarious" dance.

6:00 p.m.

Excitement mounts (not). Uncle Eddie and Vati turned up on Uncle Eddie's pre-war motorbike. Vati leaped off the bike in a way that might have caused serious injury to a man of his years.

Mum and Dad practically ATE each other. Erlack!! How can they do that? In public.

I think Dad was crying. It's hard to tell when someone is as covered in facial hair as he is. He hugged me and went, "Oh, Gee... I... oh, I've missed you! Have you missed me?"

I went, "Nnnyeah."

Then Mum gave me a look and I pretended my stomach

bug was quite bad. We'd "agreed" that we would do the stomach bug scenario early on, so as not to arouse suspicion tomorrow morning. I was beginning to feel quite ill, actually. It's weird having him back. At least Mum more or less ignores me. Vati tends to take an interest in, well, exam results and so on.

7:00 p.m.
More and more people arrived. The drive was full of cars and old drunks. Mum and Dad were holding hands. It is so sad to see that sort of thing in people who should know better. I wondered if I should tell Vati he was in a love triangle with George Clooney. But then I thought no, can't be bothered.

12:30 a.m.
What a nightmare! All the so-called grown-ups got drunk and started "letting their hair down". Well, those of them that had any.

Uncle Eddie was spectacularly drunk. He put one of Libby's rattles with a sucker bottom on his head, to look like a dalek. Libby laughed a lot. Uncle Eddie was going,

"Exterminate, exterminate," for about a million years. But then Libby wanted it back and Uncle Eddie couldn't get the sucker off his head. All the drunkards had to pull on it together, and when it eventually came off Uncle Eddie had a round purple mark about a metre wide on his forehead. Which actually was quite funny.

1:00 a.m.
I went down to tell them that some of us were trying to sleep, so could they turn down Abba's Golden Hits, please. I saw them "dancing". God it was so sad. Dad was swivelling his hips around and clapping his hands together like a seal. Also he kept yelling, "Hey you! Get off of my cloud!!" like a geriatric Mick Jagger, and as Mick Jagger is about a million years old you can imagine how old and ludicrous Dad looked. Very old and ludicrous, that's how.

Mum was all red and flushed – she was TWISTING with Mr Next Door and they both fell over into a heap.

Wednesday October 20th

12:30 p.m.

Up at the crack of midday.

Mum in the kitchen in her apron making breakfast for us all. Oh no, sorry, I was just imagining being part of a proper family where that sort of thing happens. In Nicolson land the M and D are still in bed, even Libby was in there with them. I tried to get her to come into bed with me last night but she hit me and said, "No, bad boy, I go with Big Uggy!" (That's what she calls Dad – Big Uggy.) Angus was somewhere with the sex kitten and I was just... alone in my room. In my bed of pain. Because my ankle still hurt, not that anyone cared. Very, very alone as usual.

As alone as a... er... an elk.

You never see elks largeing it up with other elks, do you? They are always on their own, just on a mountain. Alone.

Ah well, I decided to take a Buddhist viewpoint and just be happy that everyone else is happy...

12:45 p.m.

Doorbell rang.

I called down, "The doorbell to your home is ringing."

No reply from the drunks.

The doorbell rang again. It would be Mr and Mrs Across the Road wanting to search the house for Angus and the Burmese sex kitten.

Ring ring.

I yelled as I hobbled down to answer it. "Don't worry about the fact that I have a limp and a very serious stomach complaint that makes me too sick to go to school... I will get up and answer the door. You recover your strength from lifting glasses up to your mouths!"

Silence. Well, just a bit of snoring from Libby.

I opened the door.

It was the Sex God.

At my door.

Looking like a Sex God.

At my door.

The Sex God had landed at my door.

I was wearing my Teletubbies pyjamas.

He said, "Hi."

I said, "Hhhnnnnngggggghhh."

1:00 p.m.

I got dressed as quickly as I could. The Sex God said he would meet me by the telephone box so we could go for a walk round Stanmer Park. I dithered for about five minutes about lippy. I mean, if there is going to be snogging, is it worth putting it on? But then, if you don't put it on, does it look like you are expecting to snog, and is that too much pressure for boys who might go springing off in an elastic band way again?

Ooohhhh, I could feel my brain turning to soup. I knew I'd say something so stupid to the SG that even I would know it was stupid. That's how stupid it would be.

I didn't take any chances with the nipple department. I wore a bra and a vest. Let them get out of that if they could.

I must be calm. Om. Om. OhmyGodohmyGodohmyGod. My tongue seemed too big for my mouth. Do tongues grow? That would be the final straw if I had a tongue that just lolled out of my mouth. Shut up, brain!

1:25 p.m.

There he was, leaning against the wall! He was just so cool. His hair was flopping down over one eye.

When he looked up I went completely jelloid. He said, "Hi, Georgia. Come here."

And I said, "My dad has grown a little beard and I thought I was going to be lonely as an elk."

What in the name of pantyhose was I talking about? I'd be the last to know as usual.

The SG HELD OUT HIS HAND... to me!!!! Something I had dreamed of. Do you know what I did? I shook it!!!

He really laughed then, and grabbed hold of my hand. We walked to the park. Holding hands. In public. Me and a Sex God. I honestly couldn't think of anything to say. Well I could, but it would only have made sense to dogs. Or my grandad.

In the park we sat down on the grass, even though it was a bit on the nippy noodles side. Unfortunately I did feel like going to the piddly-diddly department, but I didn't say.

He looked at me for what seemed like ages and ages, and then he kissed me. It was all surf crashing and my insides felt like they were being sucked out. Which you wouldn't think was very pleasant. But it was. He put his hand on my face and kissed me quite hard. I felt all breathless and hot. It was brilliant. We whizzed through the scoring system for snogging in record time. We got to number four (kiss lasting over three minutes without a break), had a quick breather and then went into five (open mouth kissing) and a hint of six (tongues). Yesss!!!! I had got to number six with the Sex God!!! Again!!!

Eventually we had a bit of a chat. Well, he chatted. I just couldn't seem to say anything normal. Every time I thought of something to say, it was something like, "Do you want to see my impression of a lockjaw germ?" or "Can I eat your shirt?"

He had his arm round my shoulder, which was good because then he got profile rather than full-frontal nose. He said, "I haven't been able to forget you. I've tried. I tried to be glad when you started seeing Dave. But it didn't work. I even wrote a song for you. Do you want to hear it?"

I managed to say "Yes" without putting on a stupid French accent or something. Then he sort of pulled me backwards on to him so that my head was resting on his lap. It was quite nice, but I could see up his nose a bit. Which I didn't mind, because he is a Sex God and I love him. It's not like looking up Cousin James's nose, which would make anyone immediately sick. But then I thought, if he looked down and saw me looking up his nostrils, he might think it was a bit rude. So I settled on closing my eyes and letting a half-smile play around my lips.

Then he started singing me the song he had written for me. There weren't many words – it was mostly, "And I really had to see her again." And then melodic humming and yeahing. Unfortunately he was sort of jiggling his knees for the rhythm so my head was bobbling about. I don't know how attractive that looked.

4:00 p.m.
The Sex God has left the arena. He wants us to be, like, official snogging partners after my fifteenth next month. He's going to tell his parents.

I am irresistible.

I am truly a BABE magnet.

Even in my Teletubbies jimjams.

Even without mascara on.

Life is fabbity fab fab!!!!

Yesssss!!!!!! And triple hahahahahaha-di-haha!!!!

5:00 p.m.
M and D eventually got up. I didn't care because I am in the Land of the Very Fab, in fact beyond the Valley of the Fab and into the Universe of Marvy.

Vati is in a hideously good mood. He keeps looking at things and going, "Aahh-h" and hugging me. I wish he would get back to normal. I wonder how long it will be before he drops this "happy family" nonsense and gets all parenty.

6:00 p.m.
An hour, that's how long.

I was on the phone when it started. Telling Jas about SG. I said to her, "Yeah, come round and I'll tell you all about it. It is so FAB. How long will you be? OK. Good. Yeah anyway, he just turned up in his car. He looked BRILLIANT – you know those black jeans he has got, the really cool ones with the raised seam that..."

Vati had gone into the kitchen to get a cup of tea. He came out, stirring it. Jas had just asked me what sort of jacket SG was wearing and I was beginning to tell her when Dad interrupted and said, "Georgia, if Jas is coming round why are you talking to her on the phone? Phones cost money, you know."

Oh, I wondered how long it would be before the fascist landed. I said to Jas, "Have to go, Jas, I may already have wasted two pence. See you soon."

7:20 p.m.

In my room, daydreaming about my wedding. Can you wear black as a bride? Dad came up and suggested we have a family "chat". I know what that means, it means they tell me what they are going to do and expect me to go along with it, and if I don't they call me a spoiled teenager and send me to my room.

But I don't care any more. I said to Dad politely, "Look, why don't we just skip the boring middle bit where I have to come all the way downstairs and you tell me what to do and I say no I don't want to and then you send me straight to my room. Why don't I just stay in my room?"

He said, "I don't know what you are talking about. Come into the front room. And what's wrong with your eyes? They look all bunged up, have you got a cold?"

"It's Vaseline, it makes your eyelashes longer."

He said, "Can't you stop messing about with yourself?"

As I went downstairs I was thinking he should try messing about with himself a bit more. He never had what you might call good dress sense but it's so much worse since he's been in Kiwi-a-gogo land. Today he's wearing tartan slacks which is a crime against humanity in anyone's language. Also he has clipped his beard so that it is just on the end of his chin. No side bits and no moustache, just a beard thing... on the end of his chin. When we went in the room Mum kissed him on the cheek and stroked his beard... How disgusting.

Anyway, I don't care because I am going out with a Sex God and life is fab. I said, "OK, I am sitting comfortably. Rave on, El Beardo."

El Beardo said, "Great news!!! I've been offered a cottage in Scotland, I thought we would all go there for a week together as a family. Spend some quality time there together. Mum and Libbs, Grandad, Uncle Eddie, we could even ask Cousin James if you'd like a bit of company your own age. What do you think?"

Sacré bloody *bleu. Merde* and poo!!! Is what I think.

Fortunately the doorbell rang and Mrs Huge Knickers and me scampered up to my room. My room, which as usual, was full. Libby was in my bed with scuba-diving Barbie, Charlie Horse, Angus and Naomi.

I said, "Go play downstairs with Daddy, Libbs."

But she just stood up on my bed and started dancing, singing, "Winnie Bag Pool, Winnie Bag Pool." She got to the bit where she takes off her panties, but I noticed they were suspiciously bulky, so I said, "Stop it, Libbs."

And she said, "Me let my legs grow."

"No, leave them on."

Too late. I thought Jas was going to faint. She doesn't have a clue what it's like to have a little sister. Me and Jas went off to the utility room for a bit of privacy. I was dying to tell her all about my snogging extravaganza, but she went raving on about Tom: "We went to the country."

Oh good Lord. Still I thought I'd better pretend to be interested otherwise I would never get to talk about myself. I said, "What for?"

"You know, to be on our own in nature."

"Why didn't you just go and sit in your room with some houseplants instead of tramping all the way to the country? You only snog there, anyway."

"No we don't."

"Oh yeah? What else do you do?"

"We looked at things."

"What things?"

"Flora and fauna and so on. Stuff we do in blodge. It was really interesting. Tom knows a lot of things. We found cuckoo spit and followed a badger trail."

I clapped my hands together and started skipping round the room. "Cuckoo spit!!! No!!! If only I could have come with you! Sadly there was a Sex God I had to snog."

Jas got all huffy and pink. It's hilarious when Jas gets miffed, and a reason in itself to make her irritated. She goes all red and pink apart from the tip of her nose which is white. Very funny, like a sort of pink panda in a short skirt and huge knickers.

She was all sulky, but then I put my arm round her. She said, "You can stop that."

I said, "I feel a bit sad though, because I'm so lucky and I can't help thinking about Dave the Laugh. He was a really nice bloke, and you know... er... a good laugh. It's sad that I have broken his heart."

Jas was poking around in Dad's fishing bag, which is not a good idea as he sometimes leaves maggots in there which turn into bluebottles. She said, "Oh, I meant to tell you. He's going out with Ellen. Tom and I are meeting them later at the pictures."

Midnight

Bloody *sacré bleu*. Dave the Laugh was supposed to really like me. How come he is going out with Ellen? How dare she go out with him? He is only just my ex.

1:00 a.m.

Still, I am going out with a Sex God. So I should be nice to everyone.

1:05 a.m.

Dave was a laugh, though. Even if he didn't make me go jelloid.

1:10 a.m.

I definitely go jelloid with the SG. Mmmmm, dreamy. But he doesn't make me laugh, he makes me stupid.

1:15 a.m.

I wonder if Dave the Laugh did that nibbling thing with Ellen?

1:20 a.m.

Looking through the window. Angus and Naomi are lurking

about on Mr and Mrs Next Door's garden wall. Angus is just dangling his paw down at the poodles. I hope there is not going to be group sex. (Whatever that is.)

1:25 a.m.

Perhaps I could have a jelloid boyfriend and an ordinary one for laughing with.

1:30 a.m.

Good grief! What in the name of pantyhose is going to happen next?!?

Georgia's Glossary

aggers · Agony. Like I said, no one has the time to say whole words, so aggers is short for agony. The unusually irritating among you might point out that aggers is actually longer than agony. My answer to that is – Haven't you got something else to do besides count letters?

billio · From the Australian outback. A billycan was something Aborigines boiled their goodies up in, or whatever it is they eat. Anyway, billio means boiling things up. Therefore, "my cheeks ached like billio" means... er... very achy. I don't know why we say it. It's a mystery, like many things. But that's the beauty of life.

Chrimbo hols · No one has the time to say long words, so Chrimbo is Christmas and hols is holidays. As in snog fest (snogging festival).

conk · Nose. This is very interesting historically. A very long time ago (1066) – even before my grandad was born – a bloke called William the Conqueror (French) came to England and shot our King Harold in the eye. Typical. And people wonder why we don't like the French much. Anyway, William had a big nose, and so to get our own back we called him William the Big Conk-erer. If you see what I mean. I hope you do because I am exhausting myself with my hilariosity and historiosity.

crèche · Kindergarten. Nursery. Playschool. Working muttis leave preschool children so they can "enjoy themselves" making things. A sort of day prison for toddlers.

dalek · In England we have this hilariously crap TV show called Dr Who where this bloke in a scarf goes time travelling. His archenemies are these senselessly violent creatures (no, not Angus surprisingly). They are called daleks. They're a form of robot. They have weird mechanical voices and a sort of gun sticking out of their head bits. They say, "Exterminate, exterminate!" Well, I told you it is crap.

DIY · Quite literally "Do It Yourself"! Rude when you think about it. Instead of getting someone competent to do things around the house (you know, like a trained electrician or a builder or a plumber), some vatis choose to do DIY. Always with disastrous results. For example, my bedroom ceiling has footprints in it because my vati decided he would go up on the roof and replace a few tiles. Hopeless.

duffing up · Duffing up is the female equivalent of beating up. It is not so violent and usually involves a lot of pushing with the occasional pinch.

geoggers · Geoggers is short for geography. Ditto blodge (biology) and lunck (lunch).

get off with · A romantic term. It means to use your womanly charms to entice a boy into a web of love. Oh, OK then – snogging.

gob · Gob is an attractive term for someone's mouth. For example, if you saw Mark (from up the road who has the biggest mouth known to womankind) you could yell politely, "Good Lord, Mark, don't open your gob, otherwise people may think you are a basking whale in trousers and throw a mackerel at you!" Or something else full of hilariosity.

goosegog · Gooseberry. I know you are looking all quizzical now. OK. If there are two people and they want to snog and you keep hanging about saying, "Do you fancy some chewing gum?" or "Have you seen my interesting new socks?" you are a gooseberry. Or for short a goosegog, i.e., someone who nobody wants around.

gorgey · Gorgeous. Like fabby (fabulous) and marvy (marvellous).

Jammy Dodger · Biscuit with jam in it. Very nutritious (ish).

jelly rabbit · Jelly made into a rabbit shape. Children like this sort of thing. You make some jelly and pour it into a rabbit-shaped mould. When it is set the child amuses itself by eating its bottom with a spoon. Or scooping out its eyes. Or, in Libby's case, by placing it in my bed.

Knickers · Amercians (wrongly) call them panties. Knickers are a particular type of "panty" – huge and all encompassing. In the olden days (i.e., when Dad was born) all the ladies wore massive knickers that came to their knees. Many, many amusing songs were made up about knicker elastic breaking. This is because, as Slim, our headmistress, points out to anybody interested (i.e., no one), "In the old days people knew how to enjoy themselves with simple pleasures." Well, I have news for her. We modern people enjoy ourselves with knicker stories, too. We often laugh as we imagine how many homeless people she could house in hers.

jimjams · Pyjamas. Also pygmies or jammies.

lippy · Oh come on, you know what it is! Lipstick!! Honestly, what are you like?!

loo · Lavatory. In America they say "rest room", which is funny, as I never feel like having a rest when I go to the lavatory.

mincers · Cockney-type people in London use rhyming slang so that other (normal) people will not know what they are talking about. I don't know why – that is the beauty of the Cockneys. Mincers is short for mince pies, which rhymes with eyes. Get it?

Neighbours · A really crap daytime soap opera set in a suburb in Australia. Kylie Minogue was in it.

nub · The heart of the matter. You can also say gist and thrust. This is from the name for the centre of a wheel where the spokes come out. Or do I mean hub? Who cares. I feel a dance coming on.

nuddy-pants · Quite literally nude-coloured pants, and you know what nude-coloured pants are? They are no pants. So if you are in your nuddy-pants you are in your no pants, i.e., you are naked.

panstick · Stick of makeup that you use to cover up spots with. Or in my mutti's case to cover up the ravages of time and a careless attitude to skin care.

physio · A sort of massage. Short for physiotherapy. For instance, if you had a muscle that really, really hurt and that you wanted left alone, a cruel person (Miss Stamp) would insist on giving you a violent pummelling to make it better. Ha.

rate · To fancy someone. Like I fancy (or rate) the Sex God. And I certainly do fancy the SG, as anyone with the brains of an earwig (i.e., not Jas) would know by now. Phew – even writing about him in the glossary has made me go all jelloid. And stupidoid.

Reeves and Mortimer · Are a comedy double act. They are very mad indeed. But I like them.

rucky · A rucksack. Like a little kangaroo pouch you wear on your back to put things in. Backpack.

shirty · Flustered and twitchy and coming on all pompous.

Slack Alice · A Slack Alice is someone who is all stupid and nerdy. The sort of person who is always pulling their knickers up because they are too big (i.e., Jas).

umby · Umbrella. Also "brolly". Mary Poppins used to say "gamp" for umbrella. But what I say to that is – who cares?

wet · A drippy, useless, nerdy idiot. Lindsay.

whelks · A horrible shellfish thing that only the truly mad (like my grandad, for instance) eat. They are unbelievably slimy and mucuslike.

Here's a sneaky peek at my next book...

'Knocked out by my nunga-nungas!'

Saturday October 23rd
Scotland
In a crap cottage in nowhere
10:30 a.m.

Vati is back as Loonleader with a vengeance. He came barging into "my" (hahahahahaha) room at pre-dawn, waggling his new beard about. I was sleeping with cucumber slices on my eyes for beautosity purposes so at first I thought I had gone blind in the night. I nearly did go blind when he ripped open my curtains and said, "Gidday gidday, me little darlin'" in a ludicrous Kiwi-a-gogo twang.

494

I wonder if he has finally snapped? He was very nearly bonkers before he went to Kiwi-a-gogo land and having his shoes blown off by a rogue bore can't have helped.

But hey, El Beardo is, after all, my vati and that also makes him Vati of the Girlfriend of a Sex God. So I said quite kindly, "Guten morgan, Vati, could you please go away now? Thank you."

I think his beard may have grown into his ears however, because he ignored me and opened the window. He was leaning out, breathing in and out and flapping his arms around like a loon. His bottom is not tiny. If a very small pensioner was accidentally walking along behind him they may think there had been an eclipse of the sun.

"Aahh, smell that air, Georgie. Makes you feel good to be alive, doesn't it?"

I pulled my duvet round me. "I won't be alive for much longer if that freezing air gets into my lungs."

He came and sat on the bed. Oh God, he wasn't going to hug me, was he? Fortunately Mutti yelled up the stairs, "Bob, breakfast is ready!" and he lumbered off.

Breakfast is ready? Has everyone gone mad? When was the last time Mum made breakfast? Anyway, ho hum pig's

♡ 495

bum, I could snuggle down in my comfy holiday bed and do dreamy-dreamy about snogging the Sex God in peace now.

Wrong.

Clank, clank. "Gergy! Gingey! It's me!!"

Oh blimey O'Reilley's trousers, it was Libby, mad toddler from Planet of the Loons. When my adorable little sister came in I couldn't help noticing that although she was wearing her holiday sunglasses, she wasn't wearing anything else. She was also carrying a pan. I said, "Libby, don't bring the pan into..."

But she ignored me and clambered up into my bed, shoving me aside to make room. She has got hefty little arms for a child of four. She said, "Move up, bad boy, Mr Pan tired." Then she and Mr Pan snuggled up against me. I almost shot out of bed, her bottom was so cold... and sticky... urghh.

What is it with my room? You would think that at least on holiday I might be able to close my door and have a bit of privacy to do my holiday project (fantasy snogging), but oh no...